BOONE

ETERNITY SPRINGS:
THE MCBRIDES OF TEXAS

BOONE

EMILY MARCH

THORNDIKE PRESS
A part of Gale, a Cengage Company

LIBRARY OF CONGRESS CIP DATA ON FILE.
CATALOGUING IN PUBLICATION FOR THIS BOOK
IS AVAILABLE FROM THE LIBRARY OF CONGRESS.

ISBN-13: 978-1-4328-8960-9 (hardcover alk. paper)

Published in 2021 by arrangement with St. Martin's Publishing Group

Printed in Mexico
Print Number: 01   Print Year: 2021

Maddie P. Maddie P.
Nana loves her Maddie P.
She's the sweetest girl in Texas
and her Mommy will agree.
Maddie P. Maddie P.
Welcome to the world, my love.
Our 2020 saving grace.

CHAPTER ONE

Boone McBride tried hard to keep the commandments attached to Thursday-night Beer League softball in Eternity Springs, but it wasn't always easy. Oh, he didn't have trouble remembering to bring the beer when it was his turn or leaving his cell phone in his car at the ballpark. He wasn't tempted to skip games or yell at the umpire or covet a different position than the one he drew from a ball cap at the beginning of the game, as was the team's custom. What gave Boone trouble was the team's first commandment: Thou shalt not ogle thy buddy's wife.

Considering that he was a single man and all of the Base Invaders' women were as hot as Austin in August, keeping the first commandment required considerable effort.

It didn't help anything that the bleacher smoke show observed no reciprocal rule. Some of the things those women said to a man on the field could make a batboy blush.

Not that the women were vulgar. There were, after all, children present. Lots of children. So many children, in fact, that one had to question just how many home runs were hit each night in Eternity Springs. But Boone would bet the keys to his Maserati that they spent the days between games googling baseball innuendos. They didn't spare him either. In fact, as the only single man on the Base Invaders, he seemed to get attention from all of them.

The commandments said nothing about being an ogle-ee, so Boone, being Boone, played to the crowd during his turn at bat.

He approached home plate using what he thought of as his gunslinger walk — molasses slow, thighs spread, his arms swaying. A confident swagger. A few steps from home plate, he glanced toward the bleachers and gave the ladies a wink and the bat in his right hand a slow, 360-degree swing. Wearing his cockiest grin, he took his place in the batter's box.

The whistles and catcalls elicited a grouchy scoff from the catcher. With the hint of his native Australia in his tone, Devin Murphy said, "You're a dick, McBride."

"Add an adjective to that noun, and

8

you've got it right." Boone took position, bat up, weight forward, knees flexed, which served to pull the material of his softball pants tight over his ass. "I'm a swingin' dick."

He let the first pitch sail by.

"Strike," called the umpire, Harry Falwell, a retired ball coach from Indiana who obviously needed new glasses.

Boone gave him a look but kept the umpire commandment.

"I think we're good without the adjective," Devin commented.

"Waiting for my pitch." On the pitcher's mound, Josh Tarkington began his windup, and Boone added, "Then I'm hitting a homer."

The ball headed for the plate. Boone liked it. *Thump.* Bat connected with ball, right on the sweet spot. He stood and watched it sail over the fence before turning to tip his cap to the cheering bleacher brigade.

"Oh, go run your bases," Devin snarled. "Better enjoy it. Unlike the rest of us, it's the only home base you'll see tonight."

"You're a dick, Murphy," Boone replied before tossing down his bat and making the trek around the bases.

The Base Invaders won the game 9 to 6.

Boone hung around for the postgame

beer, fielding dozens of questions about his cousin Jackson's destination wedding to the lovely Caroline Carruthers, which was scheduled for a week from Saturday here in Eternity Springs. Folks were abuzz because Jackson's ex-wife and the mother of his daughter, Haley, was a pop music celebrity who performed as Coco. She was going to sing at the rehearsal party on Friday night, an event to which all Eternity Springs residents were invited. Around eight thirty, he climbed into his Land Rover and made the short drive to his office.

Celeste Blessing had asked for an appointment, and with both their schedules, the best they'd been able to do was nine tonight. He had a little paperwork to finish up before she arrived, and he'd no sooner walked inside than his landline began to ring. That was curious. Who would be calling his business number instead of his cell at eight thirty on a Thursday night?

He checked caller ID and froze. The familiar number sent a chill of apprehension down his spine. WAGGONER, THOMPSON, AND COLE.

Boone's stomach sank. To call his personal history with the Fort Worth law firm unpleasant was like saying the water of Hummingbird Lake was a little chilly in February. They were directly connected to the darkest days of his life, and not very long ago, any type of communication with them would have him breaking out in a cold sweat. His hand hovered over the receiver as he debated letting the call go to voicemail. It was well past business hours, after all.

No. He was a swingin' D, right? He wasn't going to duck a freakin' phone call from Fort Worth. "Screw it," he muttered and picked up the receiver. "Boone McBride."

"Boone? This is Ellen Woods."

Boone's brows arched in surprise. Ellen Woods had been a colleague of his at the DA's office. "Ellen. Nice to hear from you. Except, you're calling from WTC? Don't tell me you've gone over to the dark side."

She laughed. "No, I'm still fighting the good fight. I've been here for a meeting. I had an empty conference room and time to reach out to you, but my phone is about to die, so I'm using theirs. Boone, something rather unusual has come up. It involves you."

He took a seat in his desk chair and said a wary, "Okay."

"Yesterday Sarah Winston reached out to me for help. She's been trying to reach you. She thinks you're dodging her calls."

I am. He'd dodged three calls from Sarah Winston today.

Boone picked up a pencil and began tapping its eraser on the desk. "She's still with Child Protective Services, isn't she?"

"Yes. She —"

"Tell her I said no."

"Boone —"

"Tell her to talk to Jenkins or Moffat. They're tough as nails on child abuse cases. Either one of those guys will do a fabulous job for Sarah."

"But —"

He interrupted. "Okay, look. I'll do this much for her. Tell her I'll read over what she's done before they go to trial, but I'm not working the case."

"Boone McBride, would you please zip your lips long enough to let me get a word in edgewise? Sarah is not looking for legal help. That's not why she's been calling."

"Oh." He set down the pencil. "I'm sorry. The last case she brought to me was brutal. These days I'm sticking to writing wills and contracts for real estate deals."

"She told me that. That's a shame, because you have a particular talent working with victimized youth. Children adore you. Your heart is so big."

Boone stifled a snort. If he had a big heart,

12

it was due to all the scar tissue.

Restless now, he rose from his chair and walked to his window where, if he stood in the right spot, he could see the chimney in the master bedroom of the new house Jax Lancaster had built for him up at Hummingbird Lake. He'd moved in a week ago, and he'd opened the last box earlier today. He was close to being ready for the wedding guests arriving next week.

With his gaze locked on his home, his haven, he said, "I hate to rush you, Ellen, but I have somewhere I need to be soon."

Home. Sitting on the dock, getting a worm wet. Short of rolling around his bed with a beautiful woman, it was his favorite way to wind down at the end of a summer day. "What is the message Sarah wants you to pass along?"

"You need to call her. There's a baby, Boone. A newborn. He could be yours."

Boone took just a second to do the math, and then burst out laughing. Last fall he'd been having an affair with a ski instructor over at Wolf Creek. The affair ended by Thanksgiving, but they'd remained friendly. They'd had lunch together just two weeks ago, in fact. He'd been monogamous during the affair and celibate since. "No, Ellen, take my word for it. A newborn child cannot possibly be mine."

"He's officially a Safe Haven baby who was surrendered at a fire station. He arrived with a letter from the mother naming you as his legal guardian. She said she wanted you to adopt her baby, but she didn't know how to find you."

Boone went still. "Excuse me? Say that again?"

"Someone who knows you surrendered a newborn at a fire station."

"Who?"

"We don't know. She didn't say. That's what the Safe Haven law is all about."

Boone knew that, of course. Texas law provided that a parent could leave a baby up to sixty days old with an employee on duty at any hospital, emergency medical services provider, or child welfare agency and not be charged with abandonment. Parents were encouraged to give information about the child's health, race, date of birth, place of birth, and the parents' medical history, but it wasn't required.

Ellen continued, "Sarah did say there was a separate, personal message for you."

"A message? What does the message say?"

"I don't know. Sarah didn't share that with me. Call her, Boone. Tonight. You have a ticking clock situation here with this. Do

14

you need her number?" His former colleague rattled it off, and then ended the call
saying, "This could be a good thing for you,
Boone. Good luck."

"Goodbye." He disconnected the call and
stood frozen as walled-away memories
began chipping at the mortar in his mind.

Boone fought back. He couldn't allow any
breach in his defenses. *That way there be
dragons.*

A Safe Haven baby. Holy hell. Ellen
thought that bringing a child into his life
could be a good thing?

"Not hardly," he muttered. Not according
to his history. He'd been down this road
before. Traveling it brought only heartbreak
and pain. "No. Not going there. Never
again."

He returned to his desk and took a seat.
He didn't phone Sarah Winston. Instead he
phoned Josh Tarkington to schedule a
tune-up for his Maserati. After that, he took
a call on his cell from Brick Callahan and
answered a handful of questions related to
Jackson and Caroline's wedding at the
Callahans' North Forty property on the
shore of Hummingbird Lake. Upon ending
the conversation with Brick, Boone phoned
the Mocha Moose Sandwich Shop and

15

placed a pickup order for dinner on the way home.

He no sooner set the phone down than it rang again. Sarah Winston. Why had he ever given her his cell number? He let out a string of curses that would do a bronc buster proud and then answered the call.

He let her go through the entire story before he began asking questions. "Why is this even a possibility? I know how the system works. This is highly irregular, to say the least."

"That's true. But Boone, you are a hero to everyone in our office. In the courts too. Throw in the fact that you are related to half the judges in Texas, and three-quarters of the politicians on both sides of the aisle want you to run for office — nobody is going to interfere. You've long been a champion for victimized children. You helped so many people. And what happened to you —" She paused a moment and softened her voice. "What happened to you and Mary was tragic. People want to help. This can be treated like a private adoption."

He closed his eyes and massaged his brow. "I appreciate the sentiment, Sarah, but I don't need this."

"Really? Are you so certain of that? You're personally and professionally fulfilled by

16

writing wills and contracts?"

"The world needs ditch diggers too, Danny."

"What?"

"*Caddyshack.* And I don't need to defend my choices."

Besides, his work was more than contracts and wills. He was working his butt off managing the family trust with all the Enchanted Canyon projects. He stayed busy as hell. "I don't want or need a baby. If I did, I'd go out and get one the old-fashioned way."

"Fair enough. Be the baby's guardian, then, if not his father. Find him a family. He needs you."

"That's ridiculous. I don't need to be involved. Infants are a snap to place." *As long as the mothers don't change their minds.* "You probably have dozens of approved adopters who'd love nothing more than to bring a Safe Haven newborn into their home. Hell, I'm not even on the list anymore. Plus, I live in Colorado!"

"Lucky baby gets to avoid the Texas summer," she responded. "They say we might reach a hundred and ten later this week. That's brutal for this early in the season. Colorado's not a problem. I had everyone up and down the line check off on this

17

before I ever called you. Like I said, Boone, you have lots of friends."

"Yeah, and like the old yarn goes, with friends like these who needs enemies. You're not listening to me, Sarah."

"His mother chose you."

That stopped him. "About her. Who is she? Ellen said she left me a message?"

"I don't have a name. What I do have is a folded note with your name on the outside." Sarah Winston waited for a beat before adding, "It's written in gel ink. Pink gel ink."

Pink gel ink. Boone closed his eyes as his defensive walls collapsed, and he was catapulted into his past.

It was the one case that haunted him. The one case he'd totally blown. The system — Boone — had failed a sweet, vulnerable twelve-year-old girl who could not speak of the abuse, but who had managed to write it down. Seven handwritten pages with hearts dotting her i's. Cruel, sickening abuse.

Detailed in pink gel ink.

With dread crushing his chest, he cleared his throat and asked, "What does the note say?"

Softly, gently, Sarah said, " 'You owe me.' "

"Oh, God." Boone closed his eyes. He massaged his brow with fingers and his thumb. "I need to think. I'll phone you tomorrow."

"Promise?"

"I promise."

The call ended, and he sat without moving, haunted by his ghosts, his emotions a maelstrom. He only vaguely heard the knock on his door. Only vaguely heard the hinges creak as the door opened.

"Boone?" Celeste Blessing said as she approached his desk. She was a lovely older woman with kind, periwinkle eyes and a ready smile. Her silver hair was cut in a modern bob, and her signature angel wing earrings dangled from her ears. "Is everything okay?"

The concern in her voice caused a sudden lump to form in Boone's throat. He swallowed it. "No. No, Celeste, it's not. I just received some disturbing news."

"Oh, dear. I hope all of your family members are okay?"

"Yes. This has nothing to do with my family."

"That's reassuring, especially with Jackson's wedding next weekend."

Boone nodded absently. The wedding. Oh, holy hell. His entire family was descending upon Eternity Springs in less than a week. What would he tell them?

19

Nothing, that's what. After what had happened last time, no. Mom, especially, couldn't know about this until everything was settled. Permanently settled. The stress would kill her. He wasn't at all that sure that it wouldn't kill him.

He did his best to lock away all his turmoil. He had business to do. "So, Celeste, what did you need to see me about tonight?"

"It's nothing." She wrinkled her button nose and shook her head. "We'll deal with that another day. Why don't you tell me what's bothering you, Boone?"

The soft, golden lamplight illuminating the office gave her an ethereal glow. Her smile was compassionate. Her gaze offered gentle encouragement.

Boone had lived in Eternity Springs long enough to know that intelligent people listened whenever Celeste Blessing spoke. She was a wise woman, and Boone valued her opinion.

So he told her. The good, the bad, and the heartbreaking.

It took him forty minutes and two glasses of scotch. When he finally finished, he felt drained. "I guess I'll go to Fort Worth tomorrow, but I don't know what I'll do when I get there. I'm a mess, Celeste."

Celeste tossed him a lifeline. "I have a suggestion. Go to Texas tomorrow, but rather than Fort Worth, go to Enchanted Canyon. You owe it to yourself and to that sweet little baby to take a little time with this decision. Make peace with it."

Enchanted Canyon was the Hill Country property not far from the small town of Redemption that he, together with his cousins Tucker and Jackson, had inherited from a distant relative. They had refurbished a nineteenth-century cathouse, and now Celeste's cousin Angelica was the innkeeper at their Fallen Angel Inn resort. Boone's lips twisted in a wry smile as he quoted part of the marketing tagline Celeste had insisted on. "You're saying I should go 'Where troubled souls find peace'?"

"Exactly. Take the weekend and do some hiking and climbing. A little swimming."

"Maybe a bit of spelunking," Boone said, warming to the idea. "Tucker has found a couple of caves he told me to explore."

"I find caves particularly intriguing," Celeste said. "Shelter is a basic need of life. I believe your cousin spends an entire morning on sheltering in his wilderness school's Survival One Oh One class, doesn't he?"

"He does."

"Caves have offered shelter to man and animal throughout the millennia. On the

21

other hand, they also pose the risk of entrapment." She paused significantly before adding, "There are all sorts of caves in this world, aren't there?"

Boone's chair creaked as he settled back into it. He had the sense that this little tableau might just become a momentous occasion, one of the instances when Celeste Blessing shared a life-changing bit of wisdom.

However, he also knew from friends who had been the recipients of Celeste's wisdom that sometimes interpreting her advice could be tricky. "You're speaking of something beyond rock formations, I assume?"

"I am. It's important that one not limit one's perception of caves to being those made of fissures and breaks in stone. Caves can be shelters of one's own making that offer protection from life storms that threaten survival. Necessary places that offer respite and protection. However, those same shelters can, over time, transform into deep, dark, cold places that no longer shelter, but entrap. Instead of offering protection, they prevent. They prevent one from seeing that the storm has passed. They hold one back from rejoining the world."

Boone stretched out his long legs and crossed them at the ankles. He laced his fingers atop his belly. He could follow this. "Are you saying that I'm burrowing in my cave, Celeste? That I've spent the past five years hiding in Eternity Springs, holed up licking my wounds?"

"Honestly, no," she replied, surprising him. "Give yourself some credit, Boone. I think you've spent the past five years healing."

That made him sit up straight.

"You think so? After I blathered out my sob story tonight?"

"I do. But being healed of spirit and being at peace are not the same thing. You won't find peace until you face your ghosts. Enchanted Canyon is a good place to do that."

He nodded. "Okay. I hear you. I'll head to Redemption first thing in the morning."

"Excellent." Celeste rose from her chair and pinned him with a piercing look. "You found your light, Boone McBride. Once you face your ghosts in Enchanted Canyon, I believe you'll be ready to live again, ready to risk your heart again."

"From your mouth to God's ears," he murmured prayerfully.

"Yes." A twinkle flashed in her blue eyes. "Now one more thing before I go. It's something for you to think about in the coming weeks and months. We spoke of caves, of caverns. Of dark places of the soul. You know them."

"I do," he agreed, nodding.

"What was the light that guided you from the darkness? Who and what lit your way? Think about it, Boone. Though your path was solitary, you were never alone."

He shifted uncomfortably. He and God hadn't been on the best of terms the past few years. "It's difficult to keep the faith when you're drowning in grief."

"I'm not speaking to faith here, although I'd suggest that in times of grief, faith can be a true comfort. I'm referring to family and to friends. You have been blessed with the unflagging support of family and friends. Whether you called on them or not, as you sheltered from your life storm, your family and friends were a Zippo in your pocket."

Zippo? It took him a moment. "A lighter? Not a match?"

"I'm a modern woman," she said with a shrug and walked toward the door. When her hand was on the knob, she turned. Her voice held a new note of gravity as she said, "Not everyone has a Zippo. Remember what I say to you, Boone McBride. Be a Zippo. Be a light. That is how you will earn your wings. Be somebody's light."

CHAPTER TWO

On the first Sunday in June inside a Colorado Welcome Center not far from the Nebraska border, Hannah Dupree stood before a trifold pamphlet rack and searched for a safe space. She could feel the storm approaching, the wildness beginning to hum inside her and gloom starting to descend. Most days, she managed to pummel it back, but tomorrow was, well, tomorrow.

She picked up a cartoon tourist map. The drawing of what looked like a diving board made of rock and the words LOVER'S LEAP caught her notice.

As she studied the map, a little laugh escaped her. One could take the road over Sinner's Prayer Pass to pay a visit to Heartache Falls before taking a header off nearby Lover's Leap to go splat in a town called Eternity Springs. Which had a resort called Angel's Rest.

"Sounds like my kind of place," she murmured. Taking it as a sign from above, she purchased the map, plotted a digital route on her phone, and returned to the highway. She was a little over ten hours away. If she drove through the night, she'd be there for the dawn.

Eternity Springs. It would be her safe space as she battled the demons waiting to pounce.

By the time she found her way over Sinner's Prayer Pass, she recognized that she should have picked someplace closer. Exhaustion tugged at her. She'd slept maybe four hours out of the last forty-eight. With any luck, she'd find her safe spot in Eternity Springs and sleep through this entire cursed day.

It was still dark when she pulled off the road onto a scenic overlook. Below, pinpoints of glow from streetlights and signs added some illumination. For the most part, the valley remained cast in shadow. Hannah reached for the tourist map and reviewed the landmarks. Almost there, thank goodness. But where to go once she arrived?

Hummingbird Lake. She should go to Hummingbird Lake.

Hannah had a complicated relationship with lakes. She was drawn to them, found comfort from them. She could stand at the shore and not feel so alone. At the same time, she loved nothing better than to throw rocks and rage at them.

The idea of Hummingbird Lake felt right. She'd go there. Decision made, she pulled back onto the road and began the descent into the valley via a series of switchbacks down the mountain. Hummingbird Lake. The name rolled off her tongue. She couldn't wait to see it once daylight broke. Hummingbird Lake drew her. She'd find a place to sit beside its shore and fight her way through today.

It might have happened, too, had not the next switchback revealed a scene right out of her nightmares. Strobing light bars. *BLUE WHITE RED. BLUE WHITE RED. BLUE WHITE RED.*

Hannah slammed on her brakes. Her grip tightened around the steering wheel. Her breath came in shallow pants.

Rap. Rap. Rap. Hannah all but jumped from her skin. *Rap. Rap. Rap.* "Ma'am?"

The window. A man was tapping on her window with a flashlight.

The deep voice continued, "Would you lower your window, please, ma'am?"

A badge. He wore a badge.

A little moan escaped her. She started rocking back and forth, back and forth, as she melted into the memories. BLUE WHITE RED. BLUE WHITE RED. *Screaming. Someone is screaming. But it's quiet. Too quiet. Deadly silent.*

White light shone at her face. "Ma'am, I'm Sheriff Zach Turner. Are you all right? You don't look well. Let me help you. Will you step out of the car, please?"

Her gaze locked on thick brown hair and kind blue eyes and the badge he held up to her window. One of Zoe's doctors had been named Zach. He'd been good. Caring and kind.

Hannah lifted her hand from the steering wheel and buzzed down the window. "I'm sorry, sir. I was a little blinded by the lights. There's an accident?"

"We have a rockslide up ahead." He shined his light around the interior of her car and asked, "Are you all right, ma'am? Would you step out of the car, please?"

He probably thinks I'm high on something. "Certainly."

"I'll need your license and registration too."

Keeping her gaze turned away from the flashing emergency lights, she removed her license from her wallet and registration from the glove box, then opened the door and stepped out into the chilly night air. She handed him the cards, saying, "I haven't been drinking, Officer. I'm not impaired. I'm just tired, although this cold air has shaken off the cobwebs. Do you want me to do a field sobriety test?"

Without waiting for his response, she lifted one foot off the ground and balanced. Muscle memory from years of yoga classes doing the work once again. "Want me to do the walk and turn?" she asked half a minute later.

He gave her a grin and tipped his hat. "Not necessary. Just doing my job, ma'am. Now, let's see how I can assist you. Where are you headed?"

"Eternity Springs."

He nodded. "You're in luck. It'll be hours before we get this road cleared, but one of our landowners has opened up his private road. We can get you to town without too much of a detour. No more than half an hour."

"Good."

"We have a map." He picked a clipboard up off the ground and slipped a square piece of paper from beneath the clip. Handing it to her, he said, "It's a good road, well marked, follow the signs to Eagle's Way. From there, he has a series of flashing arrows, state-of-the-art electronic signs that point your way to Eternity Springs. It'll take you around the south end of the valley, and you can enter town from the west side. The speed limit is thirty-five, but I'll ask you to take the curves slower than that. It's a dark road." He gave her a boyish smile and added, "Frankly, I don't have the manpower for another accident tonight."

"Thank you." Hannah climbed back into her car.

The sheriff shut the door for her, then leaned down to speak through the lowered window. "Welcome to Eternity Springs, Ms. Dupree. Sorry for the delay. I'll have one of my guys lead you to the private road. It's a quarter mile back."

He turned his head and gave a whistle. A moment later, a car pulled up beside her, and the driver said, "This way, ma'am."

BLUE WHITE RED. BLUE WHITE RED. BLUE WHITE RED. She was supposed to follow the car? The colored lights? Hannah didn't know if she could do it.

With any luck, he'd lead her right off the mountain.

"A quarter mile," she murmured as she rolled up the window and shifted into drive. A quarter mile, that's all. She could do this. Appropriate, in a way, with blue, white, and red leading her into the dark. Today, of all days, back into the dark.

A hysterical little laugh escaped her.

She made it, driving the quarter mile in a trancelike state, and when the lead car made a U-turn and waved her on, she kept going. She drove at a safe speed, her attention focused on the road, and yet she couldn't free herself of damned blue, white, and red flashes. It didn't help anything that after she reached Eagle's Way, the arrows the sheriff had mentioned didn't flash amber like one would expect from road signs. These flashed white.

Hannah's mind filled in the red and the blue.

Finally, the private road intersected a state road. She slowed to a stop and checked the map the sheriff had given her. A right turn would take her to Eternity Springs. Left led to Lover's Leap.

She laughed aloud. Reaching into the backpack lying on the passenger seat, she felt around inside it for the tourist map. How did it go? Sinner's Prayer Pass, then Heartache Falls. Lover's Leap and . . . splat . . . Angel's Rest. Her safe space.

Hannah turned left. A few minutes later, she spied the sign for Lover's Leap, where she turned into the parking area and parked her car. She once again perused the tourist map, decided that a visit to Heartache Falls would be redundant, then googled the time for sunrise. Eighteen minutes. Was this timing or what?

She reached for a black fleece jacket in her backseat and pulled it on, and then grabbed her backpack and stepped outside. She walked to the picnic bench that her headlights had illuminated, sat on the table, and waited for dawn.

"Get this party started," she said toward the eastern sky. Get it started, so she could get it behind her.

Now that she'd reached her spot, the energy that had fueled her trek across Colorado and masked her exhaustion began to seep away, leaving her weary to the bone. Weariness, in turn, weakened her defenses.

Despair wrapped around her like a shroud of ice. Was this the moment? Would she finally be able to cry?

Her gaze was locked on flashing lights across the valley. *BLUE WHITE RED. BLUE WHITE RED. BLUE WHITE RED.* It hypnotized her and carried her away into the past.

Lost in memory and misery, she missed the sunrise. She didn't see if the sky turned golden or pink or purple, but that was nothing new. Hannah hadn't truly seen color for years now. Her world was fuzzy fizzles of black and gray, like the screen on her late great-grandmother's black-and-white TV.

When she came back to the moment, the sun was well above the eastern mountaintop. She could see that a four-foot-high rock wall provided a barrier between the picnic area and the rock that jutted out into space. It did look a little bit like a diving board, she decided. The tourist map had it right. Lover's Leap. Now that the sun was up, Hannah could see how far below the valley floor lay. A long fall away.

She wondered if there was a story behind the name. Lover's Leap was a beautiful spot, peaceful and serene. It was the kind of place that made a woman feel small and insignificant. Her kind of place.

Small. Insignificant.

Lost. Lonely. Hurting.

Tired. Oh, so tired. Weary to the bone.

Maybe the time had come to try the next painkiller in the cabinet. The big one. The final one. Perhaps that's why she'd noticed the tourist map. She'd run through all the ordinary painkillers. Booze and pills had numbed the pain for a time, but they certainly didn't cure it.

Was she ready for permanent? Finally? She'd considered it off and on for the past three years. Three years ago, today. The anniversary. Hence her need for a safe space.

Hannah stepped over the wall.

Her gaze wandered over the snowcapped mountains that ringed the valley before dropping to the town below where Victorian two-stories and cottages lined four wide avenues and a dozen or so cross streets. She spied numerous church spires, a sprawling school, and a large park complete with baseball diamonds and an elaborate playground. A handful of brick buildings lined one of the avenues forming what she surmised to be "downtown." On the far side of the creek bordering the eastern edge of town sat a large, gingerbread-bedecked mansion surrounded by newer structures. Angel's Rest, according to the map.

The word that came to mind describing this little mountain town was *quaint*. "Eternity Springs," she murmured, testing the name. It did roll off the tongue, didn't it? "Angel's Rest at Eternity Springs."

Hannah took a step closer to the edge. For the past three years, she'd been free to go anywhere, do anything, and be anyone. She'd bounced around from one place to another like a pinball off a bumper, not seeking, but fleeing. All she'd really wanted was to end the hurt. How else to explain some of the self-destructive choices she'd made?

Painkillers. Lover's Leap. Angel's Rest. It was tempting. Oh, so tempting. Hannah needed a safe space away from the pain. A place to finally rest. She took another step forward.

Vroom. Vroom. Vroom. Vroom. The sound of the motorcycle racing toward her froze Hannah in her tracks.

Boone was half a mountain away when he saw the woman step over the stone barrier wall at Lover's Leap. "Foolish tourists," he muttered and gave his Ducati the gas, increasing his speed. He had enough balls in the air this morning. He really didn't want to deal with a careless hiker falling off the mountain to her death.

It had been an eventful few days. Friday morning, he'd spent two hours on the phone with various officials and decision makers in Fort Worth and making arrangements for a charter flight to Austin. His cousin had picked him up at the airport, and they'd driven to the property they owned outside Redemption, Texas.

Hiking and camping for two and a half days had been a good decision. He'd gone into Enchanted Canyon toting a pack and a ton of old ghosts. He'd come out of it

Sunday afternoon with his decision made, and many of those ghosts laid to rest.

Boone had flown back to Colorado last night, landing just before sunset at the private airstrip that Mac Timberlake shared with Jack Davenport in the mountains above Eternity Springs. Mac had met the plane, and he'd invited Boone to dinner at his home near Heartache Falls.

Boone might be a fool, but he wasn't an idiot. No sane man passed up Ali Timberlake's pasta alla carbonara. However, on the heels of the carb-laden meal, exhaustion had hit him like a cement truck. Rather than attempt the mountain roads in that condition, he'd accepted the Timberlakes' invitation to spend the night.

Boone had woken just before dawn to a pair of big brown eyes and a sloppy, slobbery kiss. The female bestowing her favors was a droopy-eared, red Irish setter named Beauty.

Boone didn't mind the dog's friendly greeting. He'd long thought Beauty was one of the best dogs he'd ever encountered, so when Mac announced that she was expecting a litter of puppies, Boone had begged to be on the list of adopters. The four pups were six weeks old this week. Boone had chosen a male dog and planned to take him home next week after all the wedding guests cleared out. He'd told Mac he'd take the dog next Wednesday.

This morning, he'd put that off. He was going to Fort Worth to pick up his new son that Wednesday.

Whoa. The weight of the decision settled on Boone's chest like a boulder.

Be a light. Celeste's advice from Thursday night had reverberated through his mind off and on all weekend, and it continued to do so as he descended the mountain this morning.

Be a light. He'd been exploring a cave in Enchanted Canyon when he'd finally had enough clarity of thought to realize that she'd told him something important. Something profound. Celeste Blessing had given him a road map on how to finally earn his official Angel's Rest blazon.

Soon after moving to Eternity Springs and having declared it the place where broken hearts come to heal, Celeste had started the tradition of awarding the angel wing pendant to those who had "accepted love's healing grace." Almost all of Boone's friends in town had earned theirs, and frankly, he was envious.

Damn, but he wanted his wings.

He wanted what they represented — a

whole, healthy, healed heart able to love once again.

Until now, his attempts to find love again had proved unsuccessful. He'd begun to fear it simply wasn't in the cards for him. Then Thursday night, he'd told Celeste about the baby, and she'd told him to be a light.

The baby. Be a light. Okay, the two really weren't difficult to connect once he'd cleared the cobwebs from his brain. Being a light to this baby was how his heart would finally heal.

So Boone needed to be a light to . . . whom? What was he going to name this child? He really needed a name for the little guy.

Aware that he was coming up on the turnout to Lover's Leap, he recalled the careless tourist. He really, really hoped that whoever traveled with her had convinced her to stay away from the edge.

Probably wouldn't hurt to check. He could call the tourists' attention to the warning signs and mention how a moment of carelessness last summer had tragically cost a hiker his life. Who knows, that bit of good work might be a notch for his "Be a light" meter.

Moments later, he spied a car parked at

the Lover's Leap pull-off. He parked his Ducati beside it and climbed off his bike.

That's when he got his first good look at the woman and realized he'd been wrong about her being a careless tourist. Boone recognized despair and desperation. He'd seen it in witnesses. He'd seen it in the courtroom. He'd seen it in his own wife's expression.

He saw it now in this woman's big luminous violet eyes. Despair, desperation, and brittle hopelessness.

This was no careless hiker.

This woman was a jumper.

CHAPTER THREE

As the motorcycle approached, Hannah stepped back from the edge of the cliff, took a seat atop the stone wall, and tried to look like a regular tourist. With any luck, the rider would blast on past.

As to be expected, she had no luck. The motorcycle pulled off the road and into the Lover's Leap parking area.

Suddenly, Hannah became aware of her isolation. This was the first vehicle she'd seen on this road this morning. Nonchalantly, she shifted her legs back over the wall, rose, and reached for the backpack she'd left lying on the ground. Experience had taught her to keep her gun accessible. Harming herself was one thing. Someone else doing harm was another matter entirely.

The motorcycle was a Ducati, the figure a man. He wore faded jeans, scuffed cowboy boots, and a black leather jacket. Hannah unzipped her backpack and slipped her hand inside as he climbed off the bike and removed his helmet. He was tall, well over six feet, and model-handsome. Dark hair, chiseled cheekbones, a nose with a small bump that suggested a break at some point. Intense silver-gray eyes paused on her briefly before sliding on toward the view of the valley below.

He didn't look like a killer. Neither had Andrew.

Hannah gripped her 9mm.

The guy only murmured and nodded her way as he strode past her to step over the wall the way she had a few minutes earlier. Whoa. Hope this guy didn't have the same idea she had. *Hey, I got here first.*

She watched him move toward the edge without hesitation. Nervous, she called out, "Mister? Aren't you getting a little close to the edge?"

He ignored her. Hannah tried again. "Hello! Mister? Please don't go any closer to the edge."

He finally looked around. He stood directly between Hannah and the drop-off. "I'm sorry. Are you talking to me?"

"Well, yes. It's just the two of us here."

"Oh." He glanced around, then gave her a sheepish smile. "Sorry. I'm preoccupied."

"Would you please step away from the

41

edge? You're scaring me." He was maybe two of his long-legged steps away from a fall. "You're not planning to jump, are you?"

"Jump?" His brows arched in surprise. "Why would you think that? Do I look suicidal?"

"I don't know. Does suicidal have a look?"

His silver-gray eyes pinned her. "Sometimes, yes, it does."

Whoa. Hannah blinked. He sounded like he spoke from experience.

"The trouble is that many times, it's hard as hell to spot," he continued. "That's a sad thing, because the destruction that suicide leaves in its wake for families and friends is horrific and immense. I don't care how bad things are, suicide is not a solution. It's never a solution."

"Not everybody has a family." Hannah felt compelled to defend herself.

"Doesn't matter. Suicides touch people they never know. Believe me. I have some experience with this."

Bingo. Hannah frowned in disgust. "So if you're not trying to kill yourself, then you must be stupid."

"Excuse me?"

"Why else are you standing so close to the diving board?"

"What diving board?"

She let go of her gun and felt around inside her backpack for the tourist map. She pulled it out and waved it toward his face. Suddenly, he grinned, and the force of it had Hannah swaying backward. This guy wasn't just run-of-the-mill handsome. He was hot. The kind of guy that stopped you in your tracks hot. Mesmerizing eyes that glimmered with both intelligence and sincere gentleness that gave her chest a tight tug. She hadn't noticed a man as a *man* in a million years, but she couldn't help but notice this one.

"You have my map," he said, striding toward her.

Her gaze landed on his ringless left hand for a millisecond. "Your map?"

"Well, the chamber's map. The Eternity Springs Chamber of Commerce had it produced. I'm president this year." He stuck out his hand. "Boone McBride. Welcome to Eternity Springs."

She accepted his handshake. "Hannah Dupree."

"Nice to meet you, Ms. Dupree. Mind if I ask where you picked up the map?" She told him, and he nodded. "The state's official welcome centers are awesome. If I can answer any questions you have about Eternity Springs or the area, don't hesitate to ask."

"Thank you."

He stepped back toward the edge, then glanced at her over his shoulder and gave his head a jerk. "Come look. This is the best view you'll find. You can see the entire valley and all of the lake from here. As long as you're not careless, it's plenty safe to stand here."

She hesitated. He absolutely could be a murderer ready to take advantage of the isolation to push her off the mountain. *Just because he's drop-dead gorgeous doesn't mean that he can't be a serial killer. Ted Bundy, anyone?*

Nevertheless, she stepped up beside him. He pointed south.

Hannah's breath caught. Sunlight glittered like diamonds on the surface of a sapphire lake shaped like a kidney bean and snuggled at the southern end of the valley. "Hummingbird Lake. The name rolls off the tongue, doesn't it? It's pretty."

"It's my happy place," Boone observed.

"The lake?"

"The lake, the town, the whole area. I have a friend who refers to it as a little piece of heaven in the Colorado Rockies. I can't argue with her. When I came here five years

44

ago, I was beaten and battered and close to being broken. Eternity Springs healed me."

He sat cross-legged and gestured for her to join him. Again, Hannah hesitated. Again, she acquiesced to his request. She wasn't certain why. She did not strike up conversations with strangers. Beyond placing an order with a server in a restaurant or the minimal exchange with the reception desk clerk when she checked into a hotel, she did not have conversations, period.

Maybe that was exactly why she sat down beside him. Maybe part of Hannah yearned to have some contact with another human after being so solitary for so long.

"So what brings you up to Lover's Leap so early on a summer morning?" he asked. "Did you come up to watch the sunrise?"

She parsed her words. "I was here for the sunrise from here this morning."

"This is one of the best spots around to watch the sun come up. For sunsets, I'll recommend a porch rocker at Cavanaugh House."

"Where is that?"

He pointed toward the town. "There. On the far side of the creek. The big yellow mansion snuggled up against the mountain. See?"

Hannah believed he pointed toward a

large Victorian house on the far side of the creek that ran through town. "I noticed that on your map. I thought it was called something else, though."

"It's Angel's Rest on the map. Angel's Rest Healing Center and Spa. My friend Celeste Blessing bought the property and has built a fabulous business that brought the town back from the brink of bankruptcy. She's restored Cavanaugh House, the home of one of the original founders of the town. Now it serves as the main building of what is a sprawling luxury resort. Angel's Rest is a great place to stay if you're looking."

"I actually called there yesterday and tried to rent a room. They're booked up."

"Summertime." He winced and nodded. "Plus, we have a big destination wedding here this weekend. A whole bunch of folks are coming in for it from out of town. If you don't already have a reservation, finding a room might be tough."

She shrugged. "Doesn't matter. I'll just keep moving."

"You're traveling alone?"

This time rather than hesitate, she speared him with a look. "Is that a question an intelligent woman would answer? Tell me you're not on the top ten list of charming serial killers."

"So you think I'm charming?" His grin went a bit wicked.

"I think I'm probably acting too trusting." His line about *beaten and battered and close to being broken* had lured her as sure as wisteria blossoms do bees.

"You have a point," he agreed. "Okay, more about me in an effort to put your fears to rest." He leaned up on his hip and pulled his wallet from the pocket of his jeans. He flipped it open and fished inside. "Here's my card."

Hannah accepted the plain white card with black printing and read it. TIMBER-LAKE AND MCBRIDE, ATTORNEYS AT LAW.

"I've heard all the lawyer jokes, so spare me."

Quietly, she said, "Actually, I have a lot of respect for attorneys."

"Do you, now?" he said with approval in his tone. "That's a pleasant change from what I usually hear. Yes, I'm a lawyer, and before moving to Eternity Springs, I was a district attorney in Fort Worth, so I'm on the white-hat side of things when it comes to killers. Now, however, the bulk of my practice consists of mostly of drafting and reviewing contracts. I'm single, love a good rib eye, fast cars, college football, and bespoke suits. I just moved into a new home on Hummingbird Lake, and I'll be standing as co-best-man along with my cousin Tucker at our cousin Jackson's wedding on Saturday. That's the destination wedding I mentioned. They all still live in Texas."

Trying to process all the information, Hannah said the first thing that popped into her mind. "So what brings you to Lover's Leap so early this morning?"

"Well, you want the long answer or the short?"

"Either is fine."

"Let's go with short. I have a serious life decision pending, and this is a good, contemplative place. I need to pick a name."

"A name for what?"

"I'm adopting . . ." He hesitated a moment before completing his sentence. "A dog. A pup."

"Boy or girl?"

"Boy."

"What breed?"

"Irish setter. A friend of mine's dog recently had a litter. I need to come up with a name for him. I'm really not sure where to start. I've never done this before."

"He'll be your first pet?"

Boone shook his head. "The first name I picked all on my own. It's a lot of responsibility. If I get it wrong, it'll follow him the

48

rest of his life."

"Ah. I see." Part of her wondered if he was putting her on, but she didn't think so. He seemed sincere, and his concern for his pet was endearing. "I'm an animal lover myself, but isn't it possible you're giving this decision too much weight? You could name your dog something as inappropriate as, say, Lamp. He'd go through his life happily answering to it."

"I don't know."

Hannah warmed to her subject. It was a nice distraction from her reality. "He's a dog. As long as you give him care and attention and biscuits, he'll be happy. *You'll* have to live with the choice, but he won't care. It's not like he's going to walk up to you one day and say, *Dad. Seriously? Lamp? What were you thinking?*"

Boone licked his lips. "But what if he could do exactly that? Say the little guy will one day grow up and come to me and ask why I chose the name I chose. I want to be able to support my decision."

"This is a very strange conversation to have with an attorney."

"Just go with me here, would you? I figure there's a reason your path and mine crossed this morning — that's the way things work in Eternity Springs — and I need to bounce

49

this off someone. Where do I start?"

"Maybe you should google popular names for male dogs?"

Boone scowled. "I don't want to tell him that I picked his name off Google."

Hannah did something then that she never believed she'd do today, of all days. She laughed. Suddenly, for reasons beyond her understanding, she wanted to help Boone McBride, Esquire, pick out the perfect name for his dog.

Damn, but the sparkle in those fabulous eyes combined with a smile on her face transformed fragile loveliness into fascinating beauty, the kind that made him think of classic movie stars in their heyday. Liz Taylor eyes. Katharine Hepburn burnished tresses. The patrician nose, high cheekbones, and full lips of Loretta Young.

The hourglass figure of Brigitte Bardot.

Despite all that gorgeousness, she could use some color. Her complexion was pale, not fair-skinned pale, but unhealthy pale. She wore black — black jeans, a plain black T-shirt. A black backpack sat at her feet.

She gave him an encouraging smile. "Maybe start here. Do you want a name that has meaning, or do you care more about how it sounds?"

Boone dragged his hand down his jawline rough with a three-day beard while he hauled his attention away from her charms. He wasn't sure exactly how he'd let things get so far off track. He wasn't looking for a name for his dog. He was pretty sure he wanted to call the pup Lucky. What he needed was a name for his son, but he wasn't ready to roll that out to Hannah Dupree.

The woman had scared the living daylights out of him. He'd acted instinctively to put himself between her and the cliff's edge, but had he misjudged her intentions?

Maybe. Maybe he'd overreacted. That was certainly possible. He admitted to being oversensitive where suicide was concerned. However, the fact that she had brought it up suggested that the subject had been on her mind. So he'd done a little two-step atop his soapbox and then changed the topic, gripped by a sense that he was meant to be here in this place, at this time, for this woman.

Be a light.

Maybe he needed to burn his candle on two different ends — the baby and this redheaded beauty. Or perhaps this was just a start, and he needed to stock up on batteries. He should have questioned Celeste

51

about the whole light thing. Although knowing her, she'd said all she'd intended to say about it.

Be a light.

He looked into those startling eyes. Curiosity had replaced the anguish of moments before. He wanted to fall into those eyes. "Boone?"

"Hmm?" What had she asked?

"Names. Meaning or sound?"

Oh, yeah. Names. A name for his son. He pursed his lips and considered a moment before saying, "Meaning matters. Not the meaning of the name per se, but meaning to me. Sound is important too, though. I want a strong name. It doesn't need to *mean* strength, but it needs to be strong."

"Like Rocky or Rambo or Thor?"

Rambo McBride? "Too movie-character-ish. But I think something short. One or two syllables."

"Okay, then, there's your start. What things have meaning to you?"

"Family," he said, without hesitation. "He's joining my family. Becoming my family. I should give him some sort of family name."

She glanced away at that point, but not before her eyes turned luminous with moisture. She cleared her throat, then said,

"There you go. That's an excellent start. See, wasn't that easy?"

What's the matter, Hollywood? "Not really. I have a big family with lots of children and pets and opinions. I love them. Don't get me wrong, but they will second-guess the living daylights out of this decision."

"Over what you name your dog?"

No, his family would second-guess his decision to adopt the Safe Haven baby. Come to think of it, they'd have an opinion about what he named his dog too.

Boone winced and rubbed the back of his neck. "It's complicated. Also, I tend to define family in a big-tent way. I have my nuclear family — my parents and two sisters — but I also have two cousins who are as close as brothers to me and some more distant cousins to whom I've become close since moving to Colorado. Add in the friends who are like family — I'm busting at the seams with 'em."

"It sounds lovely," she observed, a wistful note in her voice.

"I'm a lucky man." A lucky man who was looking at a very lonely woman, he surmised. The morning sunlight made the fire in her hair glisten.

He'd opened his mouth to ask her where she was from when she dusted off her hands and asked, "Okay, then, what sort of strong, short, non-movie-character names say 'family' to you?"

Okay, we'll just roll with this. He stared out at the vista spread before him, looking inward as he scooped up a handful of pebbles and began tossing them out into nothing. The idea of choosing his new son's name here, this morning, felt right under these circumstances. Almost like a coming full circle. Having come to peace with his past during his trip to Enchanted Canyon, he could spend a little time with Ms. Hannah Dupree and attempt to share the wealth.

She looked tired, but not as desperate as before. However, one thing he was damned sure certain about: He would not leave her alone at Lover's Leap. He didn't care if he had to sit here until dark.

But back to the discussion at hand. "I think the name needs to be something Texan."

"I don't know much about Texas. I've never been there, but I do know something about their sports teams. Ranger is a good dog's name. I don't know if that has any family connotation to you, however."

Hmm. Ranger. Maybe that *was* a better name than Lucky. For his dog. Not his boy.

He gave Hannah a considering look. "Never been to Texas?"

"Nope."

"You should pay us a visit. Lots to see and do in Texas. Our state motto is 'Friendship.'"

"You're a friendly guy," she observed with a wry smile.

"I am. And you're right. Ranger is a good name for a dog, only if I chose to name my dog Ranger, it'd be in honor of the law enforcement Texas Rangers as opposed to the baseball team. The baseball team broke my heart in the 2011 World Series, and they haven't made up for it yet. Also, the McBride family has some Texas Rangers in their past — rangers, not ballplayers. That's a definite possibility."

For the puppy, not the boy. Though he still liked Lucky.

However, her suggestion had sent his thoughts in a direction that offered interesting possibilities. "My McBride ancestors came to Texas from South Carolina in the 1870s. The first was a widower with three young daughters. His journals say he came with little more than lint in his pocket. He won a saloon in a card game, renamed it The End of the Line, married a dressmaker, and had a passel of boys. His name was

Trace. Trace McBride."

The name had been passed down through the generations in the family, but it had not been used recently. There was not a Trace McBride alive today.

"I like the name Trace," Hannah said, brushing pebbles into a little pile in the space between them.

"Me too. It's a definite possibility. Thank you for asking the right questions to help me think of it." He threw another rock, then figured he wouldn't get a better segue. "I've yammered on about my family history. Why don't you share something about yours?"

She closed up like a chickweed flower right before a rain.

Well, there's your sign. Boone figured he had two choices, retreat or charge ahead. He'd always been a hard-charging type of guy. He set his hand atop hers. "Where are you from, Hannah?"

She stared down at their hands. She didn't jerk hers away, but he didn't think she was going to respond to his question. He gave her hand a squeeze.

Her voice came soft and heavy with emotion. "New England."

He wanted to cheer. *Atta girl, Hannah.*

"I thought I heard a hint of the Northeast in your voice. Just a hint. Boston is one of my favorite cities to visit. Love watching baseball at Fenway."

She nodded. "My dad and I attended at least one game together every year until he passed in 2010. I haven't been to a game since then."

"I'm sorry." Had Boone not been a virtual stranger, he'd have given her a hug. "You're a long way from home, Hannah."

The smile that flittered on her face was so full of pain that he winced. She repeated, "*A long way from home.* No. A lifetime."

A lifetime away from home. That could be interpreted in a number of different ways. Boone seldom felt at a loss for words, but right now he was fumbling. Should he gently prod? Boldly ask? Sit and say nothing as a way of offering silent comfort?

Hard-charging guys didn't sit and say nothing.

"I may be reading this all wrong, but I really don't think so. You look like you have the weight of the world on your shoulders, Hannah. Just so you know, I've been there. Lived it. Crawled my way from one day to the next just to survive. I couldn't talk about it to the people who loved me. I wouldn't talk about it. I shut down every attempt anyone made to prod me into opening up."

Hannah said, "So can you recommend a

57

good restaurant in Eternity Springs?"

Boone McBride was nothing if not persistent, so he ignored her attempt to shut him down. "The thing is, I found that it did help to talk about it as long as the person with whom I was speaking didn't have a dog in the hunt."

"You do like dogs, don't you, Mr. McBride?"

He squeezed her hand again. "What brings you to Lover's Leap today, Hannah?"

She closed her eyes and seemed to fold in on herself. Boone held his breath.

Finally, she exhaled sharply. "Today is the anniversary of . . ." Her voice trailed off; half a minute ticked by. She cleared her throat. "Well, leave it at an anniversary. It's a difficult time, and it's possible that I could act irrationally. I haven't slept."

A chill slithered down his spine. She might have jumped. He narrowed his eyes and studied her. "Since when?"

She shrugged. "I had a hotel room, um, Saturday night. Dozed some in my car."

"I won't scold," Boone said. "Been there, done that, have the good ol' T-shirt. Tell me why you came to Lover's Leap?"

She slipped her hand out from beneath his and began tossing pebbles like he'd done moments before. "Your tourist map. Like I

58

said, I had to be somewhere today. There was a detour on the main highway due to a rockslide last night, and I ended up here just as the sun came up."

He put this together with what she'd told him earlier and said, "So you drove through the night? And the night before that?"

"Running away from myself." She shrugged. "Like I said, I catnapped. I did make use of my membership privileges at a national chain of fitness clubs to shower and change clothes when I went through Colorado Springs. I may be crazy, but at least I'm clean."

"And exhausted." When her only response was a weary smile, he added, "I have a suggestion. I haven't had breakfast. How about you join me for a meal? I happen to know a place right on the lake that serves awesome omelets. It's quiet and peaceful. If after breakfast, you wanted to sit in the sunshine and nap, no one would bother you."

"Boone, thank you. That's very nice, but I couldn't."

"Why not?"

She opened her mouth, then shut it.

Halfway there, he decided. "Look, you'll be doing me a favor."

"How so?"

"It's difficult to explain, and it may sound

a little strange because you haven't met our Celeste. Are you a spiritual person, Hannah?"

"I believe in hell," she said flatly.

The DON'T GO THERE signs flashed so brightly that they all but blinded him. Even hard-charging men knew when to slow down, so Boone proceeded carefully. "I do too. I also believe in kismet, UFOs, and guardian angels."

"UFOs?"

"I believe there's a lot going on in the universe that is beyond humankind's knowledge or understanding. I'm okay with that. I also believe that there's a reason you and I crossed paths today, and I'm not going to ignore it. Today is a dark day for you. I can be your light and help you to see your way through it. I *need* to be a light for you today."

"If this is a pickup line, I give you points for originality."

"No pickup. A lift-up. A friendly hand to hold when you need to feel not so alone." Boone rose to his feet and extended his hand toward her. "You are safe with me, Hannah. Let me be your safe space today."

CHAPTER FOUR

Hannah was exhausted. It was easier to go along with Boone McBride than to try to resist him. When he asked for her car keys, she handed them over. Honestly, if she'd read him wrong and the man actually was a Ted Bundy wannabe, well, she'd been thinking about making the Lover's Leap splat, hadn't she?

He chatted about his friends and neighbors on the drive down the mountain into town, though she only partially listened to what he was saying. Hannah felt numb, and she was content in her numbness.

"Heavenscents is the handcrafted soap shop owned by Savannah Turner," Boone said, pointing out a shop as they passed. "Whimsies Gift Shop is a great place to find some wonderfully unique items made in Colorado. If you're into art, we have Vistas Art Gallery, and the famous glass artist Cicero has a studio here too."

Art. Hannah almost laughed. What need does a woman who lives out of her car have for art?

Her interest did pick up when their route took them to the shore of the lake. Hummingbird Lake was a deep sapphire blue and, at the moment, a little choppy from the breeze sweeping through the valley from the north. Half a dozen sailboats with bright-colored sails zipped across the surface of the water. A flotilla of canoes filled with children wearing orange life jackets over yellow T-shirts paddled their way along the lake's shoreline.

Hannah leaned forward, her heart reaching out toward the lake. It was so beautiful. She'd been headed here this morning before the road closure changed her route. "Is swimming allowed in the lake?"

"It's allowed, but most people in town claim you have to be a little crazy to do it, even in the middle of summer. The water is icy."

She pulled her gaze away from the water long enough to give him a sidelong glance. "Something tells me you go swimming in Hummingbird Lake."

He gave a charming, crooked smile. "Most summer mornings, yes, I do. I'm trying to cut back on caffeine. Diving into Hummingbird Lake will sure wake a fella up."

"Hmm . . ." she murmured, turning her attention back to the lake. She spied half a dozen boat docks, twice that number of fishing piers. Most of the shoreline remained undeveloped. She wondered if any of it was public land. She remembered seeing a national forest listed on the tourist map, but she didn't recall where. Not that the map had been anything close to scale.

"Here we are."

Boone turned into a driveway that led to a sprawling, two-story wood-and-stone house built in the traditional mountain-log-cabin style. It was obviously a private home. "This isn't a restaurant."

"I promised you awesome omelets on the lake. I happen to have a wicked way with eggs and a fully stocked fridge because I have family showing up here beginning tomorrow for that wedding I mentioned."

Another time, she might have protested or argued with him. Right now, she didn't have either the energy or the desire to do more than ride along. In fact, she wasn't sure she had the power to get out of the car.

"I'll have you know that you are my first official guest. I moved into the house last week." He kept up a constant patter about design choices and his contractor and his cousins and his mother. "I know you're probably wondering why a single guy built a house this big. You have to understand that we're wall-to-wall Texans from Memorial Day to Labor Day. Our motels and inns and bed-and-breakfasts are booked with waiting lists months in advance. I can't tell you how many times friends or relatives call from the front porch of hell to tell me they've had a sudden hankering to see me."

"The front porch of hell?"

"Texas in the summertime."

She smiled. She actually smiled!

"We designed the house to sleep a lot of people, but still be functional for me to live in during the off season. Which, to be honest, gets shorter every year. Eternity Springs has been discovered. The length of our tourist season has just about doubled in the five years since I've been living here."

He stopped the car at the center of a circular drive. Before Hannah had quite managed to stir herself to move, he'd walked around to the passenger door and opened it like an old-fashioned mannerly man. When was the last time a man had opened a car door for her? High school, maybe? Andrew never did that.

Although maybe the rules had changed, and men weren't supposed to open doors

for women any longer. Female empower-
ment and all. That was sort of a gray area
to Hannah these days.

But then everything was a gray area,
wasn't it? Gray or black, anyway.

"Hannah?" he asked, jerking her attention
back to him.

His hand was extended toward her. She
took it and allowed him to assist her from
the car. He kept his hold on her hand as he
escorted her up the wooden staircase that
led to the home's main entry. Walking
inside, she stopped abruptly. "The view!"

"Isn't it great? Best lot on the lake, in my
opinion, because I'm at the point where the
lake bends. Three-quarters of the house has
a water view."

"It's spectacular," she said. The great
room ceiling was vaulted, the walls mostly
windows. A stone fireplace stretched two
stories tall. Boone had used an earth-tone
color palette, his furnishings a pleasing mix
of traditional and midcentury styles.

"Thank you. I wanted the house to blend
modern lines with old log cabin style, and I
think my architect did a great job." He
pointed out the powder room and invited
her to make herself at home. "I suggest the
sunroom. It's through the kitchen. The two
chaises facing the lake are the best seats in

the house. You want coffee? Tea? Juice?"

"Coffee, please. Black."

Hannah admired the large kitchen as she walked toward the sunroom. A master chef would be happy working here, she decided, before her first glimpse of the sunroom wiped all else from her thoughts. "Oh."

The room was octagonal in shape, with floor-to-ceiling windows. Here earth tones gave way to — summer. Yellows and greens and pinks and blues. It made her think of an alpine meadow covered with wildflowers. A pair of chaise lounge chairs sported thick, daffodil-colored cushions and called to her. She sat and stretched out, looked to her left, and made a slow sweep to the right. From this vantage point, one could see the entire lake, snowcapped mountains rising behind, and — oh, wow, that was a bald eagle soaring over the lake. The majestic sight brought tears to her tired eyes.

Music drifted from somewhere above her, a harp and other strings playing a soothing Celtic sound. Spa music, she thought. Peaceful and relaxing.

She stared at the sapphire lake, yearning, needing, and grieving. She made another left-to-right sweep, and that's when it hit her. *There's no bridge over Hummingbird Lake.*

Silently, tearlessly, Hannah cried herself to sleep.

She dreamed of the neighborhood playground, of towheaded toddlers and strawberry-blond girls whirling on a merry-go-round wearing grass-stained britches, chubby cheeks red with exertion. And giggles. Oh, God, the giggles. Around and around and around they went. It was real and wonderful, and she wanted to stay there forever.

Inevitably, the dream began to fade. Hannah fought to follow, to dissolve into the mist, but tragically, she woke. It took a moment to recall the events of the morning and for awareness of place to return. Time, not so much. How long had she been asleep?

Long enough for Boone to cover her with a lightweight throw and place a glass of water beside her. She threw off the blanket, lifted the glass, and sipped the water as she rose and went looking for her host. The soundtrack from *Last of the Mohicans* played from a hidden sound system, and the aroma of bacon lingered in the air. Her stomach growled.

Boone wasn't in the kitchen. She didn't hear any noises to suggest where she might find him either. Hannah glanced at the digital clock's red numerals, and her eyes went wide. "Three o'clock!"

She'd slept for at least six hours.

Her ponytail had loosened during her nap, and a fistful of long auburn strands had escaped the tie. Impatiently, she tugged the band from her hair and finger-combed it as she assessed the situation.

Then her gaze snagged on the bar where a sandwich and potato chips sat on a plate beneath a domed glass lid. Beside it, she spied a note written in a firm, masculine hand.

Hannah, I had to run into town to take care of a bit of business. I won't be long. I brought your suitcase in from your car and placed it upstairs in the first guest room on the right if you want to freshen up. Please, make yourself at home. The BLT is to tide you over until dinner. I'm planning on steak unless you don't eat beef. We didn't cover that in our conversation. I have pasta as a backup. Hope you enjoyed your nap!

Boone

"He brought in my suitcase?" she murmured. The man was nothing if not assuming.

Her stomach growled again, and she eyed

the sandwich. She did love BLTs. When was the last time she'd eaten? She lifted the dome from the lunch and took a seat at the bar facing the lake.

The water and mountains beyond looked different in the afternoon light. Just as beautiful, but softer, and even more peaceful. The sailboats were gone, as were the canoes. Hannah wanted — actually, she needed — to walk down the gently sloping lawn and sit on the end of the fishing pier. First, however, she would take advantage of Boone's absence to grab a shower. She didn't feel as weird about getting naked in a stranger's house if the stranger wasn't around.

The sandwich was delicious, and the shower, divine. Hannah walked down to the fishing pier feeling better than she could have imagined when the sun rose this morning. She sat cross-legged at the end of the pier, stared at the blue water, and allowed the memories to wash over her.

Boone was glad to see the sandwich gone when he arrived home. He had not liked the idea of leaving Hannah alone, but he'd felt voyeuristic hanging around and watching her sleep. She'd been sound asleep, and he'd figured he'd be gone an hour at the most. He climbed the stairs and listened for the sound of the shower, but all was silent. The house felt empty.

His stomach took a nervous roll. Had he misjudged the situation? As he descended the stairs, his gaze went toward the windows. He breathed a sigh of relief when he spied her sitting on the pier.

Once again, uncharacteristically, Boone hesitated. He wasn't at all sure what was the best approach to take with the woman at this point. Should he leave her be? Should he join her and ply her with patter? Should he at least check on her and reassure himself that she wasn't about to take a header off the pier?

No, he was confident that this particular crisis had passed. Otherwise, he wouldn't have left Hannah for even a short time.

The ringing of his cell phone interrupted his musings. He identified his cousin Tucker's ringtone. He connected the call saying, "Hey, Vegas. What's up?"

Vegas was a reference to the sweet bit of family gossip Tucker had shared during Boone's trip to Texas over the weekend. In response, Tucker made a vulgar anatomical-related suggestion, then changed the subject. "So how did it go?"

"How did what go?"

"Your trip to Fort Worth."

Ah. Well. Boone had managed to bury thoughts about his own unsettled situation while in the company of Hannah Dupree. Tucker's question brought it right back to the forefront of his mind. He reached up and rubbed the back of his neck. "I didn't go."

"Oh." There was a moment of silence as Tucker absorbed Boone's answer. "You're not taking the baby, after all?"

"I am taking him. Trace. I'm gonna name him Trace."

"Trace," Tucker repeated, approval in his tone. "Good choice. The family is due for another Trace McBride."

"That's what I thought. I talked to the foster parents and my friends at CPS, and we all decided it made more sense to wait until after Jackson's wedding to make the trip to Fort Worth. The legal stuff needed a little more time, and honestly, I was afraid that if I'd gone to visit him, I wouldn't have wanted to leave him behind. Can you imagine what the family would do if I showed up at Jackson's wedding, and my plus-one was an infant son?"

"Your mom and sisters would go berserk."

"It wouldn't be right. Jackson and Caroline are the stars of the show this weekend,

71

and I want it to be perfect for them. And to be honest, I want time alone with the baby at first. Trace and I will need to bond."

Wariness in his tone, Tucker asked, "Alone? Boone, you're not going to try to do this without help, are you? A nanny or something?"

"No, of course not. Sarah Winston — she's the social worker who has taken point position on this whole thing — recommended a nanny for me. Excellent references and experience, and she wants to move to Colorado."

"You've hired her sight unseen?" Tucker asked, his tone incredulous.

"I trust Sarah. Besides, I don't really have any options. I don't know anyone here in Eternity Springs who is in a position to step up at this particular time."

After that, the conversation turned to wedding-related issues. Throughout the discussion, Boone found his attention divided between his cousin and the woman on the pier.

Anniversaries were hell. He knew that much from firsthand experience. The first anniversary, in particular, was a great big hairy bad. He wondered if today was the first for Hannah Dupree, and just whom she mourned.

Because mourn she did. Someone, not something. Boone would bet his favorite pair of Lucchese boots on that.

In his ear, Tucker's impatient voice said, "Hey? Did I lose you?"

"Sorry. What did you say?"

"I said I won't need to bunk at your place this week. I'm going to stay at the North Forty instead."

"Want to be closer to your wife?"

"Don't say that out loud," Tucker snapped. "I swear, Boot, if you don't keep your big mouth shut, I'll shut it for you."

"Boot" was the nickname his cousins sometimes used for him and reflected back to when his father threatened to put a boot in his ass. Tucker tended to use it when he seriously meant what he was saying.

"Your secret is safe with me," Boone assured his cousin. "You're actually doing me a favor. It looks like a friend of mine might need a place to stay this week, and there's not a rental unit to be had in a hundred miles of Eternity Springs. The cabin will be perfect for her."

"Her?"

Boone decided a subject change was in order. "Did I tell you I'm getting a puppy?"

The creak of footsteps on the wood planks

clued Hannah into the fact that she was no longer alone. She glanced over her shoulder and was unsurprised to see Boone McBride approaching. He carried a cooler in one hand and a pair of fishing poles in the other. Setting the cooler down, he handed her a pole.

"I don't have a fishing license."

"Not a problem. The game warden is a friend of mine, and I prepaid for a stack of 'em to cover instances just like this. The top compartment of the cooler is a tackle box if you want to change your bait. The cooler has beer, water, soft drinks."

"A combination tackle box and cooler, hmm? That's handy."

"Indispensable." Boone opened the cooler. "I'm having a beer. What's your preference?"

"I'll stick with water, thank you."

He handed her a bottle of water, snagged a beer for himself, then motioned toward the end of the pier. "Mind if I join you?"

"Please." She scooted to one side, then with a wry twist of her lips added, "It is your fishing pier, after all."

He sat beside her and spent the next few minutes opening his beer, switching a spoon for a spinner bait, and tossing his lure into the water. Once upon a time, Hannah had enjoyed fishing, having grown up in a boating family with a father who was an avid angler. She'd always found the repetitive process of casting and reeling to be soothing and peaceful. Now, though, she couldn't bear the thought of hooking anything hidden beneath the lake's surface. A stream, okay. A lake? Not in a million years.

"Not gonna fish?" Boone asked.

"No. I'm a lucky fisherman. I'd catch something, and I'm not in the mood for fish-smell hands."

"Hey, I'm a gentleman. I'll take the fish off your hook."

She shook her head. "My father taught me better. You catch it, you free it, and you clean it."

"Ah. A man after my own heart."

Hannah smiled wistfully. "I miss him."

Boone pinned her with a sharp look. "Is your father the person you are mourning today?"

The question was switchblade-deployed in surprise and sliced deep. Hannah shrank against the pain of it, sliding her gaze away from Boone. It landed on the open tray of tackle. Spying a casting plug, she reached for it and quickly, expertly, removed the swimming bait on the end of her line and attached the plug.

She cast, reeled, cast, reeled. Cast.

Boone must have figured that she wasn't going to answer his question. He cast his line away from hers, then said, "My college roommate started dating a girl from Fort Worth during our freshman year of undergrad. His name is Joe Hart. She's Ashleigh. Ashleigh introduced me to her best friend Mary, and I fell hard. Joe and Ashleigh married the weekend after we graduated. Mary and I tied the knot the weekend after that."

Guessing his age, she figured this would have been somewhere between twelve and fifteen years ago.

"Due to Mary's medical history, we knew going into it that we wouldn't be able to have children. We also knew the adoption road could be long and full of bumps, so while I went to law school, Mary did a deep dive into adoption. We knew we'd likely have a wait on our hands if we wanted an infant, but we were young, and Mary really wanted a baby."

Hannah set her fishing pole beside her on the pier. *Why is he telling me this?* She wasn't sure she wanted to know, but neither did she want to interrupt him. She was curious now.

Boone placed his pole on their pier and set about changing his tackle as he matter-of-factly continued his story. "Twice, we brought babies home. Twice, something happened, and the adoption fell through."

"That must have been terribly hard," Hannah said.

"Ripped our hearts out." Boone sent a top-water lure flying. "By then, I had my law degree and passed the bar. I worked for a little while at Ashleigh's father's law firm in Fort Worth, but defense wasn't my calling." He gave his line a series of jerks, working the lure. "I decided I really wanted to prosecute, so I joined the DA's office. It was a much better fit. I specialized in cases involving crimes against children."

Hannah involuntarily shuddered. Boone didn't notice her reaction. He was staring off into space.

"While all this was going on, Joe and Ashleigh's marriage was showing some serious cracks. Mary and I tried to be Switzerland and remain neutral, but there were times Joe was a real jerk. I'd call him on it." Boone's lips twisted in a sadly rueful grin. "Once it went so far, we had a fistfight. Only black eye I've ever had that wasn't given to me by one of my cousins, though I did get a little bit of a shiner when my friend Devin Murphy broke my nose. That's a different story, though. Remind me to tell you about it."

Hannah wished he'd go on about the broken nose. She had a feeling she'd much rather hear that story than the one he seemed intent on telling. It made her tense.

"Anyway," he continued. "What happened next with Joe and Ashleigh . . ."

Why was he telling her all of this? Was he about to share something about a crime against a child? If so, she might have to jump into the lake and attempt to drown herself after all. Or at least push him in.

Having reeled in his line without a strike, Boone threw another cast. He reeled and pitched twice more before continuing, "It's a long story worthy of an afternoon soap opera." He frowned and cut Hannah a glance. "Are afternoon soap operas still on the air?"

"Honestly, I don't know."

He shrugged, then continued. "Without sharing the ugly details, I'll say that one lesson I learned during this ordeal was that from the outside looking in, you can't understand another couple's marriage. You shouldn't try. Joe did have a good heart, however, and in the middle of his personal crisis, he came to us with a private adoption opportunity. The teenage daughter of someone who worked for his parents was pregnant and looking for parents for her child. I knew it was risky, but Mary . . ." He shrugged. "We decided to try one more time and went all in. We met the mother. She liked us. She picked us. Mary decorated another nursery. Two weeks before the baby was due, the mother changed her mind."

"Oh, Boone."

"Yeah." He reeled in his line, then made another cast. "I threw myself into another case, and I just didn't see what was happening at home. Mary stalked the girl. The day the baby was born, my wife came home, sat down in the rocking chair in the nursery that I hadn't made time to disassemble, and took a whole bottle of sleeping pills. I worked late, and she was gone by the time I came home."

Hannah gave in to the desire to touch him. She placed her hand atop his and gave it a quick, comforting squeeze. "I'm so sorry."

"Thank you. Me too." Boone continued to reel in the line. He filled his cheeks with air, then blew out a heavy breath. "There's more to the story, but I've done all the bleeding I care to right now. The point I wanted to make is this: I understand, Hannah. I know what it's like to lose someone. I know what a bitch anniversaries can be. March twenty-first will be seven years since Mary died. What year is today for you?"

Hannah hesitated. On the heels of his intimate confession, how could she keep quiet? "Three. This is the third anniversary."

Boone nodded. "Three was a tough one. One and two, you know you're going to be a basket case. Just when you think you're progressing okay on the road toward recovery, boom, the third anniversary rolls around. The pain is fresh and new again."

Now she looked at him appraisingly. "You have a point."

"I know. That's what I want *you* to know. Every anniversary is hard, but from my experience, four truly is a little easier than three."

"Thank you. You are a nice guy, Boone McBride."

"Not much of a fisherman, though," he grumbled when his cast failed to attract a nibble once again. He secured the hook through the eye on his pole, set it aside, and rose. "I don't know about you, but I'm so hungry that my navel is rubbing against my spine. I picked up a charcuterie board in town, and it's on my kitchen table, calling to me. Do you need a little more solo time, or would you like to join me?"

Hannah smiled up at him. "I never turn down cheese."

He grinned back at her and stretched out his hand to help her up.

Just like he'd been doing all day.

CHAPTER FIVE

As Boone flipped the steaks on the grill,
curiosity was about to kill him. He wanted
to know about the tragedy that she marked
with such sorrow today. He needed to know
just whom she mourned. Exactly why he
wanted answers so bad, he couldn't say.
Ordinarily, he didn't stick his nose in other
people's business.

Well, unless they were family. Family was
fair game. That's just the way the McBrides
rolled. And maybe he'd been known to get
nosy with good friends upon occasion.

Maybe he did lead with his nose reason-
ably often.

Of course, he'd learned at the feet of a
queen. He loved his mother more than any
woman on earth, but Marquetta McBride
was the queen of mother hens. She was the
empress of mother hens. Just how she managed to keep her thumb on the pulse of her
adult children's lives from her home base in

West Texas, he had yet to discover.

This reminded him that he'd better give Celeste a heads-up about the need to keep his baby news quiet until after the wedding. He'd give her a call after dinner.

Hannah had asked for her steak medium-rare, a woman after his own heart. Judging the meat to be done, he moved the steaks from the grill to a platter and carried them inside. She'd volunteered to make the salad, so he'd invited her to make herself at home. She'd not only prepared a killer wedge complete with homemade blue cheese dressing, but also set the table.

"Hey, that looks really nice. Thank you."

"You're welcome. You have beautiful things, Boone. And fresh flowers in the house!"

"That's because my mother is coming. She has a thing for fresh flowers. This will be her first visit to my new place, and I want to impress her."

"Well, I think you have that in the bag."

They made small talk over dinner, which Boone served in the sunroom where they could watch the sun go down. He continually searched for a way to slip a question or two for her into the mix. He discovered that she too liked flowers, had worked in a retail gift shop during high school and college, and liked to crochet. She'd shut down his attempts to delve any deeper into that subject, though he was able to ferret out the fact that she'd spent much of the past year in Florida.

He talked her into sharing a piece of the cake he'd picked up at Fresh Bakery on his trip to town. Watching her take her first bite of Sarah Murphy's Midnight Magnificence chocolate cake made him want to growl. She went melty and soft, closed her eyes, purred, and licked her lips.

"That's decadent," she murmured.

"You should taste Fresh's strawberry pinwheel cookies. I could eat myself into a sugar coma with those."

"I'll have to try them before I leave town."

There. An opening. Finally. "Speaking of that, are you going to hang around our quaint little hamlet for a little while longer?"

"I don't know. Honestly, I haven't thought beyond today. My time is my own to spend as I wish. This is my first visit to Colorado, so I'd like to do a little sightseeing before I move on."

"A first-timer?" Boone rubbed his hands villainously together and waggled his eyebrows. "Oh, honey, do I have suggestions for you. Put yourself in my tour-guide hands."

"Tour guide? I thought you were a lawyer."

"I am a man of many talents. There exists a companion piece to the tourist map that lured you here. Let me get it." He rose from his seat at the kitchen table and hurried to his home office, where he grabbed a United States atlas and the tourist map of Colorado that the local chamber had developed using Eternity Springs as a center for tourism in the state.

Returning to the sunroom, he took a seat in the chair next to Hannah and handed her first the cartoon tourist map. "It's not to scale, of course, but it shows all the places you shouldn't miss seeing." He pointed out the Royal Gorge, the Black Canyon of the Gunnison. The Durango–Silverton train. The Great Sand Dunes. Mesa Verde. "And this just covers sights to see. If you add in things to do — hiking and fishing and climbing, horseback riding and white-water rafting — Eternity Springs is a great place to use as a home base. Do you consider yourself more a doer or a looker?"

"Excuse me?"

"Which appeals to you the most? Taking part in activities or seeing the sights?"

Studying the map, she tilted her head as she considered the question. "One doesn't take precedence over another. I'd like to do both, I think."

"Good. You should stay here in Eternity Springs in that case. My friend Cam Murphy runs Refresh Outdoors, the local outfitter shop. He can hook you up with guides and day trips for just about any activity around. He'll put you with the right people and events for your needs and abilities."

"That sounds appealing. Maybe I'll stop by Refresh and visit with him tomorrow. Look into renting a place to stay. Do you have a recommendation for that?"

"Well, that's a bit more complicated." The sound of his phone ringing interrupted him, and he scowled. "Ordinarily, I wouldn't answer that while we are still technically at the dinner table, but that's my mother's ringtone. She and my dad are due to head this way first thing in the morning, so I probably should take it."

"Go ahead. Please."

Boone grabbed his phone from the wooden bowl in the kitchen, where he habitually dumped his pockets upon arriving home. "Hey, Mom, what's up?"

"We're going a mile a minute here. Want to have the car mostly loaded before we go to bed tonight. But something — someone, actually — has come up. Do you remember Linda Gail Pearson?"

"Blake's sister? Of course I remember her." The Pearsons had been part of the McBride family's summer running bunch out at Boone's grandparents' lake house.

"Well, she was down in Redemption with some friends over the weekend, and she ran into Jackson and Caroline. They invited her to the wedding. Her weekend is free, so she's going to ride up with us if we can find a place for her to stay. Do you have room at your inn?"

"Sure. The twins can bunk together." Boone felt sure that his sisters, Lara and Francesca-aka-Frankie, wouldn't mind sharing a room.

"Excellent," his mother replied. "I don't know if you've seen Linda Gail recently, but she's a lovely woman. She teaches kindergarten in Mineral Wells." In an ever-so-casual tone, she added, "She's single too."

Ding. Ding. Ding. Ding. Boone's interfering-mother warning alarm went off. "Mom, tell me this isn't a setup attempt."

All innocence, she said, "Now, son. Why would you think —"

"Do the names Brooke Harkens, Liz Trenton, and Andrea Hernandez ring a bell?" Boone felt the weight of Hannah's curious gaze, and he rolled his eyes. "Do I need to go on, Mom?"

"Oh, all right. It's just that I worry about you."

"You don't need to worry about me, Mom."

"I can't help it. You're alone."

"So are the girls."

"I worry about your sisters too."

"Are you trying to set them up with dates for the wedding?"

"Well, no." She gave a little chuckle and added, "Brick Callahan took care of that little task for me. A couple of friends of his from Gunnison."

Boone laughed. He couldn't help it. His mother was the Boy Scout of matchmaking. Always prepared.

She wanted grandchildren. Badly. Her heart had been crushed right along with Boone's when the adoptions had fallen through. She'd been his rock in the wake of Mary's death. While he'd never explained all the gory details behind his decision to move to Colorado, she'd supported him. She'd never brought up the subject of remarriage — until she'd discovered that Jackson had a new girlfriend. That's when she'd decided that Boone had licked his wounds long enough. She'd declared it was time he'd "met someone" and set about doing her part to make it happen.

Little did she know that her most desired prize, that of becoming a grandmother, was mere days away. Or so it appeared. With his history, Boone wouldn't count Trace's adoption as a sure thing until the documents were signed, sealed, and delivered, and the boy lived with him until, well, until he turned eighteen and graduated from high school. That history was a big part of the reason he'd decided to keep his news to himself for a while.

He didn't want his mother's heart to be broken all over again.

But neither did he want her setting him up with a date for Jackson's wedding.

Sounds coming from the kitchen attracted Boone's attention. He glanced over his shoulder to see that Hannah had cleared the table and was loading his dishwasher. "Like I said, Mom, Linda Gail is welcome to stay here at my place, but I hope you haven't led her to believe I need a date."

"What would it hurt for you to escort —"

"I already have a date to the wedding, Mom," he said, his gaze locked on Hannah. Being a light didn't mean there couldn't be something in it for him. Right? "In fact, I have a date here having dinner with me right now, and this call is interrupting it."

"You do? You do? Well, why didn't you say

so? You shouldn't have answered your phone during a date. That's rude. I taught you better than that. Apologize to your date for the both of us. Goodbye, son. We will see you tomorrow."

"Goodbye, Mom. Y'all drive safe."

"Don't worry about Linda Gail. I'll find another place for her to stay. I didn't say a word to her about you. I was saving that for the drive to Colorado."

He laughed. "Love you too, Mom."

With the call ended, he met Hannah's gaze. "My mother asked me to apologize to you for interrupting our supper."

"Our supper?" She arched a brow. "I thought it was a date."

He winced. "Heard that, did you?"

"You were standing in the doorway. I couldn't help but hear. So, do you lie to your mother often?"

His wince deepened to a grimace. "Ouch. Honestly, I very seldom lie to anyone, much less my mother. I can usually manage to choose my words carefully enough that I don't put myself in that position. Tonight, I'll admit I flew a little too close to the line. In my defense, I only answered her call because I thought it might be a time-sensitive issue. Instead, I found out she was matchmaking, so I shut it down as quickly as possible. After all, I do have a dinner guest, and who's to say it's not a date?"

"Um, me."

"Perhaps you're defining the word too narrowly. I invited you to dinner. You accepted. I believe I could successfully argue the point."

"Well, you're a lawyer. You'll argue that the lake is orange if it suits your purpose."

Boone flashed her a grin. "Won't try to argue *that* point. What I do want to do is return to the discussion we were having before my mother called. You'd just asked a question."

When Hannah wrinkled her brow in thought, Boone reminded her. "You asked for a recommendation for a place to stay."

"Oh, that's right. You said it was complicated."

"I did, and it is. Ordinarily, I'd send you to Angel's Rest because it's truly the nicest resort in this part of the state. However, I happen to know that they are completely booked until mid-August. Between the normal summer crowd and the big wedding this coming weekend, I doubt you'll find a free hotel room in a hundred miles. Luckily, I have a solution to that particular problem. C'mere."

He waved her over toward the windows,

then pointed toward the small, weathered log cabin some thirty yards away from his garage on the other side of a rail fence. "I bought that property with the thought of future expansion. The cabin has one bedroom, one bath, and a kitchenette. It's nothing fancy, but it's clean and comfortable. It's private. I was going to put my cousin Tucker up there, but he's decided to bunk somewhere else, so it's available. It's yours if you'd like to stay. I hope you will stay. Want to walk over and see it?"

Hannah's tongue circled her lips as she considered it. Boone could tell she was tempted, so he pressed, "I promise I'll be an exceptional landlord. I'll allow you your privacy, and I won't be a pest."

She shifted her gaze from the cabin to him, tilted her head, and studied him. "What's the catch?"

"No catch."

"There's something," she mused, suspicion in her violet eyes.

"Tell you what. I can use a walk after that big meal. Why don't we go take a look at the cabin before the sun goes down? You can think about it overnight, and let me know what you want to do in the morning. Okay?"

Following a moment's hesitation, she nodded. Boone hustled her out the door before she could change her mind.

He took the long way around, choosing the path along the shore because it showed the cabin in the most picturesque light. That and the trail exaggerated the distance between his house and the cottage. While they walked, he attempted to sell her on Eternity Springs. His recommendations included his favorite restaurant in town — Ali Timberlake's Yellow Kitchen — and the live music performances held each summer evening at Murphy's Pub. He talked more about the soap shop and the Christmas store and the spa at Angel's Rest. "If you need a day of pampering, you won't find a better place for it."

"I'll keep that in mind," she said.

They reached the fence that divided the two properties, and he opened the gate and motioned her through. "Oh, smell the honeysuckle," Hannah said, referring to the vines that draped the fence rails.

"It's why I decided to leave this fence, at least for now," he explained. "The flowers attract hummingbirds. I'm a bit of a bird-watcher."

"Really?"

"Really. I saw a bald eagle last week."

"I saw one today! It was glorious."

"Stick around, pretty lady. You'll see all sorts of wildlife." Boone pretended not to see her skip a step. He launched into an enumeration of the different species of animals he'd seen since moving into his new home. "Keep in mind, I've only lived in the house a few weeks, so I expect the list will be longer by the end of the month. This is a relatively isolated section of the lake, so early in the morning and again at dusk, we get lots of animals coming down for a drink."

As they approached the door, Boone pulled his keys from his pocket. The *ding-a-ling* of a small set of metal wind chimes hanging from the eaves sounded a pleasing welcome as he slipped the cabin key into the lock and paused. "I should probably give you a word of warning. When I decided not to tear the cabin down, I asked a friend of mine to handle the updates. I told you about her. Celeste Blessing? She owns Angel's Rest? Remember?"

Hannah nodded, and he continued, "Celeste gave the cabin a name and a theme. Serenity. So —" Boone swung open the door and gestured for her to enter. "— welcome to Serenity Cabbage."

As he'd expected, that stopped Hannah short. "Cabbage?"

"We couldn't decide between Cabin and Cottage. Cabbage became a joke that stuck."

Laughing, Hannah stepped inside. "Oh, my."

Boone followed her into the cabin, and as always, he was struck first by the smell. Celeste had commissioned a special fragrance from Savannah Turner to be used in a variety of items at Serenity, everything from fabric detergent to cleaning agents to candles. Thankfully, it had nothing to do with the aroma of cooked cabbage. It was a pleasing scent — fresh, welcoming, and cozy. Boone thought it might have some lavender in it, but beyond that, the fragrance remained a mystery. Savannah and Celeste called it Simple Serenity.

The next items Boone always noticed were the stuffed animals. The little dog was the mascot of Angel's Rest, named by Sarah Murphy of Fresh Bakery fame, and sold by the hundreds each year along with accessories like dress-up clothes and hats in the Angel's Rest gift shop. In addition to the plush toy itself, the shop sold Serenity T-shirts, and calendars and pens and socks and bathrobes and blankets. Celeste had installed at least one of every branded item in Serenity Cottage. The touches were subtle, but anyone who spent time here would note the message.

As a result, Serenity had a vibe that made a person want to sink down and chill.

"It's lovely," Hannah said. "Homey and welcoming."

"Peaceful and serene," he finished. "It can be your sanctuary for a while, Hannah. All you have to do is say yes."

She stroked the buttery soft throw draped over the back of a rocking chair and opened her mouth. Boone could all but see the word *yes* formed on her tongue. Then, abruptly, she closed her mouth and frowned. "Something about this strikes me as being too good to be true. What's the rent?"

"It's fair." He gave her his best, boyish, encouraging smile. "You can rent Serenity Cabbage for a month — no, make that the entire summer. You can have it until Labor Day at no charge if you'll do me one little favor."

She folded her arms, tilted her chin, and studied him. "Let me guess. You need a date for your cousin's wedding on Saturday, don't you?"

"And the rehearsal party on Friday night. It's going to be a lot of fun. Great Texas barbecue, superb live music, and the groom's dog will be the ring bearer at the ceremony on Saturday."

"I'm flattered, Boone. Truly I am. But I have to ask. Why me? I don't doubt for a minute that you know of dozens of women who'd be thrilled to be your date to this wedding — without the cabin bribe. Why not call one of them?"

"Cabbage bribe," he corrected. "And you're right. I imagine I could get someone to go with me. Honestly, up until now, I haven't wanted to take a date to Jackson's wedding. Here's the deal, Hannah. This is going to sound a little crazy to you, I'm sure, but we have this tradition thing going on in Eternity Springs. My friend Celeste — the one who decorated Serenity Cabbage — has this thing about angel wings. She gives an award. A blazon, she calls it, and you have to earn it. When you're part of the Eternity Springs community, and when most of your friends have already earned theirs, well, it makes a person want one. I want one. I'm competitive that way."

"Okay, but what does that have to do with me being your wedding date?"

"I think I was being guided by destiny when I chose to stop at Lover's Leap. I think that I was meant to be a light in the darkness of your anniversary day."

"You were that, Boone, and I thank you for it. You've been a real blessing for me today. But today is one thing; lighting up my entire summer is something else. How do you figure taking me to your cousin's wedding plays into the illumination process?"

He rubbed the back of his neck. He didn't know how to explain it to her because he couldn't explain it to himself. All he knew for certain was that he didn't want to see her drive off into the sunrise tomorrow. He wanted her here. Next door. This summer. He wanted her next door when he brought home his new puppy, Lucky or maybe Ranger, and when he brought his new son, Trace, home. And he wanted that quite badly.

What he didn't want was to scare her away. Judging by the look on her face, he was close to doing precisely that. *Step carefully, McBride.* "Look, the wedding date isn't a deal-breaker. We can negotiate a more typical rental fee if you'd prefer."

"I would."

"Okay, then. How about I check with the chamber and get the average price for a long-term summer rental in Eternity Springs? Would you be agreeable to that?" When she hesitated, he pressed, "I honestly believe you'd enjoy spending time in and around our town this summer, Hannah. I'd be happy to have you as a neighbor at Serenity Cabbage."

She grinned and shook her head. "I'm sorry, but that is such a stupid name."

"I know. It's why I love it. It's a shame to have such a stupidly named, peaceful place sitting empty all summer. Tell me you'll stay." When still she hesitated, he added, "We have Uber now. They'll deliver warm cookies right out of Fresh's oven."

Hannah pursed her lips. "Two weeks. Will you lease Serenity to me at the going rate for two weeks?"

He extended his hand. "Deal. With the option to extend."

She shook it. "Deal. Starting tonight. That way, we won't need to worry about changing the sheets on your guest bed before your family arrives tomorrow."

He wasn't going to argue that point. He was going to save his powder to make another run at getting Hannah to agree to be his wedding date. "Want to walk a little farther? If we follow the shoreline path about a hundred yards, there's a spot that offers a fabulous view of the sunset. It's shaping up to be a nice one tonight. Just the right amount of clouds to get some vivid color."

"Sounds perfect. Lead on, sir."

He led her along the lakeside path without speaking, toward the spot at the far end of the Serenity property where he'd replaced an old wooden bench with a pair of cushioned swivel rockers. Turned toward the west, one could watch the sunset. Turned toward the lake, one had a perfect view of the Callahan family's North Forty compound. With wedding guests slated for arrival beginning tomorrow, the property bustled with activity, Boone saw.

"This is the spot." He motioned for Hannah to take a seat if she wished while he picked up a pail half full of flat stones that he collected whenever he spied one. He had a dozen such pails parked along the shoreline of his property because Boone loved to skip rocks. "Looks like we've timed this pretty good," he observed as he selected a stone. "The sky should be spectacular in the next ten minutes or so."

He selected a rock and sent it skipping across the glassy surface of Hummingbird Lake. Three skips. Silently, he offered the pail to Hannah. She accepted the challenge.

"You're good," he said after she'd slung a five-hopper.

"Once upon a time, I lived on a lake. I found this activity the perfect blend of relaxation and challenge."

"A woman after my own heart. We're a perfect match." He handed her a second stone. "Which reminds me. Look straight across the lake. See where they've built an arch right at the water? It's the best sunset spot on the lake. That's where my cousin Jackson will marry Caroline about this time on Saturday. Now that we have the Cabbage situation settled, mind if we revisit the wedding date question?"

Her second stone skipped four times. "You are persistent, aren't you?"

"A dog with a bone, my mama says. So, yeah. I am persistent. I want you to be my date to the wedding events. You'll be doing me a solid if you agree. In fact, it could be argued that doing so would be the flip side of the light-destiny thing."

Reaching into the bucket for another stone, she paused and met his gaze, frowning in confusion. "I don't understand. Is Saturday an anniversary for you? Are you saying that you need a light of your own?"

"No. Hannah. What I need is protection."

"Against what?"

"Not what. Who. My mother. I failed to anticipate the effect that Jackson's marriage would have on the woman, and she doesn't even know about my other cousin Tucker's big news. This call tonight was a tip-off. I have a Matchmaking Mama problem, and I need to nip it in the bud this weekend. Now, you're going to repeat the suggestion that I call someone local, but here's my argument against that. It's a numbers problem. As in, we don't have them. The truth is, I've already gone out with every eligible woman in Eternity Springs. All four of them. All four of them agreed that we are great friends, but not potential lovers. And my mother knows this."

"You keep her updated on your dates?"

"No, but Mom made a visit to Angel's Rest on a girls' weekend trip with friends in April. She grilled Celeste, who spilled the beans."

"Ah."

"Say you'll come, Hannah."

He knew she was relenting when she fixed her gaze on the North Forty. "I don't have anything appropriate to wear to a wedding. I wouldn't know what to wear to this one."

"Angel's Rest has a boutique. Ask for Lisa. She'll get you fixed up." He sent the stone he held flying, a high arc, rather than a flat skip. Then he caught her hand in his and brought it up to his mouth. He kissed her knuckles. "Please? I promise to show you a good time, and I'll be a perfect gentleman."

"A perfect gentleman?"

The doubt in her eyes put a bit of devilment into his. "As perfect as you want me to be."

"Very perfect." The dryness of her tone and the surrender in her smile telegraphed his victory. "Okay, I'll do it."

"Perfect." Boone winked, then gestured toward the sky and repeated, "Perfect. Perfection."

The western sky was a blaze of yellow, orange, and scarlet fading to rose, pink, and purple. "Yes," Hannah breathed. "What a glorious sky."

They watched silently, standing side by side, their hands linked, as the sun sank below the mountain ridge and colors faded shadows. But just when the brilliance appeared to be over, a brief, bright flare of gold burst against the evening sky. "Wow," Hannah said.

Boone released her hand, wrapped his arm around her shoulders, and gave her a hug. "I think Nature just blew you a kiss to celebrate the end of your anniversary day."

"Not Nature," she replied, blinking rapidly. "Sophia and Zoe. They are Sophia and Zoe."

CHAPTER SIX

Boone silently repeated the names. *Sophia and Zoe.* Girls. Little girls, he'd bet. *Ah, Hannah Dupree, you break my heart.*

Swiftly deepening twilight cast her face in shadow but failed to hide the anguish in her watery eyes. "Want to tell me about Sophia and Zoe?"

She filled her lungs with air, then blew out a heavy breath. "I don't know. I haven't talked about them in three years. I'll just cry."

"Cleansing tears can be good."

"Maybe." She gave a thready laugh. "Even cleansing tears make a mess. I don't have any tissues."

"See, maybe this is meant to be. I'm one of those old-fashioned guys who still carry a handkerchief, and it's still as pristine as it was when my laundry girls delivered it."

Hannah gave him a sidelong look. "You have a laundry girl?"

"Girls, plural. Distant cousins of mine — Meg and Cari Callahan. They're young teens, twins, who are saving their pennies to buy their first cars. I pay them to iron for me. They're still learning when it comes to my shirts, so we mostly do handkerchiefs. If I don't go through enough of them in a week, I catch hell." He reached into his back pocket and then handed her a neatly folded handkerchief. "You'll be doing me a solid if you'll mess this up for me."

She brushed her thumb across the initials embroidered into the cotton square. "I was a sucker for monogramming. They told you for safety's sake not to put your children's name on their clothes, but at least once each year I had matching dresses monogrammed with their names for portraits. My favorites were little red polka-dot Minnie Mouse dresses. I don't know the name of the font, but it shouted Disney. It was the year we took them to Disney World. They wore mouse ears in the photos. They were so proud of them."

"I'd like to see the portraits."

Again, her thumb brushed the monogram. When she spoke, her voice was tight. "I kept the albums. They're about all I kept. I don't think I can show you. Not yet."

"That's okay." He gave the hand holding

his handkerchief a gentle, comforting squeeze. "What can you share with me?"

"Sophia was seven. Zoe, five. Sophia had my red hair. Zoe was blond. They both had their father's brown eyes. Sophia wanted to be a dolphin trainer when she grew up, and Zoe loved to color. They both adored ice cream and kittens and making leaf forts in autumn. They both thrived being outdoors, especially if it involved anything to do with water. Sophia had learned to water-ski. Zoe was determined to learn that summer."

Tears ran freely down her face at this point. Boone tugged the handkerchief from her hand and used it to dab at her cheek. She smiled, took it back, and wiped her eyes. Hoping to learn more about Hannah along with her daughters, he asked, "You had a boat?"

She nodded. "Two. A runabout and a sailboat. We had a summer place on a lake in New Hampshire."

Tidbits. He liked tidbits. But Boone decided a shift in the direction of the conversation was in order, because the haunted look had returned to Hannah's gaze. "I have an eight-year-old niece who we had to coax into the swimming hole in the Texas Hill Country, where her father lives. She loves to swim, but only had

106

experience in pools. She'll tell you she's a girly girl at heart, but she's learning to get grubby. Leaf forts were a new experience for her, too, this past year. It's been fun watching her tumble into love with the outdoors."

Hannah nodded. "That was Sophia. Zoe, on the other hand, loved digging in the dirt almost as much as she loved coloring."

"I have a friend who is a nut over adult coloring books. I don't see it myself."

"Coloring can be therapeutic."

Boone nodded. "I can see that. Probably the same way origami was for me."

"You're a paper folder, are you?"

"I make a mean swan. I can tie balloon animals too."

"Seriously?" She closed her eyes. "I learned to tie balloon animals for Zoe's fifth birthday party. We were at a mall, and a store was having a promotion. A girl wearing a cat costume tied balloons and passed them out to the children. It's all she could talk about afterward. She wanted balloon animals at her party, but the only person I could find dressed like a clown. She was scared of clowns and wanted a cat."

"So you learned?"

"YouTube is a mother's friend. I can't tell you how many bags of balloons I went through before I got the process down."

Sounded to Boone like she'd been a good, loving mother, and Boone almost said it aloud. Caution held his tongue. He didn't know how her children had died. It could have been an accident, one for which she was responsible or held herself accountable, and his observation might wound in that case.

So instead, he asked, "Was the party a success?"

She nodded. "It was a big success. I could have started a side business entertaining at children's birthday parties."

An opening. "Oh, yeah? What was your main business?"

She didn't answer right away. When she finally did speak, Boone sensed she was leaving something out.

"I was a mom. After Sophia was born, I was a stay-at-home mom. I loved the job. I was good at it." Her voice sounded raw, but fierce as she added, "I was a very good mother."

"Hannah . . ." Boone hesitated. Indecision rarely plagued him, but he wanted to get this right. "Hannah, do you want to tell me what happened to your girls?"

Silence stretched. A full minute passed. Then two. Boone realized he was holding his breath, so he quietly released it and managed not to gasp when she suddenly said, "They drowned."

How? He bit back the word as she quietly began to cry. Boone wrapped his arms around her and held her. "Bless your heart." His voice was thick with emotion as he added, "Ah, Hannah, that's so hard. Just so hard. I'm sorry."

She remained stiff at first, but as he gently swayed her back and forth, she relaxed against him and wept. He lost track of how long they stood there, her shoulders quaking, him murmuring comfort and encouragement, but by the time her tears ceased and she took a half step away from him, full darkness had fallen. "I'd thought I was done with tears," she said.

"These were the cleansing kind," he replied, confident he was correct. "You needed them."

"Maybe I did." A square of white fluttered in the minimal ambient light as she lifted his handkerchief and wiped her eyes. "It's the first time I've talked about them, the first time I've wanted to talk about them. I think I needed that, especially today. Thank you for understanding that. Thank you for offering me the opportunity."

He reached for her, and his fingers

brushed her arm just above the elbow. Sliding his hand down the length of her arm until he found her wrist, he clasped her hand and brought it to his lips for a courtly kiss across her knuckles. "It was my pleasure."

Then he pulled his keys from his pocket, switched on the mini-light he carried on the key ring, and guided Hannah through the darkness, lighting the way toward her new home, her fresh start.

Be a light.

Hannah fell asleep as soon as her head hit the pillow that night, and she slept almost until noon the following day. When she finally woke, she climbed from her bed, feeling as if a heavy weight had melted off her shoulders overnight. She made coffee and sat on the deck, watching the sailboats on Hummingbird Lake.

Zoe had loved sailboats and sailing. Sophia preferred being in the water. Both girls could swim like fishes. Some days knowing how much her girls loved the water gave Hannah comfort. Other days, it caused her anguish.

This morning — well, actually afternoon — the desire to plunge into her memories washed through her. In the past, such an activity would destroy her for days, but today she sensed a strength within herself. She wanted to test it.

She picked up her phone, swiped to the photo app, and lost herself in her previous life. When she finally put the phone down an hour and a half later, her cheeks were tear-streaked, but her heart felt just a little bit lighter.

Now she needed to move. She showered and dressed and headed into town to find a grocery store and maybe drop by the outdoors business that Boone had told her about.

She did a slow drive-through of the town to acclimate herself. Four avenues named after trees ran north and south. The cross streets were numbered First through Eighth. The Angel's Rest resort occupied a large plot of land on the eastern side of Angel Creek. Refresh, the outdoors shop, sat at the north end of town along the road that led to Gunnison.

Hannah decided to start there. She pulled into the parking lot, walked past a line of ATVs available for rental, and entered the shop where the first things that caught her notice were the fly-fishing rods standing in the SALE endcap shelving. The idea of fishing for trout in a shallow mountain stream appealed to her. The motion of an experienced angler laying a fly atop the water was a ballet of grace and art. Of course, if she cast a fly rod, rather than a dance, it'd be a slapstick comedy of tangled line and lost hooks.

She was smirking when a man with sun-streaked hair and brilliant green eyes approached her with a friendly smile. "Welcome to Refresh Outdoors. My name is Cam. What can I help you with this afternoon?"

"Well, I'm not certain. This is my first visit to Colorado, and I'm fact-finding today. I'm interested in the guided tours you offer. I'll be in this area for the next couple of weeks, and I want to do more than simply sight-seeing. I'm looking for an adventure or two."

Cam's eyes gleamed. He avariciously rubbed his hands together and teased, "New meat. I love it. We will fix you up, Ms. . . . ?"

"Dupree." She extended her hand. "I'm Hannah Dupree."

He shook her hand. "Nice to meet you, Hannah Dupree. We have a conference area in the rear left corner of the shop. If you want to have a seat there, I'll gather my flyers and schedules, and review your options with you. You'll find coffee and tea and a selection of cookies from Fresh, my wife's bakery. Feel free to help yourself. I'll join you in a couple of minutes."

"Thank you."

Hannah poured herself a cup of coffee, her attention divided between the half dozen photographs gracing the walls and the plate of cookies beneath a glass dome at the center of the table. Last night's chocolate cake had come from Fresh Bakery. Some of the cookies looked like the strawberry pinwheels that Boone had recommended.

But the photos. Oh, the photos. They were action photos: a skier on a snowy mountain against a bluebird sky, a yellow raft airborne over a white-water river, a climber hammering a pin into a sheer cliff wall high above the ground, ATV riders kicking up dust on a mountain trail, a hang glider soaring above an alpine meadow carpeted with yellow wildflowers, and a snowmobiler kicking up powder into a sky brilliant with sunset.

Hannah took a strawberry pinwheel and moved to study the photographs. They were artistic and alive and made one want to be the person on the skis and the snowmobile and in the raft. The hang glider and climber, not so much. Hannah didn't have a death wish. Not today, anyway.

Cam approached carrying a binder and

stack of brochures. "Do you like the photographs?"

"I do. They're fabulous."

Cam beamed with pride at the compliment. "My son-in-law took them."

"He's a talented photographer."

"He is that. Chase used to make his living doing adventure photography, but now he pretty much limits himself to taking portraits. These were a Christmas gift for me."

"It makes me want to ride a snowmobile."

"Wrong time of year for that, I'm afraid. I can hook you up on an ATV tour. Or a white-water tour if you'd prefer a boat. Are you interested in either of those?"

"I am."

They spent the next twenty minutes discussing various guided tours his company offered, and Hannah's experience in the areas in which she stated interest. During their discussion, Cam received a cancellation for the next day's scheduled half-day fishing trip with his best guide. Hannah claimed the opening on the spot. She also booked a trail ride through a nearby national forest for the following week.

"We run a rafting trip on the Gunnison that includes enough white water to make it interesting, but not so much that it's above your comfort level. We have an open spot on Saturday afternoon."

Hannah shook her head. "I can't. I'm going to a wedding here on Saturday."

Cam sat back in his chair. "The McBride wedding?" When she nodded, he continued, "You should have said so. Jackson and Caroline have arranged a set of special tours specifically for the entertainment of their wedding guests. You should have received word about them along with your bracelet in the welcome bags you received when you checked into your hotel. Here." He rose from his seat. "Let me get that information for you."

He returned quickly and handed her a four-color brochure. "As a McBride/Carruthers guest, you have two complimentary tours to be chosen from a selection of six offered by Refresh. Pick whichever you like. We have space available for all of them. If you want to join the wedding fishing trip tomorrow, I'll cancel your private —"

"No," Hannah interrupted. "No, thank you. I'll keep what I've booked. I wouldn't feel right about joining the wedding trips because I'm not a real guest. I'm going as a plus-one as a favor for a friend who didn't want to go solo."

The businessman shrugged. "That's not a problem on my end, Hannah, and I'm sure

Caroline and Jackson would think the same. A guest is a guest. Not only that, but your participation in the Destination Eternity Springs program will also benefit our little town."

"What's Destination Eternity Springs?"

"It's a new destination wedding marketing project that our chamber of commerce is developing. We're using Jackson McBride's wedding as our test run. You should ask your date to get you a gift bag. Inside it, you'll find a bracelet designed for us by a local artist, along with a list of participating businesses. Wear the bracelet when you frequent the merchant, and you'll receive a little gift. In the case of Refresh, it's the tours. At my wife's bakery, you'll get a dozen brownies."

"I had her chocolate cake last night. If her brownies are anything like her cookies and cake, I'd better make sure not to skip my cardio while I'm in Eternity Springs."

"Sarah is a magician."

Hannah had noticed a gift bag on the front doorstep when she'd backed her car out of the garage this afternoon. Bet Boone had left one of those wedding bags on her front step. "Thanks for the tip and the tour bookings. I'll sit down tonight and figure out my schedule and book the rest of my tours after the fishing trip."

"Sounds good. I won't be here tomorrow — it's Poppy's play day with my youngest kiddo and grandson — but my manager will be happy to fix you up."

Hannah let him coax her into taking one more cookie on her way out, and she decided to make a stop at the Angel's Rest Boutique for something to wear to this wedding before she shopped for groceries and returned to Hummingbird Lake. If she needed to build a shopping trip to a larger town into her schedule, better learn that now before she made any more plans.

A few minutes later, she pulled into the crowded Angel's Rest parking lot and searched vainly for a space before following a sign directing visitors to overflow parking. Based on the parking situation alone, Boone had been telling her the truth about occupancy rates. After parking, she followed a path toward the large Victorian mansion that appeared to be the resort's headquarters. It was a beautiful, gingerbread-bedecked building painted a cheerful lemon yellow and trimmed in white. Wicker rockers and bistro sets lined the wraparound porches on the first and second floors. She heard metal wind chimes tinkling and, from off in the distance, the sound of children's laughter. The fragrance of roses perfumed the air. Hannah's steps slowed as she took in her surroundings, enjoying the moment. This place had a good vibe.

Just ahead of her where the single path split into three, she paused to read the resort map on display. The boutique was in the same building as the spa, off to the right and down near the creek. Hannah took the proper path, and moments later a door chime pealed as she stepped into the shop.

A woman of indeterminate age looked up from the pages of a magazine behind a sleek, modern checkout counter. She wore her silver hair short. Gold earrings shaped like angel's wings dangled from her ears, and her blue eyes and brilliant smile signaled warmth and welcome. "Hello. Welcome to the Boutique at Angel's Rest."

"Thank you."

"Are you looking for something in particular?"

"I was told to ask for Lisa?"

"Ah. I'm afraid Lisa is out this afternoon. I'm Celeste. I'll be happy to assist you."

She was the friend Boone had mentioned, Hannah deduced. "I'm Hannah. I've been invited to a wedding here this weekend. I don't have my go-to little black dress with me, so I need a replacement. Unless black is inappropriate for weddings in this locale. Do you know? Can you help me?"

"I'll be thrilled to help you, Hannah. I'm sure we have something you'll love. I assume you're speaking of the McBride/Carruthers nuptials?" Hannah nodded, and Celeste continued, "It's going to be a beautiful wedding. Are you a friend of the bride or the groom?"

Hannah gave an embarrassed smile. "I haven't met either of them, I'm afraid. I'm going as the groom's cousin's date."

"Not Tucker, I'm sure. So, Boone? You are dating Boone McBride?"

"No. No. I'm not dating him. I'm just going with him to this wedding. As a favor."

"Ah."

Celeste's friendly eyes gleamed with speculative interest, and Hannah wished she'd kept the whole date thing to herself. She braced for more questions, but Celeste surprised her. "Well, you'll have a wonderful time. Boone will make sure you enjoy yourself. Aside from being a handsome devil, he truly is a special man and a treasure for our community. We're fortunate he decided to move to Eternity Springs."

"He's been very nice to me, but I don't know him well."

"That sounds like an invitation to dish,"

Celeste said, the speculation in her eyes warming to a mischievous twinkle. "What would you like to know about our little mountain town's most eligible bachelor?"

Hannah held up her hand, palm out. "To be clear, eligible doesn't matter to me. I'm only a visitor to town. I'm not in the market for a relationship." *Been there, done that. Total devastation.*

"But you *are* curious about Boone?"

She shrugged. "He's interesting. I don't think he understands the word *no.*"

Celeste laughed. "A force of nature, that's our Boone. When he sets his mind to something, there's no naysaying him."

"I can see that."

"He loves nothing better than a good argument, but he's one of the most generous people I've ever met. The man truly has a heart of gold. He's loving and loyal and dedicated to his causes. But just so you don't think I'm the president of the Boone McBride fan club, I will add that he has a reputation as a ladies' man."

"That doesn't surprise me."

"I don't think it's exactly fair. He's a healthy, single, social man who enjoys spending time with women. Why wouldn't he invite a similarly unattached woman on a date? To a person, they said he was nothing but a gentleman — even if he is a bit of a scoundrel."

"Can a guy be both a scoundrel and a gentleman?" Hannah asked.

"Boone can," Celeste said, moving out from behind the counter. "Now, enough gossip. Let's see what we have that might suit you." Her gaze skimmed Hannah up and down. "You're a size four?"

Hannah shook her head. "Eight." Although she had lost weight. "Maybe a six."

Celeste clicked her tongue. "We will see. Now, do you need something for both the rehearsal and the wedding?"

"Probably. Again, I'm not sure what's appropriate."

Celeste launched into a vivid description of what Hannah could expect on Friday night. She spoke about award-winning barbecue and Texans and a "lovable old codger" named Branch and a private concert by Coco.

"*The* Coco?" Hannah repeated. "The pop star?"

"Her roots are in country music, but yes. She's Jackson's ex-wife, and they share a child. A sweetheart of a little girl. Haley. She's the flower girl."

"Oh! Of course. That terrible plane crash." Hannah wasn't much of a celebrity follower, but she did read the front page of tabloids and magazine covers while standing in line at the grocery store. "And Coco is singing at her ex-husband's wedding? I thought theirs was an acrimonious divorce."

"Oh, it was, but tragedies have a way of changing people."

Hannah couldn't argue with that. She'd seen it firsthand in work she'd done as a licensed therapist a million years ago, back before Sophie had been born.

"Coco has come a long way, and she and Jackson work hard to work together as Haley's parents. She'll be singing at the rehearsal barbecue in a gesture of goodwill. She won't sing at the wedding. The wedding is Caroline's day."

"That's nice," Hannah murmured. Her attention was on the word *barbecue.* "What does one wear to a rehearsal barbecue in Eternity Springs, Colorado, that includes a private performance from a Grammy winner?"

Celeste laughed. "It's unique, I'll agree. If I may suggest a way to tackle this, let's find your dress for Saturday first. Then we can play a little bit for your Friday-night outfit. Do you have a budget?"

Hannah named a figure, and Celeste nodded. "Excellent. We can work with that.

Now, I have a basic black for you to try, but I want to show you a couple of others too, dresses that are perfect for a summer lakeside wedding. The styles are quite different, one classic, one more romantic, but I think they'll look fabulous on you. If you'll follow me?"

Celeste led her into a large showroom with a dozen or so racks. "For the sake of space, we display one of each item. Let me show you what I have in mind for you."

She removed a simple black fit-and-flare style dress from the rack. It was similar to one Hannah had given to Goodwill during the purge of her belongings following the funerals. Hannah held it up against her and turned toward one of the full-length mirrors in the shop. "That should do fine."

"It's totally appropriate, but . . ." Celeste pursed her lips and studied Hannah for a long moment before she nodded. "That dress reminds me of a column I'm writing for our local historical society. Are you familiar with the mourning practices of the Victorian age, Hannah?"

Hannah drew back. Now, that was a question out of left field. "Um, not really, no."

"I know that it is perfectly acceptable to wear black to weddings these days, but I'll admit to being a little old-fashioned about it. I'm originally from the South, and I still won't wear white shoes before Easter or after Labor Day. I became interested in the custom of wearing black for mourning from books I read. Historical romance novels set in that era." Smiling sheepishly, she added, "They're a guilty pleasure of mine."

"Personally, I like the Scottish Highlander stories," Hannah replied. The two women shared an understanding smile.

"Anyway," Celeste continued, "I did some research into mourning fashion for my column. In Victorian times, women were considered to be vessels of grief, and as such, they had strict etiquette rules to follow after the loss of a family member. Different rules for the mourning of a spouse, children, a parent, a cousin, or an aunt or uncle. The custom got a kick start after Queen Victoria's beloved Prince Albert died."

"I recall that she mourned him until she died."

"She did. Theirs was a true, tragic love story. But back to fashion. Family members and only family members wore black — and it had to be a dull black, by the way. Nothing shiny or pretty or rich like this little black dress. I found it interesting that the color of full mourning was seen to shield wearers from society, allowing them time to grieve and come to terms with loss."

"What does *come to terms* mean?" Hannah asked, bitterness in her tone. "Forgetting? Getting used to it?"

"Oh, heavens, no. If I may speak from a personal perspective here for a moment, I've lived a long time. I've lost many loved ones, and I've never gotten used to it. I hope I never do. When someone I love passes, it rips my heart in two. As well it should. The death of a loved one needs to matter. You need to bleed. That emotion honors both you and your loved one, and the relationship that you shared."

Hannah considered it. Celeste had a point. A good point. "That's right. That's exactly right. No one ever says that."

"Well, some people can't think when they're engulfed in emotion. And if it's a new experience, that's understandable, but the truth is that one should be proud of one's scar tissue. It's a testament to life. If one is blessed, one will reach the end of one's life bearing the scars of many loves and losses."

"That's a lot of pain."

"And joy. Don't forget the joy. Love brings joy. One tends to appreciate joy more deeply when one has lived through intense pain."

Hannah knew the truth of that from her studies and professional practice. She had yet to experience it herself.

Celeste clicked her tongue. "Oh, dear. I've gone off on one of my flights of fancy again. I tend to do that. But back to my historical society column —"

Or perhaps, getting on with selling me a dress?

"— in the Victorian Age, full mourning eventually gave way to half mourning, and women put away their black for grays, dark blue, and . . ." She shot Hannah a significant look. Then she selected a second gown from the rack — an off-the-shoulder silk sheath dress. "Purples."

Hannah's heart gave a little lurch of yearning as Celeste gave the purple dress a fluff.

"The black is fine, but I hope you will consider this dress. The color compliments your beautiful eyes. A dear friend of mine has violet-blue eyes similar to yours — Sarah Murphy."

"The cookie lady," Hannah murmured.

Celeste laughed. "Cookie, cakes, and bread. She's quite the temptress. You'll likely meet her at the wedding."

"Hmm." Hannah's gaze remained locked on the dress. Purple. A color. A dark color, but still a color. *It's not red or blue or white, though.*

What was it Celeste had called it? Half mourning? Silly term. Like being half pregnant.

And yet, no way would she choose something, say, yellow, to wear. Yellow used to be her favorite color, but it was way too bright to suit her now. Hannah studied the purple dress. The style was something she'd have chosen once upon a time. "It's pretty."

"Feel the fabric. It's luxurious."

Hannah pursed her lips. Her wardrobe now consisted of jeans, shorts, T-shirts, and a single cotton pullover dress. When was the last time she had worn silk?

When was the last time she'd worn color?

She knew the answer to that question. She'd worn bright pink to the girls' funeral, but that was the last time she'd donned any sort of color. Three years ago, when she left what had been her home, she'd kept only a handful of items from that life. She bought new clothes as she needed them, and while she hadn't consciously decided to wear only black, that's all she bought.

What was it Celeste had said? Did black shield mourners from society? That wasn't really how Hannah had looked at it. Black wasn't a shield. It's the color you get when you combine the girls' favorite pink and her favorite yellow and the orange pumpkins they carried to collect treats on Halloween and the red dresses they wore to church on Christmas Eve. Add in the bright white of the snow where they made snow angels, and the green of grass stains on their knees, and the brilliant blue of the backyard swimming pool where the girls played every chance they got, and purple Easter egg dye on the kitchen table. The color you got when you mixed all those colors together — all the colors of life — and poured them into a grave? Black.

Black wasn't a shield. It was all she had left of life.

"It's a lovely dress, but —"

"My other suggestion for you is this," Celeste interrupted. She crossed to another rack of dresses and pulled out a chiffon froth of spring. A print of yellow roses against green leaves. It was wispy and romantic, and nothing Hannah would have selected to try, even in her other life, back when she'd worn yellow.

She physically took a step backward. "Oh, no. I couldn't. It's beautiful, but it's not my style."

Celeste arched a brow. "Maybe it's time you made a change."

From out of nowhere, tears pooled in Hannah's eyes. She repeatedly blinked, trying to chase them away, to no avail. When they spilled from her eyes and trailed down her cheeks, Celeste grabbed a tissue from a nearby box and handed it to her.

"Hannah, dear, would you please indulge me a moment and have a seat at the bistro table? When you arrived, I was just about to have my afternoon tea. Please, join me?"

Hannah wanted to turn around and flee the boutique. She'd come here to buy a dress, not spend an hour on a therapist's couch. But if she ran, she still wouldn't have a dress to wear to this stupid wedding.

Of course, she could stand Boone up. She could sneak off in the middle of the night and go on to the next little mountain town. Except he'd been so kind to her, and she'd given her word, and she *was* looking forward to her fishing trip tomorrow.

The path of least resistance was to take a seat at the bistro table. Besides, something about Celeste Blessing made her want to, well, listen.

Celeste disappeared through a door and returned moments later carrying a tray filled with two glasses of iced tea and a plate of cookies. Hannah couldn't help but smile. "Let me guess. Fresh Bakery?"

"Yes. Sarah's snickerdoodles."

It was a wonder everyone in this town didn't have diabetes, Hannah thought even as she reached for a cookie. No willpower. She had absolutely no willpower. But dang it, she hadn't had an appetite for sweets in too long to remember. She hadn't had a desire for much of anything since the day her daughters died.

Celeste said, "I believe it would be beneficial to explain our purpose here. I might mention that this resort is my baby. When I chose to add a boutique to our offerings here at Angel's Rest, I did so for a specific reason. We are Angel's Rest Healing Center and Spa. Healing is our focus, our mission, and we are here to help souls who have been injured or traumatized."

She paused long enough to choose a cookie, then continued. "Trauma changes a person from the marrow out. When healing occurs, that creates another change. We've discovered that it is an important part of the healing process for some of our guests to be able to acknowledge those changes in something as simple as a change in hairstyle or wardrobe. Whether it's a significant change or a reaffirmation of their previous sense of style, it can make a real difference."

Hannah sipped her tea. Sweet tea. More

sugar. She shouldn't be surprised because she detected a note of the South in Celeste Blessing's voice.

It was easier to think about tea than deciding about branching out from black. She polished off her cookie and took another sip of tea.

"Of course, sometimes a new dress or hairstyle is simply a new dress or hairstyle." Celeste continued pleasantly. "Nothing wrong with that either. I have no wish to pressure you, Hannah. I simply wanted to allow you to take the measure of your emotional health at this point."

Hannah straightened defensively. "What makes you think I've suffered a trauma? I'm just a customer looking to buy a dress."

"Are you? I have a talent for reading people, but if I have misread you, you have my most sincere apologies."

Celeste pushed the plate of cookies toward her. Hannah took another one. Why not? She quickly polished it off.

"Am I wrong?" Celeste asked, a gleam in her light-blue eyes that was both challenging and encouraging.

Hannah sucked the snickerdoodle crumbs off her fingers and sighed. "No."

"Shall I show you what other dresses I have in your size?"

131

She hesitated a long moment before deciding. "I'll try the black. And I guess the purple."

Celeste's beam of approval was like the sun coming out inside the shop.

In the dressing room, Hannah stripped down and donned the black. It fit nicely and was an any-occasion type of dress. She'd had a similar one hanging in her closet for years. She really didn't need to try the other one. This dress would suit.

And yet Celeste Blessing's argument about healing and change had struck a chord deep within her. Hannah eyed the purple dress as she slipped out of the black one and hung it on its hanger. *Half mourning* wasn't the right term for the place she was. Shoot, yesterday she'd been ready to take a header off Lover's Leap when Boone McBride showed up.

Boone McBride. Gray eyes, broad shoulders, kind heart. He'd survived his wife's suicide. He was filled with color, filled with life.

Her hand trembled ever so slightly as she reached for the silk sheath.

The oh-so-soft fabric skimmed across her skin like a lover's hands.

A lover's hands. Now, what had made her think of that particular simile? She couldn't remember the sensation of a lover's touch.

Hannah made a snort of self-disgust and stepped into the dress, pulling it up and on. After a few contortions, she managed to get it zipped, and then she turned to face the mirror.

It fit her like it was made for her. The dress was simple and sophisticated with short sleeves and a hem that hit just above her knees. It had a deep-vee neckline with black seaming details running from the shoulders to the edges of the slightly over-lapping collar. From the other side of the dressing room door, Celeste said, "We have a three-way mirror here if you want to see the back."

Hannah stepped out of the dressing room, and Celeste clapped her hands and beamed. "It was made for you. I just knew it."

She chattered on about using jewelry to dress it up or down. Hannah's fingers automatically went to the only necklace she ever wore — three entwined circles, each engraved with a name: hers, Sophia's, and Zoe's.

At Celeste's direction, Hannah turned this way and that, viewing her reflection from all sides. When she was shown a pair of pointed-toe, black leather flats, she tried them on without protest. They felt like butter on her feet.

"These are perfect for a lakeside wedding and reception. Heels aren't easy at the North Forty if the ground is the least bit soft. What do you think, Hannah?"

"It's a beautiful dress. I think . . . I think I'll take it. The shoes too."

"Excellent. Now we can see about finding you something more casual for the rehearsal party. All right?"

"Yes. Thank you."

Hannah headed back toward the dressing room, but just before she shut the door, Celeste spoke. "Dear, would you please do me a little favor, first? Try on the chiffon." Even as Hannah opened her mouth to protest, Celeste shook her head. "No, no. It's not the right dress for you to wear to Jackson's wedding. But try it on."

"Why?"

"To appease me. It's my favorite dress in the shop, and I haven't seen it on a single customer yet. It won't take two minutes. Please?"

Hannah couldn't say no to Celeste Blessing. Maybe Boone had taken lessons from her.

Celeste had been so kind. Like Boone. And Cam Murphy. Maybe it was an Eternity Springs thing. Hannah had somehow managed to find a bastion of kindness in America. Go figure. Nevertheless, she couldn't refuse the request. As she changed out of the purple and into the chiffon, she wondered if anyone could tell the blue-eyed angel no.

The chiffon had a side zipper, so no contortions were needed this time. Hannah didn't bother to look at her reflection before stepping out to show Celeste.

"Oh. Oh, my, I knew it. Here. Try these shoes with it." Celeste handed her a pair of heeled sandals embellished with yellow roses. They were feminine and fun and nothing like any shoes Hannah had ever worn.

"One more thing." Without so much as a by-your-leave, Celeste gathered Hannah's hair up and, with a few twists, secured it with hairpins sporting enameled yellow roses. Then she placed her hands on Hannah's shoulders and turned her toward the mirror. "Now look."

Hannah went tense. The woman in the mirror with the tousled updo was a stranger. A stranger who wore a sleeveless springtime print with a sweetheart neckline and fitted bodice and just a hint of ruffle on the hem that hit four inches above her knees. Unable to help herself, she gave her hips a little swish. The skirt swirled before settling around her legs like a cloud of rose petals.

Staring at her reflection, Hannah felt a stab of an emotion she could not name. She cleared her throat and said, "This isn't me."

"No, it's not. Not yet. But I want you to take a good look at her and remember her. She's the woman you are becoming, Hannah."

The woman I'm becoming. Hannah's heart began to pound.

"You need to recognize that you've made a significant step today in Eternity Springs, here in the Angel's Rest Boutique. You've opened yourself to color once again. Take pride in that. Take comfort in it. Take your time. Take your half steps. The whole spectrum awaits you. Whenever you have doubts, you think of this woman in roses, and you believe. A wonderful world of color awaits you."

Hannah closed her eyes.

"You aren't alone any longer, Hannah," Celeste assured. "Eternity Springs has your back."

It all sounded too good to be true. "How can you say that? I've been here one day. You're only the third person I've met!"

"It's how we roll here. Besides, I know things." Celeste chuckled and gave Hannah's shoulder a reassuring pat. "Now, let me show you what I have in mind for your rehearsal party outfit. There will be dancing. Do you have jeans?"

"Yes." After a moment's pause, she added, "Black ones."

"Even better." Celeste crossed to a rack of sportswear and pulled out a long, violet-colored, loosely woven shirt. She handed it to Hannah. "While you slip into this, I'll duck into my stockroom for the belt and the boots."

"Boots?"

"It's a Texas crowd, Hannah. But don't fret. Dating Boone McBride, you'll get plenty of wear out of them."

"Dating? One date does not make an *ing.*"

"Technically, it's two dates. Friday and Saturday. Unless you're planning to spend the night with him, in which case I guess one could call it a single date."

"Spend the night with him?" Her eyes went round. "I'm not going to spend the night with him. His mother is staying at his house!"

"Yes, of course. In that case, I guess he'd spend the night with you."

With that, Hannah abandoned any attempt to resist the steamroller named Celeste. Twenty minutes later, she walked

137

out of Angel's Rest Boutique carrying a shopping bag, and dress bag, and wearing new western-style leather boots in order to "break them in." The boots were two-toned — purple and dove gray.

The same color gray as Boone McBride's eyes.

CHAPTER SEVEN

Half an hour before sunrise, Jackson Mc-Bride buckled his eight-year-old daughter into a safety booster seat in the back of Boone's Land Rover and said, "You be good for Uncle B, Sugar Bug."

"I will, Daddy," Haley McBride said. "I'm so excited. I hope I catch a rainbow. It'll be my first time!"

"Be sure to take a picture."

"I will, Daddy."

Jackson picked up his daughter's pink plastic tackle box and handed it to his cousin to stow next to the fishing gear in the rear of Boone's vehicle. Keeping his voice soft, he asked, "You certain you're ready for this? Her emotions have been all over the place of late. She goes from adorable to mini-monster in the blink of an eye."

"We'll be fine. It'll do Haley good to have some one-on-one attention."

"Yes, it will. I'll admit I didn't expect the

wedding to be hard on her. She adores Caroline. They have a great relationship, and Haley seems to be sincerely happy that I'm getting remarried. She loves living in Redemption. Her mother gets along with Caroline as well as Sharon gets along with anybody."

"Maybe it's not the wedding. I wouldn't be surprised if what you're seeing isn't some churning of her grief. It rolled over me in waves, and at the time, I didn't always recognize it for what it was."

"Could be," Jackson said as the Land Rover's rear gate clicked shut. "I hadn't thought of that."

Jackson gave his daughter one more kiss and hug as Boone climbed into the driver's seat. The stretch of water where he intended to take Haley fishing was about a twenty-minute drive away. They should reach it just as the sun came up.

He asked her questions about her trip from Texas to Eternity Springs during the drive up into the hills. He wanted to keep things light today. Last September, Haley's world had changed when the private jet carrying members of her mother's band and Haley's beloved nanny, Poppins, crashed in the Nevada desert, killing all aboard. Jackson and his ex-wife had done everything right as far as providing counseling and comfort, but Boone knew from experience how grief could manifest in unusual ways.

A vision of Hannah Dupree ghosted through his mind just before Haley began chattering about getting grubby with her Uncle T. Technically, Boone and Tucker were cousins to the girl. Still, the McBrides didn't get hung up on semantics. *Getting grubby* referred to the wilderness adventures that Haley had shared with Tucker during the past six to eight months. Time outdoors in Enchanted Canyon had proven to be an effective therapy in the girl's recovery. It was one of the reasons why Boone had suggested this morning's fishing trip when the family got together at his house last night.

His parents and sisters had arrived yesterday midafternoon, having dropped Linda Gail Pearson off at Angel's Rest, where a room vacancy for the wedding weekend had miraculously appeared. He'd given his family the grand tour of his new home, and they'd grilled hamburgers and sat beside the lake catching up on the happenings in one another's lives. It had been a great evening, though his attention had been divided between his visitors and his new tenant. The light shining in the window at the Serenity Cabbage continued to catch his notice until he'd gone to bed.

He'd noticed Hannah's car had been gone when he'd left this morning.

Boone's conversation with Haley continued to bounce from one subject to the next. As they approached his favorite fishing spot, a stretch of water on a pristine section of land that Boone had purchased from Cam Murphy a year ago, she was telling him about the two-pound catfish she'd caught two weeks ago using bacon as bait.

"You know you won't catch anything nearly that big up here," Boone warned as he pulled the Land Rover onto the shoulder of the road in his usual spot.

"But a rainbow will be prettier than a catfish, right?"

"Guaranteed. Catfish taste pretty, but they're ugly as sin to look at, don't you think?"

"They're super ugly!"

They exited the vehicle just as the first rays of sunshine speared above the mountaintop into the eastern sky. They spent the next few minutes getting Haley into her child-sized waders and gathering up the rest of their gear. As he led her toward the bubbling stream, he spoke to her about flies.

"Why do you make fake flies instead of catching real ones like we do worms?"

"That's an excellent question, Sweet Pea. I reckon a fisherman —"

"Or fishergirl!"

He grinned. "— or fishergirl could use a real insect, but for a lot of folks, a big part of the sport is tying the flies. It's rewarding when something you've created all on your own proves to be successful."

She went silent then. He didn't think much about it until she turned to him with a stricken gaze and heartbreak in her voice. "Like 'Wishes for My Angel.' "

Boone turned his head to hide his grimace. "Wishes for My Angel" was the song about Haley's nanny that Jackson and his ex had written and recorded shortly after the plane crash. A haunting, beautiful tune, the recording had gone platinum and won a Grammy.

Following the mention of her parents' song, Haley's mood deteriorated. She went from bubbly and enthusiastic to moody and sullen. Catching her first rainbow brightened her up a bit, but the effects of that proved temporary, and she soon sank back into grumpiness. Over the next forty minutes, Boone tried all the tricks he knew, from teasing and telling jokes to ignoring Haley's grouchy attitude completely. Nothing worked, so he turned to gently probing questions. "You want to talk about what's making you sad, Little Bit?"

She shrugged.

"I know what it's like to lose somebody you love. Sometimes it helps if you talk about what you are feeling. It helps me."

Again, she shrugged.

"I have big ears and wide shoulders."

She glanced up at him with her eyes narrowed in suspicion. "Your ears are not big. They're regular-sized ears."

"You think?" Boone cupped his ear and turned it toward her. "All I know is that I can listen pretty good if you want to talk about what has made you sad."

Again, she shrugged her little shoulders. Her bottom lip quivered a tiny bit. Emotion squeezed Boone's heart. He wished he had a better handle on how to deal with children. Guess he'd better develop one fast since he was about to become a dad.

But right this moment, Haley was the one who was hurting. He circled back to a distraction attempt with some bad jokes. "Knock knock."

"What?"

"Knock knock. You're supposed to say, *Who's there?*"

"I know that, but aren't we supposed to be quiet when we're fishing?"

Boone made an exaggerated purse of his lips, then he nodded and whispered loudly, "Knock knock."

She giggled and whispered back. "Who's there?"

"Canoe."

"Canoe who?"

"Canoe hurry up and catch a fish, please? I'm bored."

Haley's grin was Boone's reward. A moment later, she whispered, "Knock knock."

"Who's there?"

"Anita."

"Anita who?"

"Anita you to catch a fish first. It's your turn!"

"Good one." Boone winked at her and added, "Think it's time to switch out a fly. The fish don't seem to be hungry for what I got."

"Me too!"

Boone supported Haley's arm as they stepped toward the creek bank. "I want to try the one that Daddy says is called a Woolly Bugger. I think that's so funny. Don't you think that's so funny, Uncle B?"

"That's pretty funny. I'm kinda partial to the Squirmy Worm myself. I think I'll try that."

Once on the riverbank, they made their

way back to the spot where they'd left their tackle boxes. "Will you help me with my Woolly Bugger, Uncle B?"

"As long as it comes out of your tackle box rather than your nose."

"Gross! I don't pick my nose. I'm a girly girl."

He winked at her. "But you do like to get grubby."

"I do with Uncle Tucker, but getting grubby is digging for worms and hiking and gathering firewood. It's not picking your nose!"

"Ah." He winked at her, and she giggled again. He sensed that the tension had eased. Spying the bubblegum-pink tackle box a few step ahead, he said, "Let's see what we can do with your Woolly Bugger."

Haley darted around him and went to pick up her tackle box. Unfortunately, she'd left it unlatched. As she lifted it, the bottom dropped, and the contents of the box spilled. Boone saw in a glance that the little girl had much more than fishing tackle in her box. She had a hairbrush and a comb, a Barbie, a roll of Life Savers, and —

"Oh, no!" Haley cried, alarm in her voice. "I had them all organized!"

Boone's gaze zeroed in on the plastic tube whose cap had come off. "Lipstick, Haley?

Does your daddy know you have red lipstick?"

"Mama gave it to me."

She's only eight. Poor Jackson. "Something tells me I'm going to be real glad that Trace is a boy."

"Who's Trace?" she asked as she knelt and began returning items to the box.

Unwilling to lie or to answer the question truthfully to this precious little blabber box, Boone deflected. "Careful there. Lots of hidden barbs in your flies. We don't want you getting stuck."

"Don't worry, Uncle B. I've stuck myself four times when I've been fishing with Daddy or Uncle T."

"Four times, hmm?"

"It's just a pinprick, and a little blood doesn't hurt. You're gonna get a few bumps, scratches, and pokes when you're out gettin' grubby."

"That's my girl." Boone bent over, plucked one of Haley's Woolly Buggers from the clutter, and then picked up her fly rod from where she dropped it. He'd just finished switching out the fly when Haley cried out.

"Ouch!" She shoved to her feet, shaking her hand vigorously. Sure enough, a fishhook speared between the knuckles of her left hand. "Ouch! Ouch! Ouch! That hurts!"

Boone moved swiftly to the rescue. "Hold still, sweetie. Let me help you." Catching hold of her flailing hand, he stilled her and assessed the situation. "It took some talent to catch yourself there." It was a barbed hook too, unfortunately, which surprised him. McBrides were strictly barbless for freshwater fishing. "Did Tucker give this to you?"

Haley bravely looked at her hand. "I think this is one of the ones Mama gave me. It's called Princess."

Boone made a mental note to talk to Jackson about the contents of his daughter's tackle box. "I see. Well, hold what you got there. I'm going to clip the end before we pull it out."

Boone released her hand long enough to open his tackle box and remove his pliers and his first-aid pack. Seconds later, Haley calmly watched bright-red blood pearl on the back of her hand as he opened an antiseptic wipe.

"Now I've poked myself five times while I've been fishing," the eight-year-old said. "I need to be more careful."

"I'll second that. However, I'll take you fishing anytime. You've stayed calm, cool, and collected. I'll admit I was a little afraid that a self-professed girly girl might get upset at the sight of blood."

"No. I'm a tough girly girl."

She was that. Therefore, Boone was caught off guard ten minutes later when a beautiful red cardinal lifted from his perch in the upper branches of an aspen tree, swooped over the creek, and in a flash of unfortunate timing dropped a payload right on top of Haley's head.

All hell broke loose.

Hannah heard the screams and dropped the fish she'd just released from the hook. She looked at her guide and said, "That's a little girl. From which direction is that coming? Can you tell?"

He shook his head. "Can't be sure. Sound does weird things in the hills."

The sense of urgency sweeping through Hannah was unlike anything she'd experienced in the past three years. "Maybe she's fishing. Or is there a campsite close? A trail?"

"This is private land." The guide winced at the shrill screams as his brow furrowed in worry. "Most likely spot is the stretch we call Goldmine. It's not all that far from here, but you can't reach it along the creek. We'd have to go up the hill and down."

"Show me," Hannah demanded as she began stripping out of her waders.

"I don't know, Hannah. Maybe —"

"That is the sound of a terrified girl. She needs help. We need to help her."

The guide nodded, shucked out of his gear, then started off. Hannah followed quickly on his heels.

The screaming didn't stop, and as they topped the hill's rise, direction proved easier to determine. In only a few minutes, they spied the pair standing in the middle of the stream. Boone McBride stood four feet away from the young girl, his hands held up and out in surrender, panic in his expression. Hannah could see that he was constantly talking to the girl.

She wasn't listening. Her hands were flailing at her head.

"That's Boone McBride and his niece," the guide told Hannah. "He's not hurting her."

No. But he didn't appear to be helping her either. Hannah's fear subsided, but her concern did not. She descended the hill as quickly as possible. Growing closer, she could make out Boone's words.

"Sweetheart, it's okay. Everything is okay. Haley. Honey. Hush now. Please, sweetheart. It's okay."

He wasn't getting through to the girl. His body language conveyed that he'd tried approaching her without success, and when he heard their approach, recognized Hannah, his silver-gray eyes pleaded for help.

Hannah didn't hesitate, stepping right into the icy mountain stream and approaching the girl. "Haley, my name is Hannah."

"Poppins!" The girl turned a wild-eyed gaze her way. "The airplane blew up, and it's dropping on me! Get it off. Please, get it off! Please, Poppins. I need you!"

"What?" Hannah shot Boone an incredulous look.

"Bird droppings," he said. "She called her nanny Poppins."

"The plane is raining from the sky!"

"Oh, honey. No." Hannah pulled Haley against her and hugged her. This was what PTSD looked like in a eight-year-old. She dusted off her professional training in psychology along with her personal mothering experience to deal with the traumatized child as she rocked and crooned soothingly. "No, sweetie. No, sweetie. It's bird poop. Just icky sticky bird poop."

"No-o-o-o!" the girl wailed. Her little arms grabbed Hannah hard.

"Yes, it is. I see it. Why don't you let me wash it out?"

151

"Yes. Get it out. Get it out, Poppins. Get it all out!"

Hannah looked at Boone. "Do you have a cup or anything I can scoop with?"

"Use this," Boone said, handing her a water bottle. "The water won't be as cold. Wouldn't hurt to rub her hair with sand first. Hold on." He dipped down and scooped up a handful of sand. "Haley? Is it okay if I touch you now?"

"No! I want Poppins to do it! I want Poppins. I want Poppins. I need Poppins."

With his mouth set in a grim line, Boone transferred the dirt from his hand to Hannah's. She offered him a sympathetic smile, then spoke to Haley. "Okay, honeybunch," she said, gently pulling the girl's arm from around her waist. "I'm going to tilt your head back, so we keep the water out of your eyes. Okay?"

Tear-filled eyes gazed up at Hannah. Haley quaked like maple leaves in autumn. "Get it all, please? Get all the people from my head!"

Hannah briefly closed her eyes as her heart broke. Boone muttered a soft but vicious curse.

Inserting a level of calm and certainty into her voice, she began to rub Haley's hair and scalp with the river sand. "Oh, sweetheart, I promise you, this is bird poop. That's all it is, and I'm getting rid of it right now. Trust me. I know how to get yucky stuff out of young girls' hair. One of my little girls got saltwater taffy stuck in her hair, and we worked for hours to get it all out."

"I don't want to stay here for hours."

"This won't take any time at all. Bird poop isn't anything like taffy. I'll have it out in a jiffy."

"It's gross."

"Yes, but it's not as gross as lice. Lice really creeps me out. My other daughter got lice one time, and that was disgusting. We worked on her hair for a long time. Now I'm ready to rinse. Are you ready, Haley?"

Haley nodded. Hannah tipped her head back and started rinsing the gunk from her hair. "Hmm. I think I might just need to use a little water from the stream. It'll be cold. You okay with that?"

"Yes, please." Haley's voice remained strained, but the panic in it had faded. She sucked in a breath when Hannah poured the icy creek water through her hair.

"There. That does it. Good idea about the sand. That helped the situation a lot. Now I'm going to wring the water from your hair, and you should be good to go." Hannah smoothed back Haley's hair, then gathered it into one long strand and began to twist.

Haley's shoulders began to shake. Hannah glanced down and saw tears slip from her eyes. They were the first tears Hannah had seen, and she took it as a good sign.

"You're not Poppins, are you?" Haley asked.

"No. My name is Hannah. I'm a friend of your . . . cousin?" She glanced at Boone.

"I'm Uncle B."

Hannah tenderly touched Haley's shoulder. "I'm a friend of your uncle's."

"A very nice friend whom I owe big time," Boone added, his expression warm and filled with gratitude as he met Hannah's gaze before shifting to Haley. "Sugar Bug? You ready to head home?"

Haley's tears were flowing heavily now. She nodded.

"We'll get to the car faster if I carry you."

She nodded again, and Boone wasted no time in swooping her up into his arms. His silver eyes met hers. "Thank you, Hannah."

"Glad to be of help."

Haley wrapped her arms around Boone's neck and buried her head against his chest. As Boone sloshed his way toward the riverbank, Hannah realized for the first time just how wet and cold she was.

Her fishing guide called, "McBride, I'll

154

get your gear."

"Thanks."

Hannah watched them go, her heart heavy, memories a dark cloud on her horizon. *Mommy! Mommy! I forgot to swallow my taffy before I took my nap! I'm all stuck. Help me. Help me. Help me. Mommy!*

Hannah had been on the scene to help Sophia that day, but not when it truly mattered. Now she heard it in her nightmares. *I'm all stuck. Help me. Help me. Help me. Mommy!*

"I'm sorry, my loves." Moving like a woman three times her age, Hannah climbed from the mountain stream and hobbled toward the base of a pine tree. She sat with her back braced against the trunk and waited for her guide's return, thinking about her girls, thinking about Haley Mc-Bride and the song her parents had written and made famous — "Wishes for My Angel."

"Angels," she murmured, adding the *s* to make it plural. Then softly, sadly, she hummed the refrain.

Boone hurried toward his Land Rover with Haley in his arms. He had experience dealing with traumatized children due to the work he'd done in Fort Worth. He'd witnessed some heartbreaking things. However, watching Haley lose it this morning had left him feeling helpless in a way he had not experienced since Mary died. He'd been unequipped to deal with the child's distress.

Haley's screams had intensified when he'd tried to touch her. Talking to her had made no difference whatsoever. She hadn't heard him. Boone had stood frozen in uncertainty when Hannah Dupree ran to the rescue.

The woman didn't look anything like Haley's beloved, deceased nanny, but something about her had clicked with Haley. Hannah couldn't have played it more perfectly, and Boone's gratitude knew no bounds.

He had a towel in the back of the Land Rover, which he used to rub Haley's head as dry as possible. Then he buckled her into her seat, turned on the vehicle, and cranked up the heat. She fell asleep almost immediately. He was grateful for that too.

As much as he hated to interrupt Jackson, who was knee-deep in wedding prep, Boone placed a call to his cousin and detailed the events of the past half hour. Jackson and his fiancée were there to meet them when Boone pulled up to the cabin at the Callahan family's North Forty compound, where Jackson was staying before to his wedding.

After Caroline had spirited Haley off for a shower and shampoo, Boone filled Jackson in on details he had not shared during the phone call. "Where did the woman come from?"

"Her name is Hannah. She was with Bill Townsend. He's one of Cam Murphy's guides, and I'm sure they were fishing on a stretch of the creek around a bend from where Haley and I were. She came over the hill."

"Is Hannah a local?"

"No."

"Then did you get her name or where she's staying? I'd like to thank her personally."

"You'll have your chance. She's my date for your wedding. The rehearsal stuff too."

"Wait a minute. You hit on a woman while my daughter was screaming in panic?"

"No. I hit on Hannah the day before yesterday when I met her up at Lover's Leap." Boone gave Jackson a brief rundown of yesterday's events and ended by saying, "I recommended Cam's guide service, which I suspect is why she was fishing where she was this morning."

"Ah. Well, good timing there, Boot. I owe you."

"Pay me back by spreading the word for

everyone to make her feel extra welcome. I'd like her to hang around town for a while."

"Oh, yeah?" Interest lit Jackson's dark-green eyes.

"Yeah." Boone's emphasis on the period at the end of the word signaled he wouldn't listen to any further prying by his cousin about Hannah Dupree. "I'm going to head home. Mom promised to make her cinnamon rolls this morning, and I imagine it's just about time for them to be coming out of the oven."

"Lucky you." Jackson's envious grin turned serious as he extended his hand. "Boone, seriously, thank you for taking care of her."

"Hey, if not for Hannah, Haley and I might still be on that creek."

"Either way, you did us a solid. This is information her therapist needs." He hesitated a moment, then added, "Maybe Caroline and I should delay the honeymoon. We could —"

Boone shook his cousin's hand while saying, "Don't do it. Her mother will take care of it. A year ago this time, I never thought I'd say this, but Coco is a good mother. And the whole McBride family will have your back when you are gone."

158

Jackson nodded. The two men exchanged shoulder slaps, and Boone returned to his Land Rover. On the drive around the lake to his home, he reflected on the events of the morning. "Damned bird," he muttered. That poor little girl. Haley had come a long way since the accident, but today's crisis proved that healing was a process.

Thank God for Hannah. She'd known just what to do, known the exact right thing to say. Experience, probably, from being the mother of little girls.

Hope he never had to deal with lice. Good thing about being the father of a boy. Put the clippers on setting one and go to town. Shave it all off.

Wonder if Trace had been born with hair? He should have asked.

The psychological harm aside, he was glad that Haley wouldn't need to deal with a head-shaving situation right before her father's wedding. He could only imagine the drama that would entail.

Yep, glad he was the father of a boy. A baby boy.

Oh, holy Moses.

Boone had hit the ground running after his trip to Texas, so he hadn't had time to dwell or brood or panic. Probably a good thing. He was good about juggling a dozen different things at once, but he couldn't add a baby into the mix. He needed to compartmentalize his thoughts and feelings about the baby.

After the wedding, once his family left Colorado and Boone was free to return to Fort Worth, he would turn his thoughts toward Trace. "One step at a time, McBride. One step at a time."

He pulled into the drive leading to his home and saw his twin sisters disappearing into the trees on the trail that led around the lake. Maybe he was too late for warm cinnamon rolls after all. Didn't matter. If his mother's cinnamon rolls were a ten right out of the oven, they were still a nine point nine after they'd cooled.

Damn if his mouth didn't begin to water as he pulled into his parking place and switched off his Land Rover. Moments later, he strode into his kitchen, kissed his mother's flour-specked cheek, and glanced toward his oven, where the red numerals of the timer read less than a minute. "Do I have impeccable timing or what?"

The thought echoed through his mind Friday evening when Hannah Dupree responded to his knock on the front door of Serenity Cabbage. "Wow. Hannah, you look fabulous."

"Thank you. So the outfit is appropriate? I shopped at the boutique you recommended, and the owner helped me pick it out."

Boone gave her a slow once-over, allowing his appreciation to show. She wore skinny jeans with a long, gauzy purple top, belted at the waist. "Well, I'll be honest, Hannah. Caroline Carruthers is a beautiful woman, but I'm afraid you might outshine the bride."

"Do lines like that ever work for you, McBride?"

He shrugged and gave her a roguish grin. "It's not a line if it's true." She rolled her eyes and smirked, then said, "Thank you for the flowers. They're lovely. As were the ones from your cousin."

"Jackson sent flowers?"

"He did. And a dozen cookies too."

"Cookies! Shoot, I never thought of cookies. From Fresh?"

"Yes. Those things are everywhere. It's like you're all a bunch of cookie pushers — and I'm quickly becoming an addict."

He escorted her to the car. Then, after sliding into his seat, glanced at her while starting the engine, noting her smile of bemusement. "What?"

"I was trying to remember the last time a man opened the door for me."

"Uh-oh. Did I just step on your toes by opening your door? Break one of your principles? I grew up in West Texas, and my mama taught me that opening doors for ladies is good manners. It's a hard habit to break."

"No. No complaint. It's nice. So tell me about your mama, and the rest of your family too. They'll all be here tonight?"

"Yep." Boone decided to take the long way around the lake to the Callahans' North Forty, so at the end of his driveway, he turned right onto the road that circled the lake. He began answering her question. "I have two younger sisters, twins, Lara and Frankie — Francesca. My father's name is Parker, my mother's Marquetta, but she goes by Quetta. They live on a ranch in West Texas. Lara is a math nerd who works in Silicon Valley, doing something for a tech start-up that is beyond my capability to understand. Frankie is a makeup artist in Hollywood. She's made some spectacular monsters. You should see the Halloween parties she throws."

"I scare easily. Probably better that I don't."

He gave her a sidelong look. "Scaredy-cat,

are you?"

"I am. Monsters give me nightmares. I saw *Gremlins* in the movie theater and didn't make it past the thirty-minute mark."

"What about psychological thrillers?"

"They're even worse. I am a Hallmark movie girl all the way."

Boone winced. "Oh, man. I guess I'll need to keep the engagement ring in my pocket after all. I can't marry a Hallmark movie girl."

"Planning the wedding already, were you?" she asked drily.

"Fair warning," he replied, thinking about his cousin Tucker. "McBride men tend to do that. And hey, I'm taking you to meet my parents on our first date, so it should be obvious."

"Good thing we know from the first that we're not compatible. So what's your favorite movie?"

He rolled his tongue around his mouth and considered it. "That's a hard one. I can't say I have a single fav movie. I probably have a top five. *The Natural* is one. *Braveheart.* I watch *Caddyshack* at least once a year. Love *Saving Private Ryan* and *Seven Brides for Seven Brothers.*"

"All good — wait. *Seven Brides?* Seriously?"

"Seriously. Good music, beautiful women, and a totally politically incorrect theme. What's not to love?"

She was gawking at him. Grinning, he explained further. "The twins performed in summer musicals each year. Those girls can really sing. You couldn't live with them and not learn the songs, so when a lunch buffet of bad enchiladas ran through the cast one day, they recruited my cousins and me to perform for the matinee."

"You're a singer too?"

"Not at all. But we did know how to fight. We had a good time. It's a nice memory, and if you perchance hear one of us call another a lily-livered chicken-hearted lick-spittle, you'll understand why. That's a line we've never forgotten." That solicited the laugh he'd expected. He gave her a quick glance and asked, "What about you? Do you sing?"

"Only if I'm trying to scare raccoons away."

They spent the rest of the drive exchanging what Boone thought of as ordinary first-date, get-to-know-you small talk. Upon their arrival at the North Forty, he met her gaze and said, "Well, Ms. Dupree, ready or not. Prepare to meet the family."

164

Hannah couldn't say exactly what she expected upon her arrival at this McBride family event. But being hugged and kissed on the cheek by a Grammy-winning popmusic star wasn't it. Nevertheless, that's precisely what happened. Coco was demonstrably grateful for Hannah's help with Haley.

The singer set the tone.

Boone's parents, his sisters, his cousins — he had lots of cousins when you included the people named Callahan — all made a point to thank her and make her feel welcome. People came at her so fast that she didn't have time to think about being on a date. Not that this was a real date. It was, however, the most social activity she'd had in the past three years.

The rehearsal itself was touching, with her friend from the boutique, Celeste Blessing, making the presentation of official Angel's

Rest blazons to the bride, groom, and flower girl — Haley. Boone was jealous. The music was fabulous. The food, delicious. To Hannah's complete surprise, she had a very nice time.

Another surprise awaited her when the time came to leave. Rather than take the car he'd driven to the event, Boone led her down to the lake where half a dozen motorboats were docked. "If you're okay with getting out on the lake, I figured it'd be a nice evening to take the water route home. You up for that?"

Hannah considered the idea. Was she up for a boat ride? She hadn't been on the water since the girls died, but once upon a time, boating had been one of her favorite pastimes. Was she ready to take a boat ride? *That push–pull of the lake.*

Well, she'd already crept out on this limb. Might as well toddle on out to the end. "Sure. That sounds nice."

"Great." He gestured toward a beautiful wooden runabout, a luxury brand she recognized. "This one is mine."

"Oh, wow, Boone. One of the doctors on our lake had one of those. I always wanted to take a ride."

"It's your lucky day."

He stepped into the boat and offered her

his hand for balance as she stepped into the cockpit. She asked, "What about your car?"

"My folks will drive it home. I wasn't sure how you'd feel about the idea, so I planned options. They drove *Escape* over here, and now we'll just switch vehicles. I didn't want to bring you over here by the water. I grew up with three women in the house. I understand the importance of having good hair the first time you meet people."

"Smart man," she observed. "*Escape* is a good name for a boat."

"You don't have to sound so surprised."

"Serenity Cabbage?"

"Careful. You'll hurt my feelings."

He took a seat behind the wheel, pulled his phone from his pocket, and sent his text. Then he started the engine and nodded to Hannah's offer to cast the lines.

The engine roared, then purred, and the *Escape* pulled away from the North Forty dock.

It was a beautiful summer evening with temperatures in the sixties and a non-existent wind. The cruiser cut through the water like a dream. "Why a wooden boat, Boone? I picture you as more of a go-fast guy with a Formula or a Fountain. I know you like fast cars. I've noticed a Maserati in the multibay garage of yours."

"Running a speedboat on this lake would be overkill. Plus, the neighbors would hate me because they're so loud. The truth is that a wooden boat fits Hummingbird Lake."

"It's a great boat. Is the wood mahogany?"

"Yep. Wait until you see it in the daylight. The grain is gorgeous. I managed to track down some old Connelly wooden skis that complement it nicely. I've actually been on the lookout for an antique boat for a winter restoration project. Love me some classic beauty." He paused a moment, then added, "You belong in this boat on this lake, Hannah Dupree."

She felt her cheeks flush. She took Boone's comment as a compliment, not a come-on, and she was rusty on reacting to those. So she let it pass without a response, turned her face into the breeze, and lifted her face toward the starry sky. The moon was a fingernail rising in the east. She picked out the Big and Little Dippers, then asked, "Do you know the constellations?"

"Not really." He eased the throttle back to neutral and switched off the engine, allowing the boat to drift.

"Stargazing is actually an interest of mine. I took a class in college and got hooked."

He opened a box built into the transom

and removed something Hannah couldn't see. Then he sat upon the cushioned sundeck, scooted back, and lay down. He patted the seat beside him. "Come, show me."

Hannah hesitated only a moment before lying down beside Boone McBride. He switched on the item that he'd removed from the box and handed it to her. "You keep a laser pointer in your boat?"

"I have them stashed about lots of places. They come in handy. So show me the stars, Hollywood."

She sat up. "Hollywood?"

"Yeah. You remind me of all the classic movie stars rolled into one delicious package."

Oh. Well. Hannah ran from that by lying back down and speaking in a professorial tone. "I'm going to point out the Summer Triangle. We're looking for three bright stars. The first is here. Altair, in the constellation Aquila, the Eagle. See it?"

"I do."

"Next is Deneb." She drew a line with the pointer to another bright star. "Deneb is in the constellation Cygnus, the Swan. Finally, here's Vega in the constellation Lyra, the lyre. Cygnus is a horizontal cross of five bright stars. In dark sky conditions, Cygnus helps you find the Milky Way. There's too much light here tonight to see it."

"I know of a great dark sky spot only half an hour from here. If you're interested, I'd be happy to take you up there one night."

"I'm definitely interested. I love the Milky Way. It's been many years since I've seen it, though."

"It's a date." Before she could protest the terminology, Boone continued, "I recall a few of the stories that are connected to constellations, but I don't know Aquila or Lyra or . . . what was it? Signa?"

"Cygnus. As far as the Summer Triangle goes, in Japanese mythology, the celestial princess and goddess Vega fell in love with a man named Altair. Because Altair was a mortal, her father didn't approve and forbade them from seeing each other. The two lovers were separated by the Celestial River — the Milky Way. According to the legend, once a year a bridge of magpies forms, represented by Cygnus, and the lovers can be together again."

"That's not as tragic as some of the mythological stories."

"True."

"So what else do you have?"

"Hmm. Scorpius." She used the laser to trace the star path. "Antares is the big red star. It's something like eight or nine hundred times bigger than our sun."

"You do know your star stuff, don't you? I'm impressed."

"It's not very useful."

"Don't knock yourself. My brain is a font of useless information. Though I do a few useful things too."

Hannah grinned into the darkness. From what she'd seen, she was pretty sure Boone McBride's IQ was off the charts. "Give me an example. One of each. Start with useful."

"Okay. Give me a moment to think. I want it to be impressive. Hmm." He swiped the laser pointer from her hand and began playing with it, bouncing it from star to star while humming the *Jeopardy!* theme song. Finally, he said, "I know how to start a friction fire."

Hannah narrowed her eyes. Was *that* a come-on? Then she remembered something his cousin Tucker had said tonight. "Your cousin operates a wilderness school. I'll bet he taught you."

"I could have learned in the Boy Scouts."

Hannah's lips twisted in a wry grin. "For some reason, I can't picture you as a Boy Scout."

"I never liked those uniforms. But yes, Tucker taught me fire starting and dozens

171

of other wilderness skills. Useful information."

"Okay, then. What's your use*less* offering?"

"I can name the capitals of one hundred and ninety countries."

"Really?"

"Yep."

"I couldn't name one hundred and ninety countries, much less their capitals. Why would you want to do that?"

"It was a great bar bet in college. Plus, it made the coeds believe I was brilliant. Made it easier to get the girls."

"Something tells me you never had any trouble at all getting the girls."

He heaved a dramatic sigh. "It was a burden I stoically bore." She snorted, then laughed. "Actually, I was pretty much a one-woman man all the way through college. I fell hard and fast for the gal I married."

Hannah pulled her attention away from watching the pulsing light of a satellite moving fast across the night sky and looked toward Boone. "Tell me about her. What made you fall for your Mary?"

Hannah wished she hadn't asked the question when Boone didn't immediately answer. He dropped the laser pointer onto his chest, then laced his fingers behind his neck. Hannah had opened her mouth to say *Never mind* when he said, "She had a troubled family background. Her dad was an alcoholic and verbally abusive. She never admitted it, but I think he hit her a time or two. The night we met, we went to a frat party with our friends. While I was at the bar getting us a couple of beers, some guys cornered her and got too friendly for her comfort. I chased them off. Might have been some fisticuffs involved."

"Is that when your nose was broken?"

"Noticed that, hmm? Yep, ruined my good looks. Both times."

"Twice?"

"The first time I was twelve and going around with my cousins. The second time was not too long ago during a valiant matchmaking effort between Devin Murphy and his true love, Jenna. You met them tonight."

"The guy with the Australian accent. The outfitter's son."

"Yep. Another story for another day." Boone picked up his laser pointer and switched it back on. He idly traced star paths as he reflected. "I put the frat rats on the floor pretty fast that night. Not difficult because they were already blitzed. That fact didn't matter to Mary. From that moment on, she thought I hung the moon. I was her hero and her champion. She introduced me to her friends as her knight in shining armor."

"I'll bet that made you feel good."

"I soaked it up. It made me feel like I was ten feet tall." A contemplative note entered his voice as he added, "Mary needed me. The longer we were together, the more she leaned on me, and the more I liked it. My buddies thought I was crazy, but donning that armor suited me. In hindsight, I think that's why I was so unhappy practicing corporate law and why the move to the DA's office worked for me. I really liked being the guy people turned to for help." He hesitated a moment, then added, "Until it exploded in my face."

"Why do you —"

"No," he interrupted. "No more. Not tonight. So, what did you think of Jackson's ring bearer?"

Hannah didn't resist the change of subject. She laughed out loud, then said, "That was a surprise. I've read about people who include their pets as part of their wedding party, but this is the first time I've seen it. River is a well-trained dog, and he and Haley looked so cute together walking down the aisle."

"Let's hope they do just as well tomorrow. I don't know which worries me more — the fear of Haley having another out-of-the-blue meltdown or River getting distracted by a squirrel and taking off."

"He's not actually carrying the real wedding rings, is he?"

"Nope. River's part is all for show. Which reminds me . . ." He sat up and slid back into the driver's seat. "Probably ought to begin making our way home. Tomorrow is going to be a long day, and for me, it begins bright and early."

Hannah followed his lead and slid down from the sundeck. He put the boat in gear and idled forward, cutting smoothly through the calm surface of Hummingbird Lake. Despite his mention of his early morning, Boone took his time cruising home. They didn't speak, but the silence between them was comfortable. Hannah relaxed and sensed that she'd sleep well tonight. She'd been mildly tense about attending the party, and even though she'd enjoyed herself, she was glad to have that event behind her.

"This is so peaceful," she observed. "I've missed nighttime boat rides."

He reached over and patted her hand. "I'm happy to take you out on the lake anytime you wish."

"Thank you." Hannah leaned her head against the cushioned seat back, stared up at the sky, and absorbed the peace. She thought of her girls and imagined Zoe sitting in her lap with Sophia snuggled up against her side. When she saw a star go shooting across the sky, it seemed like a message from heaven.

All too soon, Boone guided his boat into a slip of a boat dock. Hannah sat up and looked around. "I'm lost."

"We're in a protected little cove that's hidden from the main body of the lake. It's also not readily visible from either the house or the cabin." Boone climbed from the boat and went about securing the lines to the cleats. "I keep a few other toys here you're welcome to use — canoe, paddleboat, a little one-man sailboat. Life jackets are in the deck box. Key to the box is beneath the fake rock just to the right of the walkway."

"That sounds lovely."

Hannah waited until he had the lines tied off to pick up her purse and rise. Boone offered her his hand. She took it and stepped from the boat. Uncharacteristically, she lost her balance, teetered, and tumbled into his arms.

"Well now," he murmured, his voice a deep, sexy rumble as he held her firmly against him. "Isn't this nice. Word of warning, Ms. Dupree. When an opportunity presents itself, I'm the kind of guy who's going to take advantage of it."

His signal came through loud and clear. If she didn't do something to stop him, Boone McBride was going to kiss her.

So long. It's been so long — a lifetime.

And she'd never been kissed by a man like Boone McBride.

Hannah lifted her face, and he bent his mouth to hers. Her eyes drifted shut as his lips brushed hers, testing, teasing, his touch the softest of satin, the lightest of silk. Anticipation skittered up Hannah's spine.

"Nice," he murmured, his voice a deep-throated purr before he got down to business. With his firm, hard body molded against hers, he took his time tasting and nibbling and sparking into life a yearning that Hannah had all but forgotten.

It was an entirely appropriate first-date first kiss, steamy but not hot. His hands skimmed up and down her back before his fingers sank into her hair. He held her head, and for the first time, she realized just how large his hands were. His fingers played with her hair even as his lips moved over hers. The kiss was inquisitive but not invading. Gentle but oh so exciting. He kissed her like she was fine wine, and he a connoisseur.

Hannah loved it. It was perfect. The approach, the atmosphere, the attention. She melted against him and allowed herself to enjoy it.

When he finally lifted his mouth from hers, she couldn't hold back a little sigh of dismay. His voice sounded throaty when he said, "Me too. But if I'd kept that up much longer, I'm not sure I could have kept it friendly. You pack a punch, Hollywood."

"So do you, Texas."

"Texas?"

"Big, bold, and brash."

"I can live with that." Then his left arm dropped to his side, and he stepped away. His right hand cupped her cheek, his thumb stroking softly over her cheekbone. She shivered.

"Thank you," he said simply. "I enjoyed this evening very much."

"I did too," she replied, speaking the truth.

He let his hand slide down to capture hers, and then he lifted it and pressed a gallant kiss to her knuckles. A knight-in-shining-armor gesture, she thought. Her lips twisted in a wry smile as, holding her hand, Boone led her up the walkway and onto a path that led, she soon discovered, to

Serenity Cabbage.

At her door, he tugged her back into his arms for a quick, hard kiss. "Good night, Hannah."

"Good night." Then, because her old habits died hard, as he turned and sauntered away, she added, "Sweet dreams."

He paused and glanced over his shoulder. "I don't know about dreams, but I sure intend to indulge in a sweet fantasy as I lie in bed tonight. After watching you savor that strawberry pinwheel cookie served for dessert tonight, well, I have this vision of you and me and lots of naked skin and a bowlful of that filling."

Hannah's mouth gaped in shock at the picture his words created in her mind. With a wave and wicked wink, he was gone, leaving Hannah to wonder aloud. "Knight in shining armor? Or fox in the henhouse?"

Most likely, both.

And damn if it didn't make him all the more appealing.

As the weekend's festivities progressed, Boone's success at compartmentalization weakened. With every hour that passed, his thoughts returned more often to the gigantic life change on his horizon. Saturday, he managed to stay in the moment at the wedding itself due to the gravity of the event.

The time spent in Hannah's company proved to be a great distraction, also. However, being around his parents and his sisters was becoming a problem.

On the one hand, he badly wanted to tell them about the baby. It was a significant event for him, and he wanted to share. He was scared to death at the thought of being a single dad. He was excited at the thought of it. He wanted to ask his mother's advice about feeding and diapering and sleep hygiene. He wanted to speak to his dad about the responsibilities of fatherhood and best practices for discipline. In other words, he wanted to learn Parker McBride's secret for putting the fear of God into his children with only a look.

And yet the circumstances hadn't changed from a week ago. It was still in his parents' best interests that he waited to present the adoption of his new son as a fait accompli. So he bit his tongue and bided his time and avoided looking his mama in the eyes.

Boone woke early the morning his family was due to depart. He went for a run, hoping to burn off some of the nervous energy that had been building over the past few days. His mind was full of plans and possibilities. His parents planned to leave by eight in order to arrive at the Colorado

Springs airport in time for the twins to catch a plane back to California. Boone had movers scheduled to arrive at eight thirty to switch out bedroom furniture for a crib, changing table, and other baby gear.

He hoped he'd ordered the necessary baby paraphernalia. His experience with infants was minimal. Okay, it was next to nothing.

He should probably get somebody with experience to review his list and tell him what he needed to add. After all, Eternity Springs didn't have a Buy Buy Baby where he could run in and grab what he needed.

Although, with all the babies being born here, and the tourists who shopped for their grandchildren during visits to Eternity Springs, bet there was a market for a specialty children's shop. The one in Redemption appeared to do good business, and the small Texas town where his cousins lived was similar to Eternity Springs in many ways.

He made a mental note to look into the idea at a later date. Of more immediate need, who could he hit up to review his shopping list? Heaven knew there were plenty of people in town with recent baby experience whom he could approach. Eternity Springs' recent population explosion had some folks jokingly refer to the place as

Maternity Springs.

He could call Jenna Murphy or Hope Romano or Gabi Flynn. They'd all be happy to give him advice. Or he could ask Hannah. Her experience might not be as recent as that of his local friends, but he wasn't worried about having all the new bells and whistles in baby gear. He wanted to confirm that he had the basics covered for a newborn. Fundamentals didn't change. Babies needed beds and bottles and blankets. Diapers and wipes and — clothes. Oh, crap. Boone halted in his tracks. He hadn't ordered any clothes!

That was a foolish oversight, but nothing insurmountable. He'd pick up what he needed in Fort Worth. Now to figure out what he needed.

He worked the problem for the rest of his run, but the aroma of fresh-brewed coffee and frying bacon distracted him as he entered the kitchen and found his mother at the stove. "You're up early."

She glanced up at him and smiled. "I was hoping to have a chat with you. We've hardly had any opportunity to visit this trip."

"Let me grab a quick shower, and then I'll help make breakfast. Okay?"

"Make it quick. Your dad will be up in twenty minutes."

"All right."

A little concerned about why his mother might want to speak to him privately, Boone took one of the quickest showers of his life and returned to the kitchen wearing shorts and a T-shirt. "Is something wrong?"

"What? Why would you ask that?"

"You wanted to talk to me before Dad got up. Tell me nobody is sick."

"No one is sick. We're fine. I didn't mean to worry you. I just wanted a chance to visit with you without all the interruptions we had this weekend."

"It's been a busy weekend."

"Yes, and a wonderful weekend. It's so good to see Jackson happy again. I wish his parents were here to meet Caroline. I know they'd have loved her, but I'm sure they watched the festivities from celestial seats."

"I don't doubt it, Mom."

As she used a pair of tongs to flip the bacon she was frying, she casually asked, "So what's up with Tucker and Gillian? I haven't seen so many sparks fly since the bonfire your father built in 2012."

"That was one great bonfire." *Eagle eye Quetta. That's my mom.* Boone poured himself a cup of coffee. He needed to watch his words here. He wouldn't betray his cousin's confidence. Still, Tucker's love life might be the distraction he needed to keep the conversation away from himself. "I think Tucker definitely has a thing for Gillian Thacker."

"I like Gillian very much. Do you think there might be a future there with Tucker?"

Boone sipped his coffee. "Well, I would definitely bet on a present. If it makes it to the future is anybody's guess."

"Hmm," Quetta McBride said. "Well, if Tucker decides he wants her, I'll put my money on him. He might not be quite up to your standard when it comes to pursuing what you want, but he's close on your heels."

Boone wouldn't bet against Tucker either.

"And speaking of what you want," his mother continued as she removed crispy bacon from the frying pan onto a platter. "Dare I get my hopes up about Hannah?"

"No," he fired back quickly. Too quickly, because she pinned him with a suspicious look.

"What's wrong with her? I liked her very much too."

"Nothing's wrong with her. As far as I know. I guess something might be wrong with her, but I don't know it yet. I don't know her well enough to have discovered it."

"Well, I'm a good judge of character, and I think she's lovely. Quietly classy. Not a snow bunny gold digger like that last girl you introduced to us."

"C'mon, Mom. The only reason I introduced you was due to some spectacularly bad timing." It had been one of the most embarrassing moments of his life. What were the chances that his parents would book the same intimate bed-and-breakfast near Wolf Creek ski resort as he, and exit their room at the exact moment Boone was unlocking the door to his room with his date's hand in his pants?

Quetta McBride's lips twitched as she reached for her own coffee cup and took a sip. "Well, I'm glad to see you dating a woman your age."

"I don't discriminate based on age," Boone defended. He'd dated plenty of women older than he. But then he'd dated plenty of women, period. That probably was not a direction he wanted to take the conversation, so he said, "Anyway, Hannah is not a permanent resident of Eternity Springs."

"Unless you decide you want her to be one."

"Mother." Boone snitched a slice of bacon off the platter and got his knuckles slapped for the effort. "Your confidence in my ability is gratifying but misplaced."

She made an unladylike snort.

"Okay, I'll admit to being dogged in my pursuits, but anything between Hannah and me is truly in the puppy stage. I don't want you to get your hopes up where my love life is concerned, Mom. I have bigger fish to fry at this particular moment."

As soon as the words left his mouth, he knew he'd made a mistake. Dang it. This was why he'd tried to steer clear of his mother this weekend.

She pounced like a cat. "What fish? You have another project cooking, don't you, son? I knew it. You've been avoiding me all weekend. What is it this time? A new business in Redemption? That's it, isn't it? Have you come up with the idea that will bring you home to Texas? You know if you settle in Redemption along with Tucker and Jackson and you all marry and start families, your father and I might need to buy a vacation home down there. It would be so lovely to have family around us once again. Why I wouldn't be surprised if your sisters moved —"

"Mom. Whoa." Boone held up his hands, palms out. "Slow down. You've leaped in a seriously wrong direction. I don't have any

186

more plans for businesses in Enchanted Canyon."

"Seriously?" Her smile drooped. "Not even anything with Ruin?"

Boone hesitated. Ruin was the ghost town at the far end of Enchanted Canyon, an outlaw conclave occupied in the latter part of the nineteenth century and part of the McBride family's recent inheritance from a distant relative. Boone sincerely believed it was a gold mine waiting to be worked. Tackling that project had been next on his to-do list after helping to launch Tucker's Enchanted Canyon Wilderness School.

All that changed with a phone call from Fort Worth.

The phone call he couldn't mention to his mother. Yet. "Ruin is on my list, but I'm going to have my hands full in Eternity Springs this summer."

"So you do have a project," she stated.

He said the first thing that popped into his mind. "Maternity Springs."

"Excuse me?"

Well, he'd jumped into this pool. He might as well start swimming. "It's a new retail business. I don't know if you've noticed, but we've had a serious population boom here in town. Our residents have nowhere to shop. Plus, we have tons of grandparents who are in the market for those NANA WENT TO ETERNITY SPRINGS, AND ALL I GOT WAS A LOUSY T-SHIRT shirts. Stock some stuffed bears and elk and raccoons I think we can sell a bundle of souvenirs during tourist season. Then the rest of the year, we can sell to residents. People prefer to shop locally, if at all possible."

Despite being an off-the-cuff idea, he floated it with enough detail that his mother obviously bought it. Warming to his subject, he elaborated, "I picture something about the size of Claire Lancaster's Christmas shop. Have rooms set up like nurseries. What do you think?"

She pursed her lips, tilted her head to one side, and considered his idea. "I like it. Cute name, but I think you should add something to it. Like, Children's Shop. Maternity Springs Children's Shop. That way, people will know you sell more than just maternity clothes."

"Great suggestion," he replied, meaning it. And seeing his opportunity, he followed up by asking, "So what sort of things would you suggest we stock in our children's store?"

She set down her tongs, folded her arms, and accused him in a snippy tone. "You mean the grandparent gifts? Now, how would I possibly know?"

"Moth-er," he whined like a ten-year-old.

Her expression softened. She reached out and up to cup Boone's chin, and they shared a smile. The fact that she felt she could tease him about the subject of grandchildren demonstrated how far they'd come in recent years. At that moment, he was tempted — oh, so tempted — to tell her about Trace. However, the memory of her devastation in the wake of his failed adoption attempts stilled his tongue. He had good reasons for his silence. He couldn't forget that.

That said, he didn't need to miss this chance. "Not grandparent gifts. Basic stuff for babies. Like clothes. What are the basic clothes you need when you bring a baby home?"

"Why? You won't run this business yourself. You'll have a manager in charge of buying, won't you?"

"Sure. It's just food for thought."

She shrugged and added more bacon to the skillet. As she placed the plate of bacon into the oven and returned to the stove, she spoke about swaddles and onesies and sleepers. Boone resisted taking his phone from his pocket to make notes. The conversation moved on to the summer tourist season in both Redemption and Eternity Springs. When she made a move to bring the discussion back around to Hannah Dupree, he wasn't nimble enough to ward her off.

"What does she do for a living?"

Well, he wasn't sure, but she was living on life insurance proceeds if he had to make a guess. That's nothing he wanted to share with his mother. "I don't know. She hasn't volunteered, and I haven't wanted to ask."

"She told me she graduated from Brown."

"An Ivy Leaguer, hmm? Well, that's an interesting tidbit. Good job, Mom." He paused a moment, then asked, "So what else did you weasel out of her?"

"I didn't weasel. I politely inquired during a social conversation. And I didn't learn much of anything else, I'm afraid. She's sharp. She deflected most of my questions with ease and experience and grace. She impressed me. You should keep seeing her, Boone."

He was saved from replying when his father entered the kitchen along with one of the twins. The opportunity for a private conversation with his mother ended. Boone made biscuits, Frankie scrambled eggs, and his dad went to pour orange juice. They all gave Lara a hard time when she arrived just in time to sit down to eat. It was a talent of hers. Of course, family rules meant that she always had to take point on cleanup. It was an ordinary, everyday family interaction, and it gave Boone a bittersweet sense of regret for days gone by. He hated to see them leave. When would they next share a moment like this with the whole family together for breakfast?

And of course, next time, there'd be another face at the table.

Excitement and anticipation replaced the regret roiling inside Boone as he rose to help his sister with the cleanup. He was itching to get this day going. He loved his extended family, but he was ready to enjoy his nuclear family. Trace. Time to get this daddy show on the road. "This goes against tradition, but Lara, I have this. Y'all go on and finish packing."

"Are you sure, son?" Parker McBride said. "We're just a tad behind schedule."

"I'm sure." He made a shooing motion with his hand. "Y'all get." He winked at his mother and added, "I think I'll try to set up a dinner date."

Not with Hannah, but with Sarah Winston. The plan was for Boone to fly down to Texas later today, meet Trace tomorrow, and

191

set the legalities into motion. He, his son, and his son's nanny would return to Colorado as soon as the State of Texas checked off on it. Hopefully by early next week.

However, now that tomorrow was almost here, he had the notion of moving tomorrow up to today. With any luck, before he went to bed tonight, he'd be able to meet his new son.

Boone was wiping the table with a damp paper towel when his cell phone rang. It was early for anyone to be calling, so he checked the number. Sarah Winston.

Immediately, his stomach made a slow, sick roll. He didn't believe that he'd conjured Sarah up by thinking about her a few minutes ago. Something was wrong. Why else would she be calling this early if something weren't wrong? Even the hour's time difference wouldn't justify a simple looking-forward-to-seeing-you phone call.

He tossed the paper towel into his trash can and stepped out onto the deck. With his throat tight, his muscles tense, he asked, "Sarah? It's early for a call."

"I know. I'm sorry. I wanted to give you as much time as possible. Boone, we have a problem."

CHAPTER NINE

Hannah slept a little later than usual and dawdled over her morning coffee, thoroughly enjoying the peace of the sunny summer morning. She had plans to rent a Jeep from Refresh Outfitters and play tourist today, driving the Alpine Loop up to the old mining town of Silverton. It was supposed to a beautiful trip.

She figured she'd have lunch there, poke around the shops, tour the museum, and check out the narrow-gauge train as it chugged into town.

The only problem with doing that meant that she'd likely face a barrage of children, because the train ride from Durango to Silverton was so popular with families. Best she decide ahead of time if she was ready for that.

For the past three years, she'd studiously avoided gatherings with lots of children. Between caring for Haley McBride and finding herself in the midst of a significant number of little ones at the wedding on Saturday, she was feeling a little raw.

Maybe she'd leave town before the train arrived. Give herself a little time.

Considering that she'd been little more than a traveling hermit for the past three years, she'd done okay at the wedding. She'd intermingled and conversed and even entertained with a story or two. And then that kiss with Boone. She'd done all right there too.

Feeling proud of herself, Hannah polished off her coffee, then showered and dressed. She'd just finished blow-drying her hair when she heard the banging on her door.

"Hannah! Hannah? I see your car." *Knock. Knock. Knock.* "Hannah?"

She opened the door. "Boone! What's wrong? Did someone get hurt?"

"No. It's not that. Nothing like that. Thank God. I couldn't handle that on top of this. Can I come in?"

She opened the door wide and waved him inside. He stalked forward into the living room, then halted abruptly and rubbed the back of his neck. "I need a favor, Hannah. A really big huge ginormous favor. The biggest favor I've ever asked of anyone in my life. Please say yes. I don't know what I'll do otherwise."

She shut the door and walked toward him. "Boone, I'm happy to help if I can, but you sound like you need a kidney or something."

"Shoot, I don't need a kidney. I have two of those. What I need is a woman."

She blinked. Her gaze reflexively dropped to Boone's crotch.

"That didn't come out the way I meant it. This isn't a medical emergency. Well, not my medical emergency anyway. I didn't accidentally take my father's Viagra or something. Not that he uses it. I can't imagine that he'd need it. My dad is — wait." He held up his hand palm out and then gave his head a shake. "I'm babbling. I was nervous already, and now this."

"What's wrong, Boone?"

"I need help. I'm hoping you will help me, Hannah. Otherwise, I'm going to have to call my mother. I've tried my damnedest to protect her until everything is settled legally. The last thing I want to do is clue her into the situation now. Well, that's not the very last thing. The very last thing would be my doing this thing alone. Hannah, I need you to come to Texas with me. I can probably handle things okay here at home by myself. I have friends who will help. But there's no way I can manage traveling on my own.

Please, Hannah. Say you'll help. I'm desperate."

The words *settled legally* made Hannah's antennae wiggle. Still, even as she grew alarmed, she recalled that he *was* a lawyer. Lawyers do legal things. "You want me to come to Texas with you because . . . ?"

He dragged his hand down his face. "Serena had an emergency appendectomy today."

"Serena is who?"

He sucked in a deep breath, then exhaled in a rush. "My nanny."

Hannah took both a physical and a mental step backward. "Your nanny."

"Yeah."

"You haven't mentioned children."

"I know."

Wow. Boone had talked about the wife he'd lost. He'd spoken of relatives galore and introduced her to dozens of them. He'd talked to her about a new puppy he was getting, but he'd never mentioned a *child*? What kind of man was he?

"Actually, I did mention him, but I led you to believe he was a dog. Remember? Up at Lover's Leap, I talked to you about needing to pick out a name for my new pup? I was really trying to come up with a name for the baby I'm going to adopt. I decided

196

on Trace. Trace Parker McBride. Parker for my dad. Trace is an old family name. You helped me figure it out."

"You are adopting a baby." Hannah walked into the kitchen and popped a pod into the coffeemaker as she attempted to process the information he'd just shared.

"Well, that's the plan. I have history here if you recall, so it's something I'm afraid to take for granted. Say you'll come, Hannah. Please? I'll make it worth your while. Pay you whatever you want. Please say you'll help me."

"You want me to be your nanny."

"Just until Serena recovers from her surgery. I'm going to fly down to Fort Worth a little later today. We'll return to Colorado as soon as I can make it happen. Hopefully by early next week. I'm going to buy a big, safe SUV in Fort Worth. You can make the drive in a day, but it's a long day. I think that's probably not doable with a baby."

"How old is this child?"

"He'll be three weeks old tomorrow."

Boone McBride wanted her to care for a three-week-old child. Right. As if she could care for a baby when she could barely take care of herself. She was only now acclimating to being around little ones again. "Boone, I'm sorry. No. I can't do it."

"Why not? What are your objections? Allow me the opportunity to overcome them." When she hesitated, he added, "You're great with kids. You proved that with Haley."

Hannah shut her eyes. This was just too much. Too hard. "And you don't know what a big moment that was for me personally. It's the first time I've interacted with a child since I lost Zoe and Sophia."

He deflated like a bicycle tire pierced by a nail. "Oh."

"I think being a child's caretaker is a step too far for me at this point in my life."

"Yeah. I can see that." He sighed and rubbed the back of his neck. "I should have realized it might be a problem for you." In a lower tone, speaking more to himself than to her, he said, "Crap. I really, really, really don't want to lay this on my mother."

"Sit down, Boone. Let's talk about the problem. Sometimes a second set of eyes can help reveal a solution."

He nodded and took a seat on the stool at the bar separating the kitchen from the cabin's main room. Without asking if he wanted it, Hannah set the cup of fresh coffee in front of him and set about making a second cup for herself.

"I don't know where to begin," he said.

"The beginning. How did this adoption

come about?"

He told her about the phone call from a Fort Worth colleague, about his panic and soul-searching retreat in Texas, and his decision to take a leap of faith and make another run at fatherhood. "On the morning I met you, Celeste reminded me that family and friends are a Zippo in my pocket."

"Come again? A Zippo?"

He smiled for the first time since his arrival. "Light. Friends and family are a source of light and shelter from life's storms. She told me to be somebody's light, and that's what I'm trying to do. That's how I'm going to earn my Angel's Rest blazon."

Hannah murmured beneath her breath, "Be somebody's light."

Boone traced the rim of his coffee cup with his index finger. "You were the first friend who popped into mind during my storm this morning, so that's why I came running here for help."

Be somebody's light. "Why don't you want to ask your mother for help?"

"She wants to be a grandmother more than just about anything in life. She was devastated each time the adoptions fell through, and when Mary died, it came close to breaking her. She's had some heart irregularities in the past year, so I don't want

199

to cause her any extra stress. I can't ask my sisters because those two can't keep a secret for beans. But I do have friends, both here and in Texas. I just need to figure out who to approach."

Be somebody's light. Some flicker of emotion sparked to life inside of Hannah. Was it hope or excitement or fear? She couldn't say.

"I probably should give Celeste a call and explain my problem," Boone continued. "She's Eternity Springs' ultimate problem solver. I'm sure she'll have an idea." He gave Hannah a crooked smile and added, "Celeste has a way about her. You can always count on her to offer insight into a problem, if not an outright solution. She tends to prefer to guide a person rather than tell them what to do."

Hannah reflected on her interaction with Celeste at the boutique last week. The innkeeper had a subtle way of suggestion. "I can see that. I met her cousin at the wedding. She appeared to have a different approach."

"Angelica?" Boone laughed softly. "She's different from Celeste, all right. She doesn't hesitate to give her opinion, and she has one of those on just about every topic under the sun."

200

"She told me my dress was great, but that I'd look so much better if the color was yellow."

Boone rolled his eyes. "The dress *was* great. You looked like a million bucks."

"Celeste guided me toward it."

They shared a smile, and before she could second-guess herself, Hannah said, "I'll go to Texas."

His gaze snapped to meet hers. "Seriously?"

Her heart pounded like a piston. "Yes. I won't commit to six weeks, which I'm guessing will be the earliest time your nanny would be discharged from her doctor, but I will be your travel nanny. I'll help you bring Trace home to Eternity Springs."

I'll be your light.

"A travel nanny. That's good. I can work with this." Boone closed his eyes and exhaled a heavy breath. "Thank you. Oh, Hannah. Thank you!"

He shoved to his feet and, in two long strides, moved around the bar. He threw his arms around Hannah, lifted her off her feet, and twirled her around. "Thank you. Thank you. Thank you. You are an angel, Hannah. My personal angel."

And then, because Boone McBride was

201

the very devil, he lowered his mouth and kissed her.

Boone recognized he might have taken a step too far when he kissed her again, but damn, he'd have kissed an ancient old crone with whiskers and warts if she'd just solved his problem. That said, he wouldn't have kissed an ancient old crone with such enthusiasm or fervor. Or passion.

Damn, but kissing Hannah Dupree stoked his coals.

When he'd finally begun dating again after Mary's death, he'd been content with sharing a series of casual relationships with like-minded women. He'd been in a dry spell of late, and while he missed sex, he hadn't missed it enough to go looking for it.

Hannah Dupree changed the paradigm.

For one thing, his response to her was anything but casual. The woman called to him in a way that no woman had since Mary. She was beautiful, intelligent, and witty. She was vulnerable in that way that appealed to the hero wannabe aspect of his character that apparently hadn't died with his wife. One would think that another vulnerable woman would have him running the other way, but no. Not when that woman was Hannah Dupree.

So what was different about her?

He'd put some thought into the question the night after the wedding when he'd woken from a deliciously erotic dream in which Hannah had been wearing a Dallas Cowboys Cheerleader uniform. Once he'd wrestled his libido under control, he'd figured it out. Beneath that vulnerability and the sadness swimming in those big blue eyes, he sensed a core of steel. Hannah was bent, but she wasn't broken. She was fighting her way back, and he wanted to help her.

Wasn't it handy, then, that she was willing to help him, and that she felt like heaven in his arms?

Until she wrenched her mouth away from him, and her hands, which had lifted to encircle his neck, dropped between them. She pushed against his chest. "No. Put me down."

Reluctantly, he lowered her feet to the floor.

Her tone sharp and scolding, she glared up at him. "If we do this, we are not going to do this."

He knew better than to pretend that he didn't follow her meaning, and he wasn't about to do anything to make her change her mind. "Okay. Okay."

"Hands off."

"Yes, ma'am."

"No kissing."

"It was a thank-you kiss. I'm a Texan. We're demonstrative that way."

"Yeah, well. I'm a traveling hermit. I'm not demonstrative."

"A traveling hermit? Oh, Hollywood, you're funny." He backed away, his hands up in surrender, but he added in his thick, sexy drawl, "And by the way. You demonstrate just fine."

Then without allowing her a chance to return fire, he launched into planning mode. "Pack what you need through the weekend, but don't worry about getting everything. We can always pick up what we need there. I have movers due to arrive in —" He glanced at his watch. "— fifteen minutes. It shouldn't take them more than an hour. Can you be ready to leave by then?"

"I can, but movers?"

"Guest bedroom furniture out, nursery furnishings in."

"Ah, I see."

"If you get ready and want to walk on over to the house, I'd be grateful to have your input on anything else we might need. We can get it ordered and on the way so that it'll be here when we bring him home. The order was a lot of guesswork on my part."

"Of course. It won't take me long to pack."

"Just leave your bag on the porch, and we can pick it up on the way out. Be sure to bring a swimsuit and a sweater. It's hotter than blazes in Texas this week, but air-conditioned buildings can be downright cold." He hesitated before adding, "Again, I can't thank you enough, Hannah. You're a lifesaver."

He saw immediately that it was the wrong thing to say. Pain flashed across her face like lightning. Not for the first time, Boone wondered what the story was behind her children's drowning.

While he searched futilely for the right words, a wan smile replaced the pain on Hannah's face. She said, "You'd better get back for the movers. I'll be along shortly."

Boone knew when to beat a strategic retreat. Ten minutes later, he opened his front door to Bill Johnson, of Johnson and Sons Movers. "Hey, Bill."

"Morning, Boone. You ready for us?"

"Sure am. Let me show you where to start." He led the way upstairs to the bedroom he'd chosen for Trace, explained what he required, gave them a photo and design plan, then left the men to do their work. As he packed his bag, he reflected on the harrowing forty-three minutes between the phone call from Texas, and the moment his family departed. He'd had a helluva time keeping the worry from his manner while interacting with his family. More than once, he'd come close to fessing up to his mom, but instead, he'd pinned his hopes on Hannah.

Thank God she hadn't let him down. It had been his lucky day when he'd decided to let his little Zippo shine. Doing so lit the way for both of them, didn't it? Wonder if Celeste had anticipated that. *Of course she had.*

He had his bag packed and in the back of his Land Rover when Hannah arrived. He was happy to see she carried a duffel and wore a backpack. Not that he'd expected her to beg off, but he wouldn't relax entirely until they were wheels up.

He stowed her bags before leading her upstairs, where Bill and his men were well on their way to being finished. He picked up a small leather portfolio from the table on the landing where he'd left it and handed it to her. "For notes about what I've forgotten."

He led her to the doorway of the nursery,

watching avidly for her reaction. She visibly melted. "Oh, Boone. It's darling. Just darling."

He preened beneath her approval, even as he said, "Don't give me too much credit. I found a photo I liked on Pinterest and ordered everything in the picture." He'd gone with a forest theme in earth-tone colors. The crib, changing table, and dresser were made from knotty pine, and the accessories included a moose lamp and a "bearskin" rug.

"There's more stuff in the room next door. A few toys. Lots of things that rock and swing and play music. I don't know where to put it, and I forgot all about buying clothes."

Hannah opened the portfolio and jotted a few notes. "Let's see the other room."

"It's the second door on the right." He gestured for her to lead the way down the hall. There, Hannah stopped abruptly. "A *few* toys?"

He offered an abashed grin and lifted his shoulders.

"An electric race car set? A bike? Remote control cars? Getting a little head of yourself and Trace, don't you think?"

"There's a Baby Einstein play station in there somewhere too."

Hannah shook her head, stepped into the room, and began surveying the boxes. "Did you order bottles?"

"Yes. And talk about a difficult decision. There are dozens of brands and sizes and styles. How do you know what to buy?"

"Let me guess," she drily replied. "You bought some of them all."

"Well, yeah. I can donate what we don't use to women's shelters."

She muttered something about generosity and more money than sense. At the same time, she inspected the contents of what he now considered the overflow room. Pretty soon, she was humming a tune. Recognizing it, he groaned. " 'This Old Man'? Seriously. Thanks for the earworm, Hannah. I'll be knick-knack paddy-whacking all day. That's the worst."

"No," she absently replied. " 'Wheels on the Bus' is the absolute worst."

"Great. Just great." He shook his head and signaled a retreat. "I'm going to go write Bill his check."

Bill and his crew took Boone's request for speed to heart, and they finished up twenty minutes ahead of schedule. Boone doubled the tip for each worker. "You seven men are the only people who know what was delivered to my house today. I know how small-town gossip is. There's another C-note in it for each of you if you keep the news to yourselves until I return."

"We are nothing if not discreet," Bill said. He folded his check and cash tip and slipped them into his shirt pocket. "It's all part of the job."

With the movers gone, Boone went in search of Hannah. He found her in the kitchen unpacking baby bottles and loading them into the sterilizer. "You ready to go?"

"Give me five more minutes, and I'll have this all set up for you to run when you get home."

"Sounds great."

Forty minutes later, they were in the air. It was Hannah's first trip on a private jet. They talked airplanes for a bit before conversation switched to baby gear and child-rearing challenges. However, as they drew closer to landing, Boone lapsed into silence.

The day he'd left Fort Worth, Texas, he'd intended never to return. He'd skipped weddings and funerals and the Fort Worth Stock Show — the favorite event of his youth. He'd inconvenienced his family and disappointed his friends and cut ties with his former colleagues because doing otherwise meant he'd have to go home and face his failures.

Now here he was aboard a jet approaching the landing path to Meacham Field on the north side of the city. "I'm a bundle of nerves," he admitted to Hannah.

"Not exactly what a person wants to hear from the man who employs the pilot who is landing the plane," she drily observed.

It was just the light touch of humor he needed to hear at the moment. As the Cessna landed smoothly a few minutes later, he was ever so glad to have Hannah Dupree at his side.

The heat of the summer afternoon hit like a fist when they exited the plane and walked toward the car he'd ordered. Wincing, Hannah said, "Oh, wow. I expected it to be hot, but this is crazy. You can hardly breathe, it's so hot."

"It's why what seems like half of Texas flees to the mountains in the summer. I checked the forecast. Supposed to hit a hundred and five today."

"Tell me why I agreed to leave Eternity Springs this morning?"

"Because you're my friend and you have a heart as big as this state." Then, because his fundamental nature hadn't changed, he added, "Just so you know, I think you're hot as Texas too."

She chided him with a smirk, but he thought she looked pleased with the compliment.

Soon they were on their way to the downtown hotel where he'd upgraded his reservation to a two-bedroom suite before leaving Eternity Springs. As he watched the familiar skyline grow larger with their approach, his melancholy returned. Inside himself, he felt as if someone had cranked down the air conditioner to freezing.

He had thought he'd left his ghosts behind in Enchanted Canyon when he'd decided to adopt the child. He'd spent the long weekend hiking the canyon trails and thinking about history — his own and that of people who had gone before. While poking around the ghost town that brought the Old West to life, he'd reflected on the cowboys and Comanche, and the desperadoes and fallen women who'd called the canyon home. Sinners and cast-outs with debts to pay.

Debts to pay.

He'd camped the last night in the outlaw enclave. There, he'd blown the mental safe where he'd locked away the past and allowed his ghosts to mingle with the troubled souls of an earlier time. Right there in the middle of Ruin, he'd released his memories, released the grief.

He'd faced his ghosts — the wife he'd lost, the child stolen from him by the woman he'd counted as a friend. The people and events that had shattered his heart and tormented his soul. When he'd returned home to Colorado, he'd thought he'd put those ghosts to rest. Judging by the chill running through his veins right this moment, he'd thought wrong.

His ghosts had hitched a ride and settled in, turning his blood cold as the limo driver took them past the jewelry store where he'd bought Mary's engagement ring, and the steak house where he and his wife had celebrated their final anniversary. When his gaze lit upon the office tower that housed the law firm where he'd once worked, the chill in his blood turned to ice.

Blindly, he reached for Hannah's hand.

"You okay?" she asked.

"Honestly, I don't know. This is the first time I've been back since I moved to Eternity Springs. I thought I was prepared for this, but it's more difficult than I'd imagined."

"You left here shortly after your wife's death?"

"No. I stayed for eighteen months. I left after . . ." He closed his eyes and gave his head a shake. "That's a story for another time. We're almost to the hotel."

It was true. Moments later, their driver pulled up to the hotel entrance and popped the trunk. The bellman brought a cart for their bags, Boone accepted the luggage tag, and then placed his hand at the small of Hannah's back to escort her through the revolving door into the lobby. He was halfway between the entry and the reception desk when one of those ghosts stepped into his path, and the familiar feminine voice said, "Boone. Oh, Boone. I knew this was where you would stay. Welcome home."

Ashleigh.

CHAPTER TEN

Hannah's mouth gaped when Boone marched right past the blonde as if she weren't there. His jaw had gone hard as steel, his stare was flinty. The hand at Hannah's back exerted firm pressure to propel her forward.

"Boone?" the blonde called. "Boone!"

He ignored her completely, gave his name to the man behind the reception desk, and reached into his pocket for his wallet.

Hannah took a step away from him and leaned her side against the desk, so she viewed the blonde's approach. The woman wasn't giving up, and Hannah didn't know how to feel about that. The tall, willowy woman dressed in a floral print sundress and heeled sandals attracted attention, especially when her voice rose as she said, "Boone, please. Don't be this way."

The blonde reached out and touched his shoulder. Boone visibly flinched, and Hannah decided how she felt, after all. The Mama Bear in her came out. "Okay. You need to come with me now."

She took the blonde by the arm and dragged her away. The woman attempted to plant her feet and resist, but Hannah wasn't having any of it. "Stop it. You're making a scene. He's obviously not going to talk to you now, so you need to step back and reassess."

"Who are you?" the blonde demanded, pain flashing across her eyes.

"His friend." Hannah continued to propel the woman away from Boone, searching for shelter from prying eyes. Spying a ladies' room, she headed that way.

"I'm his friend too, and I have to talk to him. I've been trying to talk to him for the longest time now."

Hannah tried to ignore the break in the blonde's voice as she opened the restroom door and guided the woman inside. She couldn't ignore the tears that flooded her brown eyes. Gentling her voice, she asked, "What's your name?"

"Ashleigh. I'm Ashleigh Hart."

Ahh. Ashleigh. Hannah remembered the name, and the story Boone had told to go with it. She was his late wife's best friend, the woman who had introduced them, and the woman whose marriage troubles were worthy of being told in an afternoon soap opera. "He's mentioned you to me."

Hope filled her expression and her voice. "He has? What did he say?"

"He told me you were his wife's friend."

"I was his friend too." Now the tears spilled down her cheek. "I need to talk to him. I need to explain. He never let me explain."

Explain what? Hannah was curious, but not interested enough to ask. "Well, it's evident that he's not going to let you explain right now either. Listen, Ashleigh. Boone has a lot on his plate right now. I think you'd be a lot better off if you wait for another time."

"There won't be another time. This is the first time he's come home, and he probably won't ever come back again. I only need five minutes. Three! I need to tell him why I did what I did and ask for his forgiveness. This is my only chance."

"I'm telling you, now is not a good time. Do you know where he lives now?"

She nodded. "A little town in Colorado."

"If it's so important to you that you talk to him, go there to do it."

"I can't. He told me that if I showed up in Colorado or at the ranch, he'd tell my father that I . . . that I . . ." She buried her face in her hands.

Caused his wife to overdose? "You can't say it?"

"He told you?" Ashleigh appeared crushed at the thought.

"Not the whole story," Hannah offered, confident of that fact. "I think —" She broke off when the door to the restroom opened and a woman wearing a hotel uniform walked inside. Her gaze scanned the two women, then she met Hannah's gaze. "Ms. Dupree?"

Surprised, Hannah said, "Yes?"

"A gentleman asked me to give this to you." She handed over a hotel portfolio with a key and the room number written on the outside.

"Thank you." Okay, then. She figured it was safe to assume that he wouldn't be waiting outside the restroom door. Good. Hannah glanced up from the folder. "Ashleigh, you're not going to be able to talk to him now, but we will be in town for a few days. I'll talk to him, okay? I'll see what I can do to help."

Ashleigh let out a little moan and steepled her fingers over her face. Hannah was relieved to see her nod in acquiescence, and even more relieved to exit the ladies' room.

217

Her role as a travel nanny didn't include therapy for broken friendships.

She found her way to the elevators and rode up to the fifteenth floor. At the door to room 1514, she hesitated. Was this her room or his? She knocked. "Boone?"

After waiting a moment without receiving a reply, she slipped the key in the slot and opened the door. "Oh."

It was a large corner suite with a view of downtown to the north and west. Two bedrooms, she judged, and then — noting the spiral staircase — reconsidered. Maybe three. It was a lovely space that felt decidedly empty. "Boone?"

He wasn't here.

Hannah sighed and went in search of her bedroom. She found her suitcase on a luggage rack in the first room she checked. A note lay on her bed where it wouldn't be missed. Boone's bold scrawl had penned: "Needed a swim. Come join me at the pool. Tenth floor."

Hannah was hot. A dip in a pool sounded good. She changed into her swimsuit and the cover-up she'd brought, then made her way to the pool deck, where she found Boone swimming freestyle in the lap pool. With steady and powerful arm strokes and controlled kicks, he displayed the form of a competitive swimmer. Bet he'd been on the swim team in high school or college. He had the build for it, with those broad shoulders and long legs. A natural athlete, she supposed. He was undoubtedly candy for the eyes.

"Would you like to order anything from the bar, ma'am? It's happy hour. Frozen cocktails are half price. I recommend our margaritas and peach Bellinis."

Tearing her gaze away from Boone, she smiled up at the waiter and considered it. A day like this deserved an umbrella drink, didn't it? "That sounds good. I'll have a Bellini, please."

"Good choice. Ours are excellent. Would you like me to serve you here or at the swim-up bar?"

"The bar is good." She needed to cool off. Not only was the temperature over one hundred degrees, watching a shirtless Boone McBride cut through the water only made her hotter.

The water felt divine, and once she had her drink, Hannah found a perch where she could keep cool while watching the show.

Boone had revealed a different side of himself today, where Ashleigh was concerned. The gallant gentleman who had interacted with her and his mother and sisters and family and friends had disappeared in a heartbeat. Or more precisely, at the sound of his name. The man had gone cold as ice in an instant.

Now he used exercise to work out his frustrations.

Hannah was glad to see him deal with it that way. Someone else she'd known would have used his fists.

No. She wouldn't think about Andrew. Just because Boone was wrapped up in a battle with old ghosts didn't mean she had to follow suit. This was his party. She was simply a bystander, maybe a facilitator if she decided she wanted to mediate between him and his ex-friend. She would not allow herself to be dragged back to a place she'd fought so hard to escape.

Hannah firmly shut that mental door and returned her attention to the Texan swimming laps. He really was delicious to look at, and she couldn't help but notice the other females around the pool watching him too.

She'd finished half of her drink by the time he ended his swim. With little visible effort, he lifted himself from the pool. Hannah had to smile when she recognized the pattern on his red, white, and blue swim trunks — Texas's Lone Star flag. When he grabbed a fluffy white towel off a lounge chair and dried first his face, then his broad shoulders, and then his lean torso, Hannah's mouth went dry as the summer heat. The hollow ache of sexual desire had her shifting uncomfortably. She sucked in a healthy sip of the frozen peach cocktail, hoping to cool off.

Across the pool deck, Boone began scanning the crowd, looking for her, she assumed. She lifted her hand and waved. He saw her and smiled that familiar, cocky cowboy grin.

Good. It looked like the exercise restored Boone's good mood.

Oblivious to the hungry stares of the women all around the pool, he sauntered toward her. "Hey."

"Hey, yourself."

He sat on the pool deck beside her and dangled his legs into the water. "You ordered a girly drink."

"Happy hour. Will you join me?"

"Well, hmm." He eyed her glass as he considered it. "I'd better stick to beer. If I start on the hard stuff now, I might not have the will to quit. I don't want to be lit the first time I see my son."

"What kind of beer? I'll get it for you. I get a kick out of the swim-up bar." He named a brand, and she handed him her drink, then swam toward the bartender. Returning a few moments later, she traded the plastic pint for her hurricane-shaped glass.

They clinked glasses, and he observed, "It's not black."

"Excuse me?"

"Your swimming suit. It's turquoise. You look great in it, by the way. I'm just surprised it's not black."

Hannah glanced down at herself. The suit was a strapless one-piece from her previous life, the one item of clothing she hadn't replaced with something less colorful. Honestly, she didn't know why she'd been toting it around in her bag for the past three years. This was the first time since she left New England that she'd had a reason to wear a swimsuit. Undoubtedly, had she gone shopping for one in the last three years, she would have chosen black.

She didn't want to journey down that mental path, so she deflected and redirected the conversation back to him. "So, Mr. McBride. What next? I don't think we rushed out of your house this morning to lounge pool-side this afternoon."

"True. I got distracted. I was already on edge. Didn't expect to get ambushed." He sipped his beer, then added, "Thanks for coming to the rescue."

"I'm here to help." Hannah studied Boone. The exercise hadn't rid him of the strain around his eyes or the grim set of his mouth. It was a different look for him, and she didn't like it. "You want to talk about her?"

"Nope. Let's talk about dinner. I told Sarah Winston this morning that I'd get back to her about where we'd meet for dinner. What sounds good to you — barbecue, Tex-Mex or Italian?"

Hannah started to tell him it was his choice. Still, she had been in that place mentally where the need to make one simple decision tripped the switch into overload, and everything shut down. And as she'd told him, she was here to help. "Barbecue."

"Excellent. I'll call Sarah and nail down the arrangements." He rose and sauntered over to the towel hut, where he spoke to the attendant, who then handed Boone his wallet and phone. While he was occupied with his call, Hannah climbed from the pool and walked over to the lounge chair where she'd left her towel, cover-up, and shoes. After drying herself and dressing, she found his warm stare watching her as he spoke into his phone.

Once again, sexual awareness sizzled through her. *Whoa.* Guess her libido had decided to reawaken with a roar. Luckily, she didn't need to worry about the consequences of the state overmuch. Experience had taught her that nothing interfered with romance like a baby. As of tomorrow, Boone McBride wouldn't have time or energy for anything more than taking care of his new son.

Pretending she hadn't noticed the heated look he sent her, she looked around for a shady spot to wait for him to finish his call. She'd no sooner sat down than the peace of the summer afternoon was shattered by a trio of squealing girls who burst onto the pool deck carrying inflatable toys, a harried woman on their heels. Hannah shut her eyes as a memory of Zoe and Sophia running toward the lake for the first swim of the season floated through her mind.

Lost in memories, she didn't note Boone's approach until he spoke. "You okay? That's a sad smile you're wearing."

"I'm fine. The laughter of little girls takes me back." Then she shook off the bittersweet memories and asked, "So what's the game plan?"

"Are you ready to get out of the sun?"

"Yes. Definitely. It's nice while you're in the water, but the heat is stifling."

"In that case, I suggest we head up to the suite. My friend has agreed to meet us at my favorite local barbecue joint at five thirty. It's a ten-minute drive from here. Does that give you time to get ready?"

"Sure."

Upstairs, they parted with a smile and retreated to their separate bedrooms and baths. Hannah eyed the luxury toiletries the hotel supplied, unscrewed the cap of the shampoo, and sniffed. "Mmm." Almost as nice as the custom products Boone supplied to the cabin.

After her shower, dressed in the white spa robe the hotel provided, Hannah dried and styled her hair, taking a little more time with it than usual. She was glad she'd brought along the makeup that Celeste Blessing had talked her into purchasing the day she'd bought her dresses for Jackson McBride's wedding. A week ago, her skin care products were limited to the lotion she picked up at the drugstore. She hadn't owned makeup of any kind. As Boone's travel nanny, she wanted to make a good impression on the social worker they would be meeting for dinner shortly.

With her hair and makeup completed, she

dressed in her favorite black slacks and the top she'd worn to the rehearsal party. She gave her image one last critical scan in the bathroom mirror, then picked up her handbag and exited her bedroom. Boone stood at the north-facing window gazing down at the city below. He wore jeans, boots, and a long-sleeved white sports shirt with the sleeves rolled halfway to his elbows.

He didn't turn around when he heard her come in, but he did speak. "Being back here is surreal for me. I look the other direction, and I can see the rooftop of my old house across the river. I look in this direction, and I see the courthouse and the office space occupied by my former law firm. I spent thousands of hours in those buildings, hours that I should have spent at home. I didn't know what was happening until it was too late. My inability to create that right balance between work and family life was one of my biggest failures. Mary died. Then I overcorrected."

Hannah didn't know how to respond, so she simply waited. After a long moment of silence, he asked, "What time is it?"

She glanced at her phone. "Ten minutes to five."

"Half an hour," he murmured. He shoved his hands into his pockets and added, "I've been running from that overcorrection for five years now. My folks think I left Texas because of Mary. Shoot, even Jackson and Tucker think that's it. That's not it. I left because of Rachel Davis, and because I was haunted by pink gel ink."

Pink gel ink?

"I think I need to tell you about Rachel before I meet up with Sarah Winston, before I meet Trace. I need to get this off my chest. Will you listen to my story, Hannah?"

"I will." She walked over the sofa, kicked off her sandals, and sat with her legs tucked beneath her.

His voice tight and husky with regret, he said, "It was shortly before the first anniversary of Mary's death that Rachel's case first came to my attention. Hannah, she was the bravest little girl I've ever met in my life. I won't go into all the details. You don't need them running around in your head, believe me. Suffice to say someone abused her horribly, and Rachel was admitted to the hospital."

"Oh, that poor child."

Boone continued to face the window, but he removed one hand from his pocket, lifted it, and began rubbing the back of his neck. "The people at CPS expected that I'd eventually end up on the case, so I got called in before she was discharged. I'd witnessed a lot of ugly things in my career, but seeing that pale, hollow-eyed girl lying in that hospital bed got me in a way no other case had.

"When she'd healed enough physically to be discharged, she still wasn't talking. Her doctors didn't want to lock her up on the psych floor, and since she had a couple of fractures, I pulled a couple of strings and got her transferred to orthopedics. We wanted to give her some time. As it happened, I was doing rehab on a shoulder injury at that time, so I spent a lot of time there myself. I started visiting her. I didn't question her. Just sat and talked about my family, primarily. Then one evening, I came in, and she wasn't in her bed. I found her exiting the physical therapy office with a notebook and a pen. I asked her what she was doing. She shrugged and returned to her room and ignored me for the next half hour while she watched reruns of *Bewitched.*"

He lapsed into silence, and at length, Hannah decided he needed encouragement to continue. She said, "I always wished I could twitch my nose like Samantha. I just don't have the muscles for it."

He glanced over his shoulder and met her

228

gaze with a crooked, sad smile. Gently, she asked, "Did she write you a message?"

He turned back to the window, and his shoulders visibly slumped. "Yep. A detailed account of the abuse. It took every bit of control I possessed not to start bawling like a baby when I read it. If she hadn't been sitting there watching, I couldn't have held back."

"What did you do?"

"Ah, leave it to the pretty lady to cut right to the heart of the issue." He turned away from the window and strode across the room to the bar. He half filled a glass with tap water and tossed it back like whiskey. The glass hit the black granite countertop with clink when he set it down hard. "I promised Rachel I would get her justice. I sat beside her hospital bed and swore it. I gave her my solemn word — and then I broke it. I failed her."

The bleakness in his expression caused her heart to twist. Hannah felt compelled to go to him to offer him a comforting touch, but his body language shouted, *Stay* away. So she tried to offer him comfort with words. "I haven't known you very long, but I am confident that I know you very well. If you failed her, it was due to circumstances beyond your control."

"Nope. See, there you're wrong. I was in complete control of my work life. What was spinning away from me was my personal life, and I allowed it to interfere. That over-correction I mentioned. I was distracted and made a stupid, rookie mistake, which ultimately allowed Rachel's abuser to get off on a technicality." Boone dragged his hands down his face, closed his eyes, and massaged his temples. "I will never forget the look of betrayal in Rachel's eyes when I told her the news."

"Was it a family member?"

"Yep. Age-old story. Her stepfather."

Hannah didn't believe Boone would have moved to Colorado without finding another way to make the stepfather pay for his sins, so she asked, "What happened to him?"

"He's dead," Boone snapped, his tone flat and angry.

Hannah's eyes went wide. "Did you . . . ?"

"No. Unfortunately. Less than a week after his case was dismissed, the sonofabitch died in his sleep. Drug overdose. Rachel didn't get justice."

And neither did you.

Hannah recognized that she was still missing some pieces here. What had happened to Rachel Davis? What, if anything, did Ashleigh have to do with the situation? Why had

230

he wanted to tell her this before having dinner with the social worker?

Hannah remembered that Ashleigh's husband had been the one who had facilitated the adoption attempt that ultimately led to Boone's wife's suicide. He'd also said it was a story worthy of a soap opera.

Rachel Davis. Ashleigh. The late Mary. The baby. Maybe even the social worker, Sarah. Somehow they were tied together, and that piece of the story, she believed, was what Boone found difficult to tell. She glanced at the clock. They still had twenty minutes before they needed to leave.

Maybe he needed a push to get it out. "What does all of this have to do with Trace?"

"Once again, you cut to the meat of it, don't you? Trace is — well, it's highly probable that Trace is Rachel's son." Boone told Hannah about the note addressed to him and written in pink gel ink that was left with the baby at the fire station. "I've seen a picture of the note. I recognize Rachel's handwriting. Nobody's sure about whether or not the baby is her child or if she acted on behalf of the infant's mother."

Hannah thought about the revelation a moment, then shook her head. "What's the piece I'm missing? Why would Rachel give you a baby?"

"Beats me. If it's actually going to happen, that is. It's possible this is her way to make me pay for letting my personal issues get in the way of professional ones. I let her down. I'm forging ahead as though that's not the case because I really can't afford to do otherwise. That said, I have serious reservations."

"Because those personal issues prevented you from doing your best in her case."

"Yes. Well, I allowed it. Unnecessarily."

"What were they? The personal issues?"

"O-o-oh," he groaned. "That is the soap opera part of the story. I don't think we have the time for it. I've told you about Rachel, and that's what I really wanted you to know tonight before we meet with Sarah."

Leave it to a man to dangle tantalizing information like that and then slam the door shut.

"Okay." Hannah unfolded from the sofa, stood, and slipped on her sandals. "Shall we go?"

He gave her a long look, and his lips stretched in a slow smile. "You are a good sport, Hannah Dupree."

She nodded. "Doesn't mean I'm not curious. You should expect me to nag you for more info at some future point."

"Fair enough." He pulled his phone from his pocket and ordered an Uber. They exited the suite and headed for the elevator. Upon reaching the lobby, Boone made a scan of the area before moving forward. Within a few moments, they climbed into their ride and made small talk during the short drive to the restaurant.

Hannah inhaled the mouthwatering aroma of smoking meat the minute she opened the car door. She realized she was seriously hungry. She hoped their dinner companion would arrive on time. "There's Sarah," Boone said, moments after entering the restaurant. He waved and headed for the round table in the corner where a middle-aged, dark-haired woman wearing a purple polo shirt and a welcoming smile sat with a glass of iced tea in front of her.

She rose as Boone approached. He kissed her cheek, introduced Hannah, then suggested they order before diving into their meeting. "Lunch was a long time ago, and I'm hungry as a horse."

With Sarah's and Hannah's okays, he ordered for the table. Brisket and ribs and chicken and something called bacon burnt ends. Slaw and mac-and-cheese and corn and beans and onion rings. And rolls.

"Just how many people do you intend to

feed?" Hannah teased when he finally sent the waiter on his way.

"Don't make fun of me. This is one of my favorite restaurants in the world, and I've missed it. Besides, we'll have great leftovers."

They spoke about the weather until the food arrived. Once Hannah got a taste of the brisket, she couldn't help but moan aloud. Boone gave her a knowing look. "See, I told you so."

It wasn't until both Sarah and Hannah had set down their forks, and after Boone had plowed his way through two plates of food and placed an order for banana pudding for dessert, that he was ready to get down to business. "Any updates on the little fellow? We are still set for a meeting this evening?"

Sarah's gaze flickered away for a moment, and Hannah's stomach sank. Boone saw it too, because Hannah saw that he subtly stiffened. "Sarah?"

"Everything is on course," she assured him. "You will meet the baby today. There are just a couple of details I need to go over."

Warily, Boone asked, "Details?"

Sarah wiped her mouth with a napkin and stood. "Excuse me, please. Before we get into this any farther, I'm going to make a quick visit the ladies' room."

While Sarah was gone, Boone signaled the waiter for the check. He asked Hannah how she'd liked her meal. That question devolved into a debate about the superiority of Texas-style barbecue in comparison with what she'd sampled in Nashville during a recent visit. He'd just coaxed Hannah into trying the pudding when Sarah returned and took her seat. Without preamble, she said, "You and I have known each other for a long time, Boone. We worked together very well as colleagues, and I have long considered you a friend. You were a champion for children here in Tarrant County. I knew I could always count on you to put the children first."

Boone traced the rim of his water glass with his fingertip. "Cut to the chase, Sarah. What's wrong? Is it Thompson? Has he decided to eff this up for me?"

"No. David Thompson isn't involved with this adoption in any way. Waggoner, Thompson, and Cole isn't handling any of the paperwork. I told you that."

"Well, the firm is involved somehow. Ashleigh knew I was coming into town today. She ambushed me at the hotel." To Hannah, he explained, "It's her father's law firm.

"Did you tell her, Sarah? How is she involved in this? Wait, did she track down Rachel Davis and convince her that I'm a head case? She has a history of that, you know. I guess I should have anticipated —"

Sarah interrupted. "No, Boone. Ashleigh isn't part of this. I don't know how she found out about your visit. It wasn't from me."

He dragged his hand across his mouth. "I think Ashleigh has —"

Sarah slapped the table. "Boone. Hush. Let me talk! The sooner I'm able to say what I've promised to say, the sooner you'll get to meet the baby."

"Promised? Promised who?"

She rolled her eyes and muttered, "Hard-headed Texan. Like I was saying, you've always put the children first. Tonight, I need you to remember that I've always put the kids first too. You know that, don't you?"

"Yes. That's why we clicked. We were always on the same page. Had the same sign on our desks."

"THE MOST VULNERABLE DESERVE OUR BEST EFFORTS," she quoted. "You gave the sign to me for Christmas one year."

"That's right. I'd forgotten."

"I have never forgotten. I will always put the children's best interests first, even if that means bending a rule a time or two. You were the one who taught me about rule-bending, remember? I can quote you exactly: *Don't be afraid to bend or twist or massage a rule, Sarah. Trust your judgment.*"

"I am not liking the direction this is going."

"Well, you should like it, because, in my judgment, becoming your child is in the best interests of this baby. So I massaged the rules a bit."

"I want this adoption," Boone said with a warning in his voice. "But if it's not legal, we are stopping it here and now."

"No worries. Everything is legal. Where I've done some bending is with the broader picture."

"Okay. Fine. I get the warning. Cut to the chase, Sarah. What is it that you want to say?"

She held his gaze for a long moment, then nodded. "Okay." She stood. "Come with me, Boone. It's time you met this child."

He shoved to his feet, reached for his wallet, and began tossing bills onto the table. "Let's do it. Where do we go?"

"They're on the patio."

Boone froze with a twenty-dollar bill in his hand. "Here? He's here? Now?"

Sarah reached out and touched his arm.

"Boone. There is one important thing for you to keep in mind. Think before you react. Everything is riding on it. More than you know."

"But he's here."

Sarah encouraged him with a smile. "The foster parents are Jared and Katie Devlin. They're waiting for you on the patio with the baby."

The twenty slipped from his fingers and floated to the table. "Now? Right now?"

"Right now."

He grabbed for Hannah's hand and held it in a grip so hard, she winced. Sarah led them toward a door Hannah had not previously noticed. They stepped onto a patio where large fans and misting machines worked to offset the heat of the evening. Boone didn't appear to notice the heat. He focused on the infant seat placed atop a table next to a burbling fountain. A man and a woman were seated on either side of the carrier.

His viselike grip on Hannah's hand tightened even more.

He took three steps toward the table before he abruptly stopped. His head jerked to one side and then moved slowly to the other as he scanned the patio. He muttered, "What the heck?"

"What's wrong?" Hannah whispered.

"Trace is wearing a hair bow."

Abruptly, Hannah understood. The pink blanket. Pink bow. Pink dress and booties.

Either the foster parents were attempting to make a political point, or Boone Mc-Bride's little boy was actually a girl.

CHAPTER ELEVEN

Boone had experience with being blind-sided.

After intercepting a pass and running it back for the winning touchdown in the semifinal round of the state high school football championships, he'd been tackled from behind by the losing quarterback and gotten his bell rung. Once when Boone was at his grandparents' lake house, a rattlesnake wrapped around a bicycle's handlebars had surprised him. The viper sank its fangs into Boone's forearm and necessitated an emergency life-flight trip to a hospital with antivenin in stock. Add in Mary's suicide and discovering how Ashleigh had betrayed him, and that just about made him a blind-siding expert.

This experience gave him professional status.

He swallowed hard and stepped forward, his gaze shifting between the man and the woman for the scant seconds he was able to keep his eyes off the baby. "Mr. and Ms. Devlin?"

"Mr. McBride?"

"Yes. I'm Boone McBride." For the next few moments, anyway. Until he stroked out or his heart blew up. Could his pulse pound any harder and faster?

The man stood. "I'm pleased to meet you, Boone. I'm Jared. This is my wife, Katie. We've been honored to take care of this little one for the past month. She's such a good baby. Just a little doll."

"A little doll," Boone repeated. It was true. She was tiny, with a heart-shaped mouth and smushy little nose and a round head full of dark hair that definitely had a reddish gleam to it. Red! "I've always been partial to redheads."

He took two steps closer. *A little doll. Not Trace. She has an innie rather than an outie.* Then, as if she sensed him, her eyes blinked once. Twice. And opened.

Boone gazed into those dark-blue eyes, and he promptly tumbled head over heels into love.

He cleared his throat. "May I hold her?"

"Of course." Katie Devlin rose and picked the baby up from her carrier, taking care to support her head. "She's just finished a bottle, so she should be content for a bit. She might even stay awake for a few minutes. Do you want to sit down before I give her to you?"

"I probably should," Boone murmured, pulling a chair out from the table and taking a seat without tugging his gaze away from the baby.

She was skinny, he thought, surveying the bare legs extending from the pastel-pink onesie with a white heart on the front. Was that normal for a newborn? Beyond welcoming new children of his friends and neighbors in Eternity Springs, he had little experience with newborns. He didn't have a ton of experience with babies either, for that matter.

As the thought occurred, he finally glanced away from the infant toward Hannah. She was standing back, not quite part of the tableau. When their gazes met, she gave him an encouraging smile and nod.

Boone turned his attention back to the baby, made a cradle of his arms, and Katie Devlin handed her over. With the baby's head nestled in the crook of his left elbow, Boone stared down into the little face, emotion clogging his throat. The handful of other times he'd held a newborn baby, he'd surveyed the face with the usual "Whose nose/eyes/mouth does he have?" exploration. This was a different experience entirely.

Despite the fact that she weighed little more than a minute, the weight in his arms was heavier than anything he'd ever known. This was responsibility. This was commitment. Nothing else in his life had ever come close.

Rather than the round, chubby Gerber baby look of older children, she had a little old woman's face with puffy eyes, a brow that furrowed, and a mouth that frowned as she squinted and grunted and snorted. And yet Boone thought she was the prettiest baby he'd ever seen. Look at that mouth — the very definition of bow-shaped. And her little ears. She had dainty ears. And those eyelashes — how could they be so long already? They twitched. Her lids opened. Her eyes were a little crossed until she focused on his mouth.

Reacting, Boone smiled. "Hello, gorgeous."

Her eyes were the blue of the mid-Atlantic on a cloudy day. He fell into them, drowned in them, until they drifted shut. Her body relaxed in sleep.

Keeping her supported and held securely against his chest, he brushed his thumb across her cheek. Soft. So soft. The most delicate skin he'd ever touched. With his index finger, he gently traced her almost nonexistent eyebrows and then the curious pattern of her hair — thick in places, but thinner in others.

"Aren't you the sweetest thing?" he murmured. He lifted her hand, studied her long fingers and tiny fingernails. "Sweet as spun sugar, like my grandmother used to say."

He couldn't say how long he sat holding her, staring at her, but eventually he realized someone was speaking his name. He glanced up. Sarah was standing in front of him, her hands clasped, her spine just a little stiff. He gathered that she'd just asked him a question. "I'm sorry. What did you say?"

"I asked if you still want the baby."

"What? Why? I'm here, aren't I?"

"She's a girl, not a boy."

"Yeah, that is a little detail I'm surprised you got wrong."

"But how do you feel about it? About having a daughter instead of a son?"

Boone scowled at Sarah, then looked down at the baby. "Well, I'm not going to name her Trace. And the whole nursery theme will need to be redone. I'm modern enough not to push a girl toward pink and purple, but a moose head on the wall and a bear rug on the floor doesn't fit this little angel."

"You put a moose head on the nursery wall?" Sarah asked, her tone aghast. Katie Devlin looked pretty appalled too.

Hannah spoke up. "It's a forest theme. They're stuffed animals. It's adorable, I promise. He saw it on Pinterest."

Jared Devlin smirked. "You don't strike me as the Pinterest type."

"I had a baby on the way. Needs must."

Sarah's voice grew insistent. "Boone. I need your attention. I need you to answer my question. Do you care that she's a girl and not a boy? Do you want a daughter?"

His hold tightened protectively around the bundle in his arms. "I want her! I want to be a father — her father — her daddy. I wouldn't be here if I didn't. I don't go back on decisions. You know that about me, Sarah. Did you really think I'd change my mind just because she's a girl instead of a boy?"

"No, I didn't." She lifted her chin, and sincerity blazed in her eyes. "I absolutely didn't."

"I might be a little mush-minded right now because this is a big moment in my life, but I'm very well aware that more is going on than meets the eye. I do want an explanation, because I know you too, Sarah. You had a reason for the subterfuge. However, all that can wait. Right now, I'm getting to know my little girl."

He returned his gaze to the baby, sleeping peacefully in his arms. "We have lots of things to figure out, don't we? Need to figure out what direction we want to go with the nursery so we get my designer working on it. You and I might need a Pinterest date. What do you say? Most important, though, Trace Parker McBride isn't going to do. You need a name. To paraphrase the great Jimmy Buffett, tell me . . ." Boone softly sang, "Little Miss Magic, who you gonna be?"

Hannah was a great big glob of goo.

Boone might not have been blindsided by the fact that this baby was a girl, but Hannah darned sure was. A girl? She'd committed to taking care of a girl?

She couldn't do it. That wasn't the deal. It was a step too freaking far. Her heart was healing — emphasis on the *ing*. Not healed. She wasn't there yet. She was a long way from being there yet.

A girl. What the heck was going on here? How could anyone have made such a basic mistake? Nobody. Somebody misled Boone on purpose. Why?

She watched him drink in the sight of the infant in arms, and her heart gave an extra-vicious twist. She couldn't help but think of the moment she and Andrew had learned they were expecting a second daughter. Andrew had been sorely disappointed and cranky about it.

His reaction had hurt. Hannah would have welcomed a boy, but she had been happy that Sophia would have a sister. All she truly cared about was that the baby be born healthy.

Yeah, well. "You Can't Always Get What You Want" by the Stones was her theme song, wasn't it?

Her mind drifted into the past, and tears stung her eyes. Her heart was hurting. She turned away, and that's when something at-tracted her attention to the teenager half hidden by a hedge. Perhaps it was the tear trailing down her cheek. Maybe it was the intensity of the stare the girl had leveled on Boone and the baby.

Probably it was the naked pain etched across her face.

Hannah knew grief when she saw it.

Vaguely, she heard Boone talking to the baby about Pinterest and nursery design.

The teenager covered her mouth with her hands and shut her eyes. That's when Hannah figured it out. This was that baby's mother.

Hannah studied the girl. No, the young woman. Older than fifteen, less than nineteen, would be her guess. A little taller than Hannah's five foot six. She had long brown hair, big brown mournful eyes, and she dressed in yoga pants, sneakers, and an oversized T-shirt.

When Boone sang to the baby, the girl turned away. She began walking away. Fast. Hannah glanced at Boone. He remained focused on the baby.

She followed the teen, who exited the restaurant's patio through a gate and headed toward a parking lot. Even as she pursued the girl, Hannah second-guessed herself. Maybe everyone would be better off if she just let this go. Nevertheless, she got close enough to call, "Rachel? Rachel Davis? Please, may I speak with you a minute?"

The girl stopped and whirled around. "What do you want? Who are you? How do you know my name?"

"My name is Hannah. I'm a friend of Boone's. I'll be helping with the baby during the trip back to Colorado. He's told me about you."

"What did he say about me?"

Uncertain whether Boone's explanation

to her had breached any professional privacy rules, Hannah chose her words carefully. "He told me he guessed that you were the baby's mother."

"Are you his girlfriend?" Rachel swiped the tear tracks from her cheeks.

"No. I'm his tenant. I'm renting a place to stay from him, and I have experience with children, so he asked for my help." She paused a moment and added, "Can we talk?"

"Why? What is there to talk about? If I'd wanted to talk to Boone, I'd have been there."

You were *there.* "So don't talk to him. Talk to me. Tell me why you chose Boone to be your baby's father."

"The kid needed someone." Shrugging, she glanced back over her shoulder toward the restaurant patio. "I knew Boone could afford a kid. Look, I gotta go. My bus will be here soon."

Obviously, there was much more to this story than the fact that Boone had money. Hannah wanted to hear it. She knew Boone would too. "Tell you what." She gestured toward the Italian restaurant across the street. "Why don't we go inside where it's cool, order something to drink — and eat if you haven't had dinner — and when we're done, I'll order an Uber for you. My treat."

When she saw the refusal forming on the teen's face, she quickly added, "Boone should know. It will help him be a better father."

Rachel pursed her lips and considered. When a moment later, she nodded, Hannah breathed a sigh of relief. A few minutes later, they were seated inside the welcome air-conditioning of the dining room. While Rachel perused the menu, Hannah sent Boone a text. *Something came up. Will meet you back at the hotel later.*

She ordered a dessert she didn't want so that Rachel wouldn't have to eat alone and waited until their drinks were served to say, "Rachel, here's the deal. I would love to hear your story, as much as you feel comfortable sharing. I'll also promise to keep your confidence. If there is something you don't want Boone to know, I'll keep my lips zipped. You have my word. I just, well, from one mother to another, I know that sometimes it really helps to have a sympathetic, nonjudgmental ear."

The teen dumped the contents of a sugar packet into her iced tea and stirred it with her straw. In Hannah's purse, her phone pinged with an incoming text. She ignored it.

"I don't know where to start," Rachel said.

"Well, you could start at the beginning. Want to tell me how you met Boone?"

She shrugged. "When I was a kid, I had this thing happen, and I met him 'cause of that. He was nice to me. I was in the hospital for a while, and he came to visit me. A lot. He'd come and sit and talk to me. No one had ever talked to me like that. He told me about his parents and his sisters and his ranch and his granddad's lake house and his cousins. He told me when I got better, he would help me learn how to ride a horse and a wake-board. It sounded like, well, heaven."

"I imagine it did."

"But the thing about Boone, he didn't only talk about the good things. He talked about hard things too. He told me his wife had died. He told me they'd tried to adopt a baby three times, and it never happened. He told me how it had broken his heart and how badly he wanted to be a daddy. He talked to me about his dreams. He talked a lot." She paused, sipped her drink through her straw, and asked, "Does he still talk a lot?"

Hannah considered the question and then nodded. "He does when he's trying to be convincing."

"He's a lawyer," Rachel said dismissively as the server placed an order of veal Parmesan in front of her.

From inside her purse, Hannah's phone blew up with incoming texts. Rachel observed, "Is that him?"

"Probably."

"Are you going to answer him?"

"Do you want me to?"

Rachel took a bite of her meal, swallowed, then shook her head. "No."

"Okay, then." Hannah took her phone from her purse, ignored the screen full of messages, and thumbed it off. She dropped the phone back into her bag, picked up her spoon, and took a small bite of vanilla ice cream.

Rachel abruptly resumed the conversation. "He kept his promise. He sent me to a summer camp where I learned to water-ski and wakeboard, and ride a horse. It was magic. He was magic. He was like my own personal Santa Claus and big brother. Everything was great until one day, it wasn't."

"What happened?"

"His" — she made air quotes with her fingers — "friend."

Ashleigh. Had to be. Hannah knew it.

Rachel inspected the bread basket the

server had left and chose a roll. "I didn't know what happened at first. I didn't know why he wigged out during my case for a long time. The 'friend' tracked me down and told me a couple of years ago because her therapist made her do it."

"What happened?" Hannah repeated.

"Well, Ralph, my stepfather —" She broke off and frowned at Hannah. "Do you know about that part?"

"Boone told me you were a crime victim, and that he made a serious prosecutorial mistake that allowed your abuser to go free."

"Yeah. Boone effed up. He was all in a rage because just as the trial started, he found out his dead wife's best friend had intentionally torpedoed the adoption that made his wife kill herself. It screwed up his head. He didn't do his job right, and Ralph got off on a technicality. That's what they called it when they explained it to me.

"Boone was just as big a wreck as me at that point. He apologized to me, but I was pretty bitchy to him. I had some anger issues going on. I ran away from home after it all went down."

"Oh, Rachel." Hannah's heart broke for her. It broke for Boone. This explained so much. "Where did you go?"

"I won't say. Someone helped me. She

253

tracked me down. I wasn't that hard to find. But that person would get into trouble, so I swore I'd never tell. I'm pretty sure Boone was behind it, but I never saw him again. I told him I didn't want to see him, and he took me at my word. He left town pretty soon after that."

Hannah digested all the information as Rachel finished her veal. She waited until the server brought the teen tiramisu for dessert to say, "That's the past. What about now? What events brought you to the patio across the street watching Boone McBride meet an infant girl whom he expected to be a boy?"

Hannah and Rachel's heads whipped around when a deep, familiar voice drawled, "I'm anxious to hear that story too. Mind if I join you?"

CHAPTER TWELVE

Boone didn't precisely panic when he realized Hannah had gone missing. He did grow confused, then concerned, and then, when he read her text, a little pissed. What the heck had her running off that way?

Once the baby grew fussy, Katie Devlin indicated the time had come to put her to bed, and the three of them departed. Boone had looked around for Hannah and figured she'd gone to the ladies' room. The confusion set in when she didn't return, and her text had raised more questions than it answered. He'd been about to apologize to Sarah and cut the meeting short to Uber back to the hotel when Sarah had touched his arm.

"I saw where she went. I think you should join them. The cat is out of the bag."

"What cat?"

"Boone, Rachel was here. She wanted to watch you meet the baby. Hannah noticed her and followed her. I saw them go across the street and into the Italian restaurant."

"Rachel. Rachel is with Hannah." He pinned Sarah with a narrow-eyed look. "So Rachel *is* this baby's mother?"

"I'm not allowed to say. Go across the street, Boone. I'll see you tomorrow at the office at ten."

He nodded and left, crossing the street and entering the restaurant. He spied Hannah almost immediately and . . . Rachel.

Rachel. All grown up.

It was a kick to his gut. The promise of beauty she'd shown at twelve had bloomed. She was a lovely young woman. A lump of emotion lodged in his throat. Damn. Rachel.

What is this all about? Had she set him up? Thank God he hadn't told his mother about the baby if this had been Rachel's effort to serve her revenge cold.

So that little girl probably wasn't going home with him to Colorado. Boone's heart broke at the thought.

Well, he wasn't one to put off bad news. Might as well face this and get it over with.

He started across the room and drew close enough to hear just as Hannah asked the million-dollar question. *So here we go.* "I'm anxious to hear that story too. Mind if

I join you?"

Both women looked at him with surprise. Hannah's expression softened with welcome. Rachel sat back in her chair and folded her arms defensively. All grown up, but still the same sadly damaged little girl whom he'd tried to rescue. She shrugged. "Feel free."

She kept her head turned away, her gaze avoiding him. She obviously wasn't going to answer Hannah's question, so Boone searched for a place to begin. He was the smooth-talkin', fast-thinking lawyer who never ran out of words and always had fifteen different ways to ask the same damned question. He knew how to build an argument and mine for a secret with subtlety and finesse.

Unfortunately, the words that came out of his mouth were an accusation. "Are you scamming me?"

Now, finally, she met his gaze. "What?"

"Is this your payback? I know I deserve one, and if this is it, you've outdone yourself."

Rachel gave him that silent you're-an-idiot smirk that teenagers perfected. "Get over yourself, McBride. I forgave you for screwing up my case before my thirteenth birthday."

257

Stunned, Boone asked, "You did?"

"Okay, maybe it was my fourteenth, but yeah. I forgave you."

Boone felt something tight loosen in his chest. He spared a glance toward Hannah, who watched him with a warm and sympathetic gaze. He cleared his throat. "Thank you. That means a lot to me."

Rachel shrugged. "It happened the way it was meant to happen."

Boone dragged his hand across his jaw. So many thoughts and questions spun through his head. Where to start? *Pick a spot, dumbass.* He cleared his throat a second time and said, "I've thought of you a lot, Rachel. Will you tell me about your world for the past five years?"

She set down her fork and said, "Dinner was good. Thank you. But if I'm going to talk, I need to walk."

Boone reached for his wallet and threw a couple of twenties on the table. "Trinity Park is one block away. Want to go there?"

"Sure."

Hannah glanced between the pair and suggested, "Why don't I let you two have time to yourselves? I'll go on back to the hotel."

Boone questioned Rachel with a glance. She said, "You'll be her caretaker. Nothing

I'm going to tell him is a secret. Come with us."

Hannah agreed and excused herself to visit the ladies' room. While Boone watched her cross the restaurant, Rachel watched him. Then she observed, "You have a thing for her."

Boone gave her a sidelong look. "It's that obvious?"

"Definitely some starry sparkle in your eyes. She told me she's just your travel nanny."

"Yeah. For now. We'll see."

"What's it like? This little town where you live — Eternity Springs?"

Boone gazed through the restaurant's west-facing windows where ripples of heat visibly radiated from the parking lot outside. "I imagine it's about forty degrees cooler right this minute, for one thing. It's early for the weather to be this hot. It doesn't bode well for the next few months. I'd forgotten how brutal the heat could be here in the summer."

"When was the last time you were home?"

"To Texas?"

"Fort Worth."

He shook his head. "This is my first time back."

"Whoa. You were serious about telling the

lawyers and judge and social workers all to go blow, weren't you?"

"Yep. I pretty much was."

"Hmm."

Hannah rejoined them. As they walked the block and a half toward the park, he responded to Rachel's question about Eternity Springs. He included those aspects he found particularly appealing because they were important for both women to hear. Rachel needed to know it was an excellent place for her daughter, and relaying the good press continued his subtle campaign to convince Hannah to stay.

They reached the park and the shade provided by the full, spreading branches of hundreds of live oaks and elms. With a thick layer of grass rather than concrete beneath their feet, the temperature felt like it dropped at least ten degrees. The evening air rang with the laughter of a group of children playing hide-and-go-seek among the trees and with the fainter sound of an orchestra playing John Philip Sousa. It must be the Fort Worth Symphony's Concert in the Park, Boone realized. He hadn't thought of that program in years. Once upon a time, he and Mary had been regulars.

Then Rachel interrupted his trip down memory lane with a kick to the 'nads when she pinned him with a narrow-eyed stare and accused, "I know it was you. You hired Lisa to find me."

Crap. Boone shoved his hands into his pockets. "Lisa Jackson is an excellent private detective. However, I thought she was more discreet."

"She's never said a word, but I knew it was you. Now you've just confirmed it."

Boone's lips lifted in a reluctant grin. "Bright girl."

"Not a girl, Boone McBride. I'm a woman. Most definitely a woman."

Chastised, he nodded. "You're right. My apologies." Then, because he thought it was important that she knew, he said, "I kept my word to you, Rachel. As much as it went against my grain, as much as it killed me to do it, I didn't check up on you. I haven't been funneling money to you. What I did do was hire Lisa to find you and put someone she trusted in touch to get services you needed. Lisa sent word that she had found you and that you were safe, but that's the last I heard until Sarah Winston contacted me about the baby and your note."

"That's kind of what I figured," Rachel said. "So you don't know where I've been living? Or with who?"

"I don't."

261

"I've been with Lisa. She took me in, and I've lived with her ever since."

Boone stopped in his tracks. "Seriously?"

"She's cool. Like my big sister."

"So you've been living in Fort Worth? Going to school?"

"Yep. I even made it to graduation. Waddled my way across the stage when I was nine months' pregnant."

There. The proverbial elephant in the park. Boone both wanted to ask and dreaded the answer. "Are you going to tell me about the baby's father?"

Rachel didn't respond right away but veered her path toward the sidewalk that ran alongside the riverbank. Boone caught Hannah's gaze and, because he could use her support, held out his hand. She took it, and he squeezed a silent thank-you as they followed the teenager.

"We were both in the marching band," Rachel eventually continued. "He played trumpet. I played the flute. He graduated last year and decided to get his basics out of the way at TCC."

"The local junior college," Boone explained to Hannah.

"He wanted to go to Texas Tech. His parents were alumni. We'd been dating almost a year when I found out I was pregnant. He was killed in a car wreck the same day. I never got the chance to tell him about the baby."

"Ah, honey." It was a stab to Boone's heart. What horrific luck. So not fair. And while life wasn't fair at all, this young woman had certainly been dealt a raw deal.

Rachel's lips twisted with a sad smile. "He was a good guy. Kind and sweet. My first. My *real* first. I think he would have wanted to get married, but it wasn't meant to be."

She fell silent, and after a moment, Hannah gently asked, "What was his name?"

"Ryan. Ryan Walton. I didn't tell his parents. They were so devastated, and it wasn't the right time. Ryan was their only child. They were older when he was born, and they thought he hung the moon — and so did I. He was a good guy. Knew everything about me. Ralph, all of it. His parents were good people too. They were kind to me, but when his mother saw me, she'd cry, so we didn't stay in touch after the funeral. It took me a little while to decide what I wanted to do about the baby. Once I made up my mind about adoption, I thought it was cleaner this way. Lisa said I'm not legally obligated to tell them. That's right?"

"Yes," Boone replied. The pain in her big Bambi eyes broke his heart.

Rachel stopped walking, picked up a rock, and threw it into the river. "I spent a lot of time thinking about my options and deciding what would be best. I figured out that I do want to be a mother someday, but it's better for me and for this baby that I am not her mom. I'm going to go to college. I'm going to study nursing. I'm good at science and math. I got accepted to TCU, and I'm going to use that scholarship you set up for me all those years ago."

Boone drew a deep breath, then exhaled in a rush. "Rachel. I am so glad to hear that. You will make a great nurse."

"I think so too. But going to college and being a single mom is just too much to tackle. She deserves better. So I decided on adoption, and once I got that far, well, I wanted to give you first choice."

"But why?"

For the first time in minutes, she looked at him. Boone read truth and confidence in her gaze. "I know what kind of a father you'll be."

It floored him. "How can you say that?"

Rather than reply to him, she turned to Hannah. "He visited me every single night that I was in the hospital. I'm sure he doesn't remember all the things he talked about, but they made a huge impression on me. He told me his family had dinner together every night. They had a big extended-family reunion every year. He and his sisters all played youth sports, and his parents went to all of their games. They went to church and did volunteer work."

Rachel's eyes grew misty and her voice thick as she added, "I remember lying in that hospital bed thinking that if someday he had children, they would be the luckiest kids on earth."

Boone had a lump in his throat, and damn if he wasn't fighting back the tears. Rachel looked like she was about to cry. Hannah, bless her heart, saved them by lightening the mood. "I met his family last weekend when his cousin Jackson got married. I liked them very much."

"I heard about that wedding," the teen replied. She looked at Boone. "It's why you didn't come to Fort Worth as soon as they called you about the baby." Then, turning back to Hannah, she asked, "Is Jackson McBride as hot in person as he is in his pictures?"

Hannah's lips twitched. "Honestly, he's hotter."

"Whoa!" Rachel said.

A teasing glint entering her eyes, Hannah added, "And Jackson doesn't have anything on his cousin Tucker." She fanned her face with her hand. Both women's eyes turned toward Boone.

"I am not begging for compliments." He folded his arms and scowled. "Tucker wears his hair too short, and I swear Jackson's hairline is receding."

"It is not," Hannah objected, giving her eyes an exaggerated roll.

The McBride cousin discussion succeeded in breaking up the overly emotional moment. Rachel continued her story with a steadier voice. "I googled you. Found out you'd moved to Colorado, that you didn't already have a houseful of kids. Found out you hadn't remarried. So I figured I'd explore the possibility of giving you the baby, but I wanted to do it on the down low. I wanted to be sure about you. So we came up with a plan."

"We?"

"Better for everyone if I don't go there."

If Boone had to guess, she had help from Lisa and likely Sarah Winston too. Probably an attorney also, someone that he knew. But Rachel was right. No sense rattling a cage and mucking up the deal she'd gone to extraordinary effort to pull off. "So the Safe Haven story — I take it you didn't surrender her at a fire station?"

"Technically yes, but it was all part of the plan. I wanted — I needed — to be sure that you really truly wanted her. I needed you to jump through a few hoops."

"You figured out some good ones. I'll give you that." Boone spied an acorn on the ground. He bent, scooped it up, and threw it. "One thing I can't figure out. Why did you have them tell me she was a boy?"

"Because one time, you told me how much you wanted a son. I thought you'd find it easier to say no to a girl. Plus, I heard what you said to the social worker after you read my note about what Ralph did to me."

"I don't remember. What did I say?"

"That you hoped you'd never have a daughter, that you'd be too afraid to have a daughter."

He didn't remember saying that, but her claim didn't surprise him. The thought of being a father to a daughter *did* terrify him. His own father always said the same thing about being a dad to the twins.

"I did what I did because I needed to be sure that you wanted my little girl." Rachel gave Boone a warm and wistful smile. "You didn't hesitate, so I knew that I was doing the right thing."

Boone was overwhelmed. So much had happened in a short amount of time, and he was having trouble processing everything. He was glad when Hannah asked a question he hadn't thought to ask. She said, "Tonight after you watched him meet your daughter, you left. You didn't plan on telling him all this?"

"No. I didn't. Not now. I thought maybe I'd write you a letter someday. I've signed all the paperwork already. The lawyer assured me you'll be able to take the baby home to Colorado within the week."

"Man." Boone rubbed the back of his neck and grimaced. "I'll be honest, Rachel. My mind is spinning, and I'm not sure that doing it this way is right for you."

Rachel's spine snapped straight, and she fired an accusatory question. "You don't want her now?"

"Of course I want her. It would break my heart to give her up. I'm talking about you. We could do this like an open adoption and —"

"No!" Rachel cut in. "I can't do that, Boone. I thought it through. I thought about it a lot. It's too hard. I need this to be a clean break."

He accepted her decision with a nod. "I get it. But if you ever change your mind, the door is always open."

"Thank you." Rachel shoved her hands in

her back pant pockets and rocked on her heels. "Look, I need to be going. I have to be at the airport early tomorrow. Lisa and I are going on a girls' trip. It's my graduation gift."

"That's nice," Hannah said. "Somewhere cooler than this, I hope?"

"Definitely. We are going to Scotland. After binge-watching *Outlander,* we decided we wanted to see if we can't find some legit guys wearing kilts."

"What is it about those things? Men in skirts, that's all it is." Boone's scowl was mostly put on. Mostly. He faced his old friend. "Rach, before you go, I need to tell you that you always were and still are one of the strongest people I have ever met. This gift you are giving me, I want you to know, I will treasure her. I will protect her. I will love her with all my heart from now until the day I die. I give you my word, and I won't let you down." His voice tight, he added, "Not again. Never again."

At that, Rachel threw herself into his arms and hugged him tightly. "I know. That's why she's yours now. I know you'll love her, and you'll love her for me too."

She went up on her toes and kissed him on the cheek, then released him and turned away, walking off quickly. But there was something Boone still needed to know. "Rach? Is there something, in particutar, you want me to give her?"

The girl stopped. "A family. Give her a family. A mother and a brother and a sister."

"Okay. I'll do my best to do that."

"And maybe a puppy too."

"Consider that done."

"Good." She gave him a wave and started off again. Boone knew then that he had one last question. "Rachel, what is her name?"

She went still. Boone held his breath. The moment drew out, and he thought she wasn't going to answer. Finally, in a thin voice, she said, "You're her father. You get to name her."

"What is her name, Rachel? What is our baby's name?"

She started running. "Damn it," Boone muttered, tears filling his eyes. Hannah rose and stood beside him. She slipped her hand into his.

Just before Rachel topped a hill and disappeared, she turned around. "Bree," she called. "Brianna Claire."

Then she was gone.

Boone rubbed the back of his neck. Hannah murmured, "Brianna Claire McBride. A beautiful name for a beautiful little girl."

The tears overflowed but damn if Boone

cared. "I'll do it, Hannah," he swore. "I'll be the best daddy in the universe. I won't let Rachel down again. I won't let Bree down."

"I have no doubt." Hannah opened her handbag and removed a clean tissue. Handing to Boone, she said, "You are going to be that little girl's light."

CHAPTER THIRTEEN

Tired as she was, Hannah had trouble falling asleep that night. Her mind bounced between reliving the events of the day and reliving events of her past. When a glance at the bedside clock revealed 1:37 in glowing red numerals, she groaned aloud and pulled the feather pillow over her head.

When she'd agreed to accompany Boone to Texas, she'd recognized that it would test her emotional stability. She hadn't cared for an infant since Zoe was born. The fact that the baby was a boy had made the mountain seem less hard to climb.

Now Trace was Brianna Claire, and cradling the infant girl in her arms had catapulted Hannah back to pre-nightmare time. She wasn't at all sure that she had the heart for this.

Maybe in the morning, she should tell Boone he needed to look for someone else for this job. She had told him her daughters had died. He would understand that being a nanny for a baby girl might be a bridge too far for her.

She tossed and turned throughout the night and awoke to Boone's knock at her door feeling lethargic. He relayed the news that breakfast had arrived. She wanted to tell him she would skip the meal, but the notion of hot coffee was a powerful lure.

"I'll be there in five," she called to him and then dragged herself from the bed. A quick shower helped, but she needed coffee bad. Boone, on the other hand, appeared rested and relaxed, and his mood was annoyingly chipper.

"I did some thinking overnight," he told her as she poured her second cup of coffee.

Me too. Little of it was good.

"After talking to Rachel, and knowing the people involved, I'm much more confident that this adoption will actually happen. If we don't run into any hiccups at the attorney's office, how would you feel about taking a detour on the way back to Eternity Springs?"

Warily, she asked, "What sort of detour?"

"Not far. To my family's ranch. I think it'll be safe to introduce Bree to my parents. I have no doubt that my mom will volunteer to fill in as my babysitter until the nanny recovers from her surgery."

"Oh. That would be great," Hannah said, relief flowing through her. "Really great."

"Not that I'm trying to kick you out of a job or anything. I promise it's cooler out on the ranch than it is here in town. Plus, my folks have excellent air-conditioning."

"No! It's good. I'm totally on board with that." She walked toward the window and stared out at downtown Fort Worth before adding, "I'll be honest. Jumping from blue to pink territory has me a bit freaked out."

His silver-gray eyes focused on her intently. "I was afraid of that. I have a confession to make. After I heard you cry out last night, I looked in on you. You were obviously in the throes of a nightmare. I didn't know whether it was best to try to wake you up or not. You settled down before I could make up my mind, so I went back to bed. I wasn't being a peeper, but I do apologize for invading your privacy."

Hannah had two thoughts. The damned nightmare again, and she'd probably looked like a nightmare when he'd peeked in. Great. "I'm sorry I woke you."

"I wasn't really asleep. I tossed and turned all night."

"Me too." Then, because she had tired-brain, she added, "We could have tossed and turned together, I guess."

"Now, that is definitely something I could get on board with," he said, his grin a wicked slash of white teeth.

Hannah held up her hand palm out. "Wait. That came out wrong."

"Sounds pretty right to me."

"Boone," she protested.

"Okay. Okay. I'll quit teasing. Just let me say one thing, all kidding aside. I'm up for tossing and turning with you anytime."

"Grrr . . . I'm going to go get ready." His laughter followed her into her bedroom.

Four days of meetings, shopping, eating at Boone's favorite restaurants, and more shopping followed. They met the convalescing nanny and spent time with Bree and her foster parents each day. She was a beautiful baby, born earlier than Boone had been led to believe, a little over a month old. Her hair was definitely red.

Boone had changed diapers and dealt with spit-up like a trooper. Hannah had avoided holding the little sweetie as much as possible. If the foster parents or the social workers or attorneys had noticed, no one commented on it.

Through it all, Boone was a combination of the Energizer Bunny and a five-year-old boy waiting for Santa on Christmas Eve.

The one instance when he was less than enthused was the afternoon of the second day in town after Hannah had done as she'd promised and spoken to Boone about Ashleigh Hart. "I don't want to hear her explanation. I don't care about any explanation she thinks she wants to roll out. The woman is dead to me."

"Obviously not," Hannah pointed out. "If you still get this worked up at the thought of speaking to her, she still has a hold on you. Let me offer you a word of advice if I may. I know firsthand what it's like to live with a grudge that has outlasted a life. Living with regrets you cannot change can ding your psyche pretty bad, Boone. My advice is to avoid it if you possibly can."

He tilted his head and studied her. "Am I correct in assuming that regret has something to do with your late husband?"

"Got it in one."

"You never talk about him."

"Maybe one day you can tell me your soap opera story, and I'll tell you mine."

"You already know most of mine."

"And you know what really matters about mine." Hannah shrugged. "Look, I have no skin in this game, so how you choose to deal with Ashleigh Hart doesn't matter to me. I just thought I'd share insight on regrets

276

because if I had to do it over again, I would."

Boone thought a moment, and sighed heavily. "You're right. I have some of those where my wife was concerned. Maybe I'll call Ashleigh and let her say what she wants to say after all the adoption legalities are done. I don't trust her not to screw this up for me too."

He frowned, gave a little shudder, then quickly changed the subject. "So do you want to come with me to buy a car, or would you rather hang by the pool? Personally, I get a charge out of haggling with car dealers, but I know not everyone thinks it's fun."

"Root canals are more fun, in my opinion," Hannah said. She chose pool time.

Finally, five days after arriving in Fort Worth, all the paperwork was officially signed and filed, and Boone took custody of his daughter. His stunning smile when his gaze met Hannah's caused her heart to do a little flip-flop. She took photos of the moment because she knew his family would want to see them.

Acting with all caution and a share of superstition, Boone had waited to call his parents with his news. He'd actually dodged three calls from his mother during the past two days. Still, since the message she'd left asking him to return the call indicated no emergency, he hadn't phoned home. He didn't want to lie to her or spoil the surprise he had planned.

"I figure I'll wait until I'm ten minutes out. Then I'll call and tell her that I have some news to share and am dropping by," Boone told Hannah as he exited the courthouse carrying his new daughter. "That'll be just enough time for Mom to get all worked up imagining what the surprise is, but not so much time that it'll stress her out."

"Sounds good, but Boone? You're about to run into a parking meter. I suggest you look up from Bree's face and watch where you're going."

He looked up and veered, saying, "Yikes. It's just hard not to look at her. She's so pretty. Isn't she pretty?"

"She's beautiful." *And you are too cute.*

Boone had used the remote to start the engine and get the air conditioner running in his new Mercedes SUV. The car seat base was strapped into the middle of the back seat, so getting Bree all set for the trip took little effort. Hannah sat in the back seat with her, and within minutes, they were on the highway headed west. The baby drifted to sleep.

"Maybe I should go ahead and call my folks," Boone said after they'd passed the city limit sign. "Now that I think about it, giving an hour's notice is probably a good thing. It'd be just my luck that they'd choose today to go into town for supplies."

"You're looking for excuses," Hannah pointed out. "You can't wait to call them."

"I'll cop to that. I'm excited. And scared. I think I need my mommy to reassure me that I can handle this."

"I can't imagine anything that would be beyond your ability to handle. You are the most capable person I've ever met."

"I'll admit that ordinarily, I'm squared away. Tackling new projects and experiences doesn't intimidate me. This is different."

"You'll do fine, Boone. You know why I know that? It's because you *want* this. You want to be a great dad, and you'll do whatever it takes to make that happen. Your actions since the first day we met have proved that to me."

"Thank you, Hannah. I appreciate that."

"Now call your mother. Make her day."

His silver eyes gleamed with excitement when his gaze met hers in the rearview mirror. "I'll do that. Now, while Bree is still asleep."

Utilizing the Mercedes's hands-free dialing, he placed the call. After two rings, Quetta McBride's scolding voice emerged from the speakers. "Well, it's about time you returned my calls."

"Hi, Mom. Sorry. I've been tied up with something."

Hannah could see his profile well enough to note the broad grin. His eagerness to share his news with his parents was so appealing. So charming. So much about this man was fascinating.

She could fall for him so easily. If she still fell. If she wasn't *not* in the market to fall.

"Well, I'll try not to take it personally that you ignored my calls. I don't know that I'll succeed."

"Mo-om. I didn't ignore you. I'm calling you now, aren't I?"

"It's a good thing you aren't twenty minutes later, or you'd have missed your chance."

"Oh, yeah? How come? Was I so slow that you decided to block my calls? I promise you, Mom, I had a good reason, a *great* reason, and you'll be so happy when you find out what it was."

She sniffed audibly. "Unless you pulled a Tucker and eloped, I'm not impressed."

"You know about that? How did you find out?"

"The good, attentive family member answered my call."

Boone laughed. "Okay, Mom. I get the hint. I apologize. Forgive me?"

"Of course. All I wanted was the apology."

"So were you calling to chat or for something specific?"

"I have news! Big news."

"Oh, yeah? Me too." His gaze flicked up and met Hannah's in the rearview mirror. He grinned as he said to his mother, "You first."

"Dad surprised me with a trip. For our anniversary! It's a cruise!"

"Way to go, Dad. Your anniversary isn't until next week, right? He gave it to you early? So, where are you going? When do you leave? How long will you be gone?"

"He gave it to me early because we're leaving today. It's the trip of a lifetime, Boone. That's why I said you almost missed your chance to return my call. We're at DFW, and they're about to start boarding our plane. We fly to Hawaii and then Asia and the South Pacific. We'll be gone for two months."

"Two months," he repeated, deflating. "Wow. That *is* big news. I'm happy for you, Mom."

"I'm ecstatic."

281

"I'm shocked. Dad always said you would have to drag him onto a cruise ship kicking and screaming. And now he's going for two months?"

"In for a dime, in for a dollar, he says." Quetta laughed. "I have to tell you, Boone, when I opened his gift, I almost fainted. This is the most excited I've been since, well, since forever!"

They were approaching an exit from the interstate and Boone put on his blinker and took it. "That's just awesome, Mom."

"I've wished that your dad would make a grand romantic gesture all my life — especially since you moved to Eternity Springs. I met all your friends and learned how so many of the husbands in town tried to outdo one another with grand romantic gestures. Now I get my own, not in small part due to you because your dad heard me go on and on about the romantic men of Eternity Springs!"

"I'm really happy for you, Mom." Boone pulled into a Dairy Queen parking lot and shifted into park. "Thank you. I'm like a little kid at Christmas."

Boone turned his head and gave Hannah a wry look. "I know what you mean."

"Now it's your turn. You said you had big news for us too? What is it?"

"No, this is your and Dad's big day. Your concentration needs to be on each other. My news can wait until you're home."

"If you're sure . . ."

"I'm sure, Mom. Go get on the plane and order a glass of champagne. Send pictures when you can."

"We will. Love you, Boone! Touch base with your sisters from time to time."

"I always do."

He rang off and sighed heavily. "Well, that was unexpected." He released his seat belt and twisted around to look at Hannah. "A two-month cruise? My father, who always said he'd rather spend his retirement un-clogging toilets than getting on a cruise ship, is putting on his boat shoes and sailing off to the South Seas for two months? Now? How's that for bad timing."

"I'm sorry, Boone."

"Talk about a letdown."

"You could have gone ahead and told her about Bree."

"I couldn't. Mom would have either bailed on her dream trip or spent the summer fretting about not being here. I'm not doing that to her."

Beside Hannah in the car seat, the sleeping baby began to stir. Hannah offered Bree the pacifier that had fallen onto her tummy.

The baby sucked and settled, and Hannah asked Boone, "So now what?"

"Well, Plan B, I guess, if we can figure out what it is. We can't go on to the ranch. I'm sure Dad will check in with the managers, and those guys and the ranch hands aren't any better at keeping secrets than a bunch of eight-year-olds. If you're up for it, we might as well head for home. We can take our time, and stop for the night when you think it's best for you and Bree."

"That sounds good to me."

"Okay. Then that's what we'll do."

But instead of pulling out of the parking lot, Boone moved the car into the drive-through line. He responded to her silent, curious look by saying, "It's a day to celebrate. There's nothing more Texan than savoring a Dairy Queen dip cone on a hot summer day."

They were five miles down the road, and Hannah was half finished with her soft-serve ice cream cone dipped in chocolate, when Boone asked, "Hannah? As I consider my options, is there any chance that I can change your mind about continuing to fill in as Bree's nanny until Serena is able to take over?"

Hannah's heart twisted. She gazed down at the infant, who chose that moment to

284

open her eyes. Big blue eyes. Just like Zoe's.

"I'm sorry, Boone. I know you're in a bind, and I wish I could help, but you can't count on me. *I* can't count on me. We're still in the top of the first inning, and I'm not sure I'm going to make it to the third out, much less the bottom of the ninth. Bree is an angel, but I need to take baby steps where babies are concerned. I simply can't be your Plan B."

Boone took it in stride, saying, "Fair enough. Didn't hurt to ask."

"No, it didn't."

"Then let me ask you something else. I will find a solution to my nanny problem, so set that aside. I respect your baby steps. But I could really use a friend right now, especially one who understands what went down the past week. Would you stay in Eternity Springs for a while and be that friend? I give you my word that any time you spend with Bree will be on your terms."

She considered it a long moment. She had to be somewhere. She still had several items on her Eternity Springs to-do list. What would it hurt to stay a little longer? He'd been a good friend to her so far. She could return the favor. "Baby steps," she said. "Maybe I'll learn to toddle."

"Who knows?" Boone's gaze met hers in

the rearview mirror. "Maybe you'll learn to fly."

Boone thought about his day care dilemma all across The Big Empty, aka West Texas. He chewed on it at every diaper change and pit stop, while Hannah took a turn at driving, and when it was his turn to give Bree a bottle.

He didn't have an answer when they decided to call it a night and check into a hotel in Amarillo. By the time morning rolled around following a mostly sleepless night of feedings every two hours, he knew he'd have to find his answer fast. So as soon as they were back on the road and with both Hannah and Bree asleep in the backseat, he did what every intelligent, Eternity Springs resident would have done under similar circumstances.

He called Celeste.

"Good morning, Boone," she said, her voice way too chirpy for his ears. "I heard by the grapevine that you were out of town. Are you back?"

"No, ma'am. On the way, though. I hope to be back by this evening if everyone manages to tolerate a long day in the car today."

"Everyone?" she asked, picking up on the one word in the sentence that was open to interpretation and or clarification.

"Yes. Everyone. Hannah Dupree, who you've met, and the new female in my life. Celeste, I'm bringing a precious cargo with me back to Eternity Springs, but the copilot I counted on helping us settle in has gone AWOL and is drinking an umbrella drink with her flip-flops propped up on a lounge chair on the lido deck."

"I'm sorry, Boone. You've lost me."

"My bad. I didn't get much sleep last night. My mind is a glob of saltwater taffy, and thoughts are having a heckuva time pushing through. My mom and dad just left on a two-month cruise. I had hoped to tap her to help with child care until my new nanny heals from emergency surgery and joins us in Eternity Springs."

Celeste remained silent for a long moment. "You are bringing home a child, Boone?"

"I am. I've adopted a little girl. She's one month old." He told her the highlights, then said, "I need help, Celeste. Hannah has been a trouper making the trip with me to Texas and back, but she's not ready to sign on for six weeks. Do you think there's someone in town who might be willing to help out a desperate new father? I can try Caitlin Tarkington's day care if I have no other options, but I'd rather have one-on-one care for a newborn."

"Oh, I imagine we can put our heads together and find a solution. When do you expect to be home?"

"Unless we have an unexpected meltdown, we should be there around five. No later than six, I'd imagine."

"Very good. Expect me at seven."

"Awesome."

"I'll bring dinner."

"Even more awesome." He told her where to find a key and invited her to make herself at home. When the call ended a few moments later, Boone felt a thousand pounds lighter. Celeste's calm had lifted a burden from his shoulders that he'd carried all the way from the Dairy Queen in Weatherford, Texas.

The rest of the trip went relatively smoothly. They made three times more stops than he would have made had he been traveling by himself, which served to remind him of the road trips his family had taken when he and the twins were young. Boone, his mom, and Frankie could go for hours without stopping. His dad and Lara? Their bathroom breaks added fifteen minutes to every hundred miles they traveled.

Hannah was an excellent traveling companion, content to mix comfortable silences with periods of conversation. She'd been as happy as he was to hear that Celeste was ready to take on the task of finding a temporary nanny for Bree. As they crossed the border from New Mexico into Colorado, their conversation moved from favorite songs of the nineties to first paying jobs. "I worked in a boutique that sold children's clothes."

"Did you enjoy it?"

"I did. I liked retail."

"Oh, yeah? So were you a business major in college?"

"No. I went a different direction, but in hindsight, I think I'd have been happier in the business school."

"Maybe you should think about managing a retail shop once you work your wander out?"

"Work my wander out?" she repeated, her smile appreciative. "I like the way that you put that."

She considered the question a few minutes, then said, "Maybe I'll do that. I'm going to have to do something. This insurance money I've been spending for the past three years won't last forever. I have enough left that I could probably invest in a small business. If I could find the right concept, location, and situation, I might just give it a go."

"Hmm . . ." Boone murmured. Mentally, he reviewed the empty spaces and needs of his town, even as his brain was shouting *Maternity Springs! Maternity Springs!* However, his instincts cautioned him to tread softly here. Understandably, children were a touchy subject where Hannah was concerned.

Movement off the road caught his notice, and he spied a herd of antelope. "Look off to the right. Bet you don't see sights like that back in New England."

"It is beautiful," she said. "The snowcapped mountains are a welcome sight after watching heat waves on the Texas panhandle plains."

"No kidding. Although, in defense of my home state, this isn't the best time of year to visit. For ten months of the year — okay, nine and a half — Texas is a great place to be. But there's a reason you run into a Texan every time you turn around in Eternity Springs during the summer."

"One hundred degrees in the shade?"

"Exactly." Bree let out a little squall at that point, and Boone laughed. "She's glad we're headed to the mountains and cooler air too."

"Smart girl," Hannah said. "Sweet girl."

In a softer voice that held a bit of a bitter-sweet to it, she added, "She's a precious gift. A priceless blessing."

Boone said, "Amen."

They reached the summit of Sinner's Prayer Pass at half past five and made the turn onto his drive at a quarter to six. Celeste Blessing sat in one of the rockers on his front porch.

"Any chance she has someone on deck to help tonight?" Hannah asked. "I don't know about you, but I'm exhausted."

"Celeste is an angel. She'll have a miracle in the works for us."

After parking the SUV, Boone helped Hannah free Bree from her car seat. Then as Celeste stood to greet them, he approached his friend with his daughter in his arms. A lump formed in his throat as he walked up the path. His own grandmother had died long ago, but this woman did an excellent job of standing in for Gammy. As a result, he was introducing his daughter to a member of his family — a notable first.

"Oh, Boone. Look at you. Look at the two of you. Isn't she beautiful?"

"I think so."

"May I hold her?"

"Of course." He awkwardly transferred Bree over to Celeste. "Hannah tells me I'll get better at this hand-off with practice."

"You will. You'll be an old pro at it within the week."

Boone wasn't so sure. To whom was he going to hand her over?

Celeste greeted Hannah and asked, "How was the trip?"

"It was actually easier than I expected. She slept most of the time and was content to be fed in her car seat. I think we stopped and stretched more for ourselves than for Brianna."

"Well, I know you must be tired. Why don't I care for Miss Precious here while the two of you go and freshen up? Dinner's in the oven keeping warm. I do love that kitchen of yours, Boone, by the way. After we eat, we can discuss my nanny plan." Speaking to Hannah, she said, "Boone explained that you generously stepped in at the last minute to help him with the trip, but that you're not looking for a full-time nanny position."

Hannah's voice was friendly but firm. "I'm definitely not."

Celeste then gave Hannah one of her extraordinary, impossible-to-refuse smiles and added, "Nevertheless, do join us this evening. Please? Since you've spent time with little Sweet Pea here, your input in our plans will be invaluable."

"Thank you. I'd love to join you." Hannah glanced Boone's direction and asked, "Want some help unloading the car? Celeste, you won't believe all he bought for the baby."

"Knowing Boone, I'm sure I'll believe it. In fact, I trusted as much."

"Hey, it's easier to have something and not need it, than to need it and not have it." He turned to Hannah. "Let's get your bag from the car. The rest of the stuff can wait. Go have some downtime and meet us back here at . . ." He glanced at Celeste. "Seven?"

"Seven is perfect."

Hannah handed off the diaper bag she'd taken from the SUV, then leaned over and pressed a gentle kiss to the top of Brianna's head. She followed Boone to the SUV, where he unearthed her bag from the mountain of packages in the back. He handed it to her, saying, "Hannah. I don't have words to thank you. What you did for me, for us, goes above and beyond the call of friendship."

"I'm glad I could help." With a glance toward the baby, she added, "The trip was good for me. Except for the heat, I enjoyed it."

"Like I said, you need to see Texas in

October. I'll take you to Enchanted Canyon. You'll love it." Before she could offer a protest, he leaned down and kissed her lightly. "See you at seven."

As happy as Boone was to be home, he watched Hannah walk toward Serenity Cabbage and nursed a real sense of regret that the trip was over.

"You need to convince that woman to settle here in town," Celeste said.

"Working on it." Boone strode back toward the house. "If you ladies are doing all right, I'll hit the shower. There's a bottle and anything else you might need in the diaper bag."

"We're fine. I've got this under control, Boone. I'll enjoy it immensely. Some of life's best moments are spent rocking a newborn baby."

"Won't argue with you there." Although come to think about it, he hadn't had the opportunity to rock Brianna yet. He'd have to rectify that as soon as he got cleaned up.

The aromas wafting from the kitchen when he entered the house almost had him detouring that way. Still, he resisted and went straight to the master suite. He lingered beneath the hot shower, letting the massage jets pound into muscles stiff from too many hours in the car.

Bet Hannah was as stiff as he. The shower in the Cabbage was functional, but it wasn't nearly as luxurious as this one. He should have offered to share.

That thought gave rise to a vision that put another spin on stiff, and he indulged in a little shower-with-the-travel-nanny fantasy. When he finally dragged himself from the shower, he was much more limber and relaxed. He dried off, wrapped his fluffy white towel around his hips, and padded barefoot into the bedroom. Rather than go to his dresser in search of underwear, he sat on his bed.

Exhaustion tugged at him. He knew he should get up, get dressed, and go relieve Celeste, but he didn't hear any screaming from either her or the baby. She'd said she had it under control. The trip to Texas and back had been long and emotional, and now that he'd had a few minutes to himself, it was catching up to him.

A glance at the clock showed that he had time to catch a little shut-eye. He'd give himself fifteen minutes. Lying back, Boone set his internal, never-fail alarm and closed his eyes.

CHAPTER FOURTEEN

Showered and dressed in jeans and the soft, oversized hoodie she'd picked up in a gift shop in town, Hannah made her way back to Boone's house a little before seven. She arrived to discover Brianna sound asleep in the bassinet in the nursery. She found Celeste outside on the deck setting out disposable plastic plates, cutlery, cups, and napkins along the bar — for many more than three.

After discussing how the older woman had managed with the baby, Hannah observed, "Whatever is in the oven smells delicious, but I have to ask. Celeste, how many are you planning to feed?"

"I expect we'll have twenty to twenty-five. Dinner is potluck, with my contribution being corn casserole.

"Twenty to twenty-five?" Hannah repeated, shocked.

"It's my nanny plan. We're throwing a

baby and babysitters' shower for Boone. Everyone is bringing one dish for us to share tonight, and a smaller portion to go into Boone's freezer. I've always said the best gift you can give new parents is the gift of sleep and meal prep. Judging by the appearance of the nursery, there's nothing anyone could give him that he hasn't already bought himself."

"That's true. Remember, the car isn't unloaded yet."

"Boone has a lot of friends in town. What he needs from us is day care, and we are ready to help. He said that his permanent nanny would not be available for six more weeks. I have a sign-up sheet, and everyone is going to take a turn or two. It's tourist season in Eternity Springs, so everyone is up to their feathers in work with little time to spare, but we all want to help him as best we can. Boone has done a lot for our community, and he's been a good friend to many of us personally. It's lovely to have an opportunity to repay his kindness."

"Baby and babysitters," Hannah mused. "That's inspired, Celeste."

"Yes, well, I do tend to be inspirational."

The women began arriving a few minutes later. Hannah had met many of them at Jackson's wedding, and other faces she recognized from the businesses in town. To a person, they were friendly and excited for Boone. The bar soon grew crowded with casseroles and Crock-Pots and cookies, of course, as everyone waited for the star of the show and her father to wake up.

Finally, Celeste arched a brow toward Hannah. "Dear, I think I might have heard Brianna beginning to stir. Boone must have fallen asleep. Would you please go wake him up so he can introduce his daughter to his guests, and we can get this party started?"

Me? Hannah glanced around the deck, looking for another volunteer, but everyone simply looked at her expectantly.

"Sure. I'll be right back."

On the way to Boone's bedroom, she peeked in the nursery. Brianna was sleeping soundly. Under other circumstances, she might be tempted to let Boone sleep too — Hannah understood his exhaustion very well. But the man had a deck full of guests, so she made her way to his bedroom and knocked lightly on the door. "Boone?"

Nothing.

She waited a moment, then knocked a little harder, called a little louder. "Boone?"

Nothing.

The third time she banged. "Boone!"

From the nursery came the cry, "Waaaaa!"

"Oh, for heaven's sake." The man was going to have to turn on his daddy radar and wake up at the sound of a crying infant. She opened his bedroom door, peeked inside, and froze.

He lay asleep on his bed, a forearm over his eyes, naked, the towel that must have been wrapped around his waist loosened and lying open. Hannah had known he was a beautiful man, but seeing him here, like this, she thought *breathtaking* the more appropriate adjective. Or maybe delicious. Definitely delicious with a dark, sun-kissed complexion and shoulders as broad as Texas. A light mat of dark hair stretched across his chest and narrowed down a flat torso ripped with cords of muscle to — whoa. Well, they did claim that everything was bigger in Texas.

"Waa . . . waa . . . waa."

He startled awake, jackknifed up, and caught her staring.

"I knocked," she declared, her tone defensive. "Three times."

He blinked once. Twice. Then his gray eyes warmed with a wicked glimmer. "I didn't hear you."

"I know. That's why I looked in." The baby cried again, which poured frigid water over the rising sensual heat of the moment.

Hannah kept her gaze focused intently upon Boone's face as she snapped, "Hurry and get dressed. Your daughter needs you. And you have guests. Lots of them."

She drew back and pulled the door shut behind her with a bit of a bang, then walked quickly toward the sound of the fussing baby. Thankfully, she hadn't worked up to wail yet, but if Bree wasn't tended to soon, that's what would happen. Better to get a bottle into her mouth before she got to the shrieking stage.

Unless, hmm. Wonder when Celeste had fed her last? Maybe Bree didn't need to eat. Hannah always kept a list of when her infants nursed and how long the feeding took. Boone needed to keep track of Bree's feedings and have it available for his babysitters.

She started talking to the infant the moment she entered the nursery. "It's okay, sweetheart. I'm here. We'll get you fixed up." She lifted the infant from the crib, clucking her tongue. "Well, I know part of the problem. You need a new diaper. We have some overflow going on. First let's see where we are with the bottle situation, and then we'll get you changed."

Boone, being Boone, had created a feeding station for the nursery, complete with a mini-fridge stocked with pre-mixed bottles of formula and a bottle warmer. Working from experience and with the baby cradled snugly in one arm, she placed a bottle in the warmer and switched it on. Then she set Brianna down atop the changing table and clicked her tongue. "You need a new outfit also. We've had some spillage here."

Just then Boone strode into the nursery wearing faded jeans, scuffed boots, and a gray T-shirt advertising Enchanted Canyon Wilderness School that complimented his eyes. "Hey. What do —"

"Here," Hannah interrupted and stepped aside. Because she was embarrassed at being caught gawking at him, her tone was snappish as she continued, "Finish changing her diaper and then offer her the bottle. She needs new clothes too, and you'll want one of the outfits we bought in Fort Worth. I'll go get the bag."

"But —"

Hannah didn't wait. She sailed out of the nursery and from the house. A woman with thick red hair and big brown eyes whom Hannah didn't recognize walked up the path carrying a Tupperware dish and a pack of disposable diapers. Hannah pasted on a smile and called, "Everyone is on the deck. You'll see the steps in front."

"Great. I'm Hope Romano, by the way. You must be Hannah. Welcome to Eternity Springs."

"Thank you. Nice to meet you, Hope."

Boone's SUV sat where he'd left it upon their arrival. It took her a little time to unearth the particular bags she wanted — a trio packed to overflowing from a boutique on the west side of Fort Worth. She toted them back inside the house to the nursery, where she found Boone seated in the rocker with Bree slurping at a bottle.

"Should she be making this much noise when she eats? She snorts like a piglet at the teat."

"I wouldn't know about piglets," Hannah replied. She let the bags drop to the floor. "Some babies are loud eaters. Boone, I think half of the female half of Eternity Springs is outside waiting to meet Brianna. Which outfit do you want her to wear?"

"Huh?"

"You're going to want to pick something soft because she's bound to be passed around a lot. Decide now if you want to go with hair bows. You need to get little girls accustomed to them early. If you present her with a hair bow, your babysitters will know you support the look, and they will too."

"Wait a minute. Hold on. Can we start over here, please? First, don't be getting all weird on me because you saw me naked. Remember, I looked in on you while you slept, so turnabout is fair play. When I'm exhausted, I sleep like the dead."

Hannah did her best to ignore the warm flush of her cheeks. "Well, you're going to have to do something about that. You might need to put Bree's bassinet next to your bed."

"Good idea. I'll do that tonight. So what's this about a crowd of women?"

"It's Celeste's plan. We should let her explain it. Have you burped Brianna?"

"No." He grimaced. "I tried once, but getting the bottle away from her was like wrestling an alligator. She won."

Hannah sighed. "Give her to me. I'll finish feeding her, and you pick out something to wear."

"Okay." He rose from the rocker, and Hannah smoothly took hold of both the baby and bottle. Boone scowled. "You make that look so easy."

"Practice." Hannah placed the baby on her shoulder and patted her back hard. Almost immediately, she was rewarded with a loud belch, and the unmistakable sound of a baby filling up her diaper.

"Again?" Boone grumbled. "I just changed her. I may need to float a loan to buy diapers."

Hannah rolled her eyes and nodded toward the bags. "Outfit."

He began rifling through the bags. "What do I pick? A onesie? A sleeper? A dress? A sunsuit? There's too much to choose from."

"And whose fault is that?" she asked drily. "Brianna is making her Eternity Springs debut, Boone. Work it. And do it in about ninety seconds. We are almost done here, and again, you have guests dying to meet this little angel."

"Ahh. Angel. That's it." He dug through the clothes until he'd unearthed a pale-pink gingham dress with a band of smocking across the bodice where little angels turned somersaults above a field of flowers. "Celeste is gonna love this one."

He'd chosen the entire outfit himself, so he knew what items he needed. White socks with pink gingham ruffles. A diaper cover embroidered with the baby's initials — a B and a C on either side of an M. And the pièce de résistance — a soft white headband with a gingham rosette surrounded by leaves shaped like angel wings.

The outfit was so over the top. That made it perfect for this particular moment. "Good job, Daddy."

"Will you do the honors?" he begged. "It might take me until midnight."

"Sure." Hannah quickly changed Bree's diaper, got her into the dress, and wrestled on the socks, cooing and talking to the infant all the while. "Now then. Let's see about this bow. It'll be easier if you hold her, Boone."

"Okay."

"Get a spit cloth first."

"Oh, yeah."

He took a plain white cloth from a drawer and tossed it over his left shoulder. Hannah handed him the baby, fixed the bow, then took a step back. Her throat went tight. She blinked back tears. "Precious. Simply precious."

"She is the world's cutest baby," Boone said, pride ringing in his voice.

And she has the world's cutest daddy. "Let's do this thing, Daddy. But give me about a fifteen-second head start. I want to see these women's reactions when you walk in."

"Okay."

As Hannah walked down the hallway, she heard him start singing to Bree, using the tune he'd made up sometime during the past forty-eight hours with words that changed depending on the circumstance. He had verses for diaper changing, bottle mixing, and getting strapped in the car seat. Now he sang, "Brianna C., Brianna C. Gonna meet my friends, Miss Brianna C. They'll ooh and ah and coo, and then we'll all agree. You are the best, my Brianna C., Daddy's world champion baby, my Brianna C."

Misty-eyed, Hannah walked out onto the deck and snagged a glass of champagne. Celeste met her gaze and arched a questioning brow. "They'll be right out."

As Boone caught sight of the crowd on his deck, his one regret was that his immediate family wasn't here to share this moment. However, his extended family had shown up in spades — the female half of it, anyway. The men must be home with the children.

There had to be close to twenty women here. He spied Nic Callahan, Sage Rafferty, Ali Timberlake, and Sarah Murphy. Kat Davenport. Maggie Romano. Rose Cicero and Shannon Garrett, to name just a few. Hannah stood off to one side with Celeste and Gabi Brogan. He saw pink and white balloons, a small mountain of disposable diapers, and a table laden with food. Wow. Just wow. Celeste had pulled this together in a few hours. He shouldn't be surprised, but he was. He was also just a tiny bit nervous — something totally out of character for him. This was a crowd of mothers and a few grandmothers known for holding "interventions" when one of them was in the process of making a big mistake. Were they prepared to pounce on him in an attempt to convince him that he'd bitten off more than he could chew?

No. They wouldn't have brought balloons if that were the case. Balloons were for celebrations, not interventions.

He drew in a deep breath. "Are you ready, Bree? It's showtime."

He walked out onto the deck with his daughter in his arms and gratitude in his heart.

The women went wild over Brianna. Everyone wanted to hold her, but Rose Cicero donned her physician's hat and suggested they limit the number to avoid overstimulation. Experienced mothers all, no one argued. Instead they came up with a game in order to choose the lucky pairs of arms and included Hannah by asking her to choose five random dates throughout the year. The person with the closest birthday got to hold Bree.

That done, Celeste presented her nanny plan, and while Boone scarfed down his supper — he loved potluck — his friends and neighbors passed around the babysitting schedule sign-up sheet. Before he'd worked his way to dessert, he had sitters from nine AM to nine PM every day for the next eight weeks.

Celeste took a photo of the schedule with her phone, then handed the paper to Boone. "You'll have to handle nights on your own, but you're a competent man. You'll manage just fine, and frankly, it's a life experience you need to have."

Well, now. Hmm. Beggars can't be choosers, he knew, but he'd been running on fumes after one night of every-two-hour feedings.

"She's right," Nic Callahan added. "Sleep deprivation is a rite of parental passage."

To a person, everyone on the deck nodded.

Boone frowned. Capable. Okay, he was that. He could handle the nights. Now that they were home, he would get Bree on a schedule. He was good at schedules. Shoot, he might have her sleeping through the night by the end of the week.

Okay, that was probably optimistic.

Speaking to the larger group, Celeste continued, "I'll upload the list to an editable Google document and send everyone the link. If you need to trade days or times, it's your responsibility to find a sub and update the schedule. We will suspend the schedule when Boone's nanny arrives in town and is ready to work. If she suffers a delay in her recovery, I'll ask for volunteers to extend the schedule one week at a time. How does that sound to everyone?"

Celeste's nanny plan was adopted by general consent. Since Boone had yet to find time in his schedule for a housewarming party, almost everyone wanted the grand tour of his home before the party began wrapping up. By eight, everyone but Hannah had departed. He'd managed to sweet-talk her into hanging around while he unloaded the SUV.

As he carried a stack of boxes into the nursery at ten past the hour, Hannah glanced up from tending to a nearly naked baby on the changing table. "Are you almost done?"

"This is the last of it."

"Good timing. This little girl is ready for her bath, a bottle, and her bassinet, I believe. I'll leave you to it." Boone stopped abruptly. "A bath? Wait a minute. We skipped that part last night, and I forgot to look it up on YouTube. I've never given a baby a bath. I don't know how to give a baby a bath. Will you teach me?"

"Oh, Boone."

"Please?" When Hannah sighed heavily, he pressed. "Baths are the most intimidating part of this process. Is there an order you should use when washing body parts? How warm should you have the water? What do you do if she starts squirming? How do you hold her to make sure she doesn't squirt right out of your arms?"

"Okay. Okay. Okay," she said. "Here's what I'm going to do. One time, McBride. I'll stay and go through the entire bedtime routine this one time if you promise not to ask me again."

"I promise."

"I mean it, Boone. No more going lawyer on me. You're too good at it."

"Thank you."

"That wasn't a compliment."

"Ouch."

Hannah wrapped the infant in a blanket and picked her up. "First lesson, leave Bree's diaper on until you're ready to put her into the water."

"Got it."

She walked into the bathroom and turned on the heater. "The room doesn't need to be hot, but you'll want it a little warmer than it is now. I know you said you forgot to buy clothes before you went to Texas, but does that include swaddles? Do you have any sleep swaddles that already have been laundered?"

"I do. The store clerk who helped me order the bassinet suggested it." He opened one of the dresser drawers, removed a garment, and showed it to Hannah along with a sheepish smile. "Unfortunately, it's blue with footballs."

"She's not going to be traumatized because she wears something that isn't pink."

"Hey, I bought quite a few gender-neutral things at that baby shop in Fort Worth," he grumbled.

Hannah ignored his grousing and continued her lecture, instructing him to set out everything he would need after the bath beforehand. He fixed a bottle of formula and placed it in the warmer. Once he had a washcloth, hooded towel, baby wash, lotion, diaper, and clothes ready to go, she had him add a few inches of warm water to the baby bathtub. He asked, "How warm?"

"Do what you think is right, and I'll test it."

He spent a ridiculous amount of time adjusting the water. He got distracted a time or two when their gazes met in the mirror, and sexual awareness sparked between them. The bathroom wasn't small by any measure, but with all three of them inside the warmed room, it felt tiny, the moment, intimate.

Finally, Brianna emitted a little squawk and brought Boone's attention back to the business at hand. "What do you think?"

She tested the temperature with the inside of her wrist. "I'm a little warm, I think."

I'm warm?

"It's warm," she quickly corrected. "The water's too warm."

"Ah. Yeah. Gotcha. Better cool things off."

He added some cold water to the bath. Hannah checked the temperature and nodded, "Okay, you're ready."

"Not at all sure I am," Boone said.

"Sure you are. Now take off her diaper and hand her to me. I'll show you how to hold her, and you can do the honors."

"I think this will go better if you do it and let me watch. I learn better by watching than by doing."

"I don't believe that for a minute," she replied. "You're chicken."

"Cluck cluck." He removed Brianna's diaper, then handed the naked baby to Hannah. She demonstrated how to keep the infant's head and back supported and lowered her gently and expertly into the water.

Boone wasn't sure what he'd expected, but loud wailing similar to infant baptisms in church probably topped his list. Instead, Brianna took her bath in stride, kicking her little legs and batting her tiny fists around. "I think she likes it."

"My girls always loved bath time."

Hannah showed Boone how to wash the baby's hair and face, smiling and speaking to Bree rather than the man standing next to her. She mentioned something he'd never heard of called cradle cap and cautioned him to use the washcloth to clean Bree's ears. "Spit-up has a way of finding its way into every crook and cranny, so don't miss getting behind her ears."

Boone watched the demonstration attentively, but even as he absorbed the information he needed to care for his daughter properly, his awareness of Hannah continued to hum through his veins.

This woman did it for him. He thought he was falling for her. That was a crazy idea. He'd known her little more than a week. He didn't fall for women in a week's time. He didn't fall for women, period. Not since Mary, anyway, and that process had taken months.

However, he and Hannah had done a lot of living in the past week, sharing big, intense life moments that taught each of them a lot about the other. Standing here watching Hannah bathe his baby, Boone felt like he knew her better than he had known his wife the day they'd married.

The thought stayed with him as Hannah finished the bath, then oversaw Boone's attempt at drying, diapering, and dressing. The swaddle sack thing didn't impress him. It seemed cruel to put a baby in a strait-jacket, but Hannah assured him that Brianna would be happier and sleep better in it.

"Okay, then. You're ready for the bottle and bed." She turned toward the door, saying, "I'll let myself out. See you around, McBride."

"Wait. Hannah, please, one more thing."

"Is it always one more thing with you?"

"I'm thirsty, and I need something to drink. Plus, I'd like to find my phone before I sit down to feed her and rock her to sleep. Knowing my luck, I'll get her almost asleep, and the phone will ring and I'll wake her up while I'm trying to find it. Tomorrow night, I'll make sure I have myself squared away before I start the bath. Please? I just need a few more minutes."

Hannah gave him a narrow-eyed glare, but she lifted the bottle from the warmer and carried it and Brianna over to the rocker. Wishing to avoid the possibility of Hannah changing her mind, Boone didn't dawdle.

He tracked down his phone and slipped it into his pocket, drank a tall glass of water, then, because being a father didn't make him less a man, he decided a nightcap was in order. He took two snifters from his bar cabinet, poured in generous splashes of his favorite cognac, and carried the glasses to the nursery. His steps slowed as he heard Hannah singing a lullaby to Brianna.

She had a sexy voice, a Norah Jones, whiskey-in-a-dark-nightclub sound that skidded across Boone's nerves. He stood in the hallway just out of sight and waited for her to finish the song about a mockingbird that he recognized as one his cousin Jackson used to sing to his baby daughter.

Jackson, a renowned singer-songwriter, would like Hannah's voice. Bet he could write a song that suited her. Propelled by a sudden urge, Boone set down the drinks, turned, and quickly made his way to the staircase, headed for the entertainment room on the second floor. Three minutes later, he was back with his acoustic guitar. The three McBride cousins had passed many hours picking out songs on guitars. Jackson could play rings around Boone and Tucker, but Boone wasn't exactly a slouch. He could hold his own making music with Hannah Dupree.

Hannah had finished the mockingbird song and was now singing the first verse of "Baby Mine." Boone knew this one because Jackson had sung it to Haley too. Boone joined her at the chorus, moving to stand in the doorway and lean against the jamb as he played.

Bree had finished her bottle, and she lay against Hannah's shoulder as Hannah patted her back. Hannah's voice skipped a few beats while Boone continued to play, and he wondered if she would stop singing. She did not, but finished the song and moved on to another, a beautiful, haunting Irish lullaby.

By the time she finished that song, tears were rolling down Hannah's face. *Oh, sweetheart.* Boone felt confident that she'd been thinking about her girls. Regret washed over him. She'd told him that being around the baby would be painful for her.

He'd been damned insensitive leaning on her this way. It was torture for her. He should have realized it. Damn, he'd been selfish and blind to her pain. *Shame on me.*

When the last notes of the final chorus faded away, she didn't start another song. Boone set his guitar aside as she rose from the rocker, carried Brianna to her crib, and lay her down. Then, staring at the sleeping child, Hannah swiped at the tear tracks on her cheeks.

Boone placed a hand on her shoulder and whispered, "Honey, I'm sorry. I'm so sorry. I'm a jerk. I didn't listen —"

She turned and placed her fingers against his lips, silently shushing him. Then she jerked her head toward the door, gesturing that they should leave.

He stepped aside and motioned for her to proceed, and then, after blowing Brianna a silent good-night kiss, followed Hannah from the room, exiting just in time to see her pick up one of the cognac glasses from the hall table. He wouldn't have been surprised to see her sail right out the door with her drink. Instead, she halted in front of the fireplace in the great room, threw back her drink like it was the cheapest of rotgut whiskey, set her glass on the mantel, and turned to face him.

Pain and pique and a hint of wildness swam in her eyes as she lifted her chin and declared, "For the past three years, I've existed. I haven't lived. Life is a gift, and it is a crime to waste even a second of it. I want to live again. I *need* to live again. Will you help me?"

"Of course. How would you like me to help? What can I do?"

"Make love to me, Boone McBride. I want you to make love to me. Now. Tonight."

CHAPTER FIFTEEN

Hannah's heart thudded. Her nerves fluttered. Her breaths came in shallow pants.

She'd obviously shocked him. She could see it in his eyes and in the fact that he almost dropped his drink.

She was more than a little shocked herself. She didn't sleep with men she'd known for barely two weeks. She hadn't slept with a man to whom she wasn't married or engaged to be married in a decade. But she wanted Boone McBride. She wanted him rather desperately.

And unless she was positively clueless, he wanted her too.

So why was he just standing there? Why didn't he say something? Do something? Yes, heat had flared in his eyes, turning them to molten silver, but his feet hadn't moved. He hadn't said a word.

When he finally moved, all he did was lift his snifter to his mouth.

Hannah almost, *almost,* bared her teeth and growled at him.

After about a million years, he spoke. "I want to make love to you right now more than I want to breathe."

Whew. Okay, so she hadn't misread him. However, there was a *but* coming. She could tell.

"But."

I knew it.

"I don't want to take advantage of you."

Take advantage of me, please!

"This seems like a spur-of-the-moment decision and somewhat out of character for you, Hannah."

"That's the point! I want to change my character. My current character has no color. I have no color. I'm so over black, and gray is not much better. I shouldn't be afraid to hold a baby, Boone. One of life's most precious moments is rocking a new-born baby."

"Celeste said something similar to me not too long ago."

"She's right!"

"She's always right."

"What does she say about sex?"

Boone physically took a step back. "Um, *that* we haven't discussed."

"Well, as someone who has gone without

320

it for longer than I care to contemplate, I can assure you that sex — well, good sex, anyway — is another one of life's precious moments. I'm confident that sex with you would be good."

"I, uh, haven't had any complaints."

"I'm not ready to be a mother or a wife again, but I want to be able to cuddle and love on a little one and go to bed with a man again. I like you, Boone. I'm hot for you. I want to live! Are you going to help me or not?"

"Damn skippy, I am."

Her breath hitched at the heat that blazed in his eyes. Setting down his drink, he crossed the room, prowling like a panther. Hannah shivered. A part of her — the dull, gray part — couldn't believe she was doing this, but the color sizzling through her veins right now was red — bright passionate red.

Then Boone placed his hands on her hips and tugged her against him and his obvious erection, and his mouth swooped down toward hers.

And because life was all about timing, and Hannah's timing was invariably bad, Brianna wailed.

Boone groaned.

Hannah moaned.

It was the sound of parents everywhere.

"This is so much my luck," Hannah muttered.

Boone kissed her forehead rather than her mouth. "I think this is probably a good thing."

"You've changed your mind."

"Not at all. I'm totally on board with doing my part in welcoming you back to life. It's gonna be my pleasure. But I think you and I will both enjoy the process more if we do this the right way."

From the nursery came, "Waaa! Waaaa! Waaa!"

"With a babysitter?" Hannah asked.

"Absolutely. And a little romance. Romance is another one of life's gifts. Let me romance you into my bedroom, Hannah. Let's do this the right way. I want to give you romance." He kissed her briefly on the mouth and added, "In addition to a mind-blowing orgasm."

She might have whimpered just a little bit before saying, "You'd better go tend to your baby."

"Yeah." He stepped away.

"I'm going home."

"Okay. I'll see you tomorrow."

"Okay."

"Hannah?" Boone said, just before disappearing down the hallway. "Be prepared to be romanced."

She floated all the way home.

He sent her flowers the next day, a big, beautiful mixed bouquet in a rainbow of brilliant colors that made her smile. The enclosed card invited her to join him for a dinnertime picnic cruise on the lake. They had a lovely time, but they didn't have sex. He left her with a kiss at Serenity Cabbage's front door at eight fifty-five, using every minute of Nic Callahan's turn at babysitting.

The day after that he sent her a cookie bouquet from Fresh and invited her to go running with him and Bree around the lake. His jogging stroller was sweet, the baby dressed in a little running suit and adorable, but that was the only exercise Hannah got. On the third day following their return to Eternity Springs, she didn't see him because she spent the day playing tourist at the Black Canyon of the Gunnison. Day four, they had a lunch date scheduled at the Mocha Moose Coffee Shop, so the knock at her door shortly after dawn was totally unexpected.

"Hannah, it's me," Boone's voice called. "Hannah, wake up. I need help!"

She raced toward the door, flung it open,

and clapped her hand over her mouth at first sight of Boone. His shoulders drooped. His eyes were red with exhaustion. His dark hair stood straight up in places where it appeared he'd repeatedly run his fingers through it. In one arm, he held Brianna.

The other held a dog, a precious little red long-haired puppy.

"I'm begging you. I'm desperate. Take one or the other? I don't care which. They've both been fed. I need half an hour. Shoot, just twenty lousy minutes will do. I was already running low on shut-eye. New baby, that's the deal, I get it. But I didn't factor in a baby when I agreed to take a puppy. I haven't slept for more than ten minutes all night. I need a little nap. Please, Hannah?"

"Wait a minute." She held up her hand, palm out. "You got a baby *and* a puppy? In the same week?"

"I told you about the pup. Remember up at Lover's Leap the day we met? I was trying to come up with a name."

"Yes, I remember. However, you also told me you were talking about a dog, but speaking about a baby that day. Trace Parker McBride."

"Yes, I was. But you suggested a great dog name. Ranger. This is Ranger. Will you take him, Hannah? Please?"

"Oh, for crying out loud. And here I thought you were an intelligent man."

He smiled sheepishly and held up both the pup and the baby.

Hannah surrendered. "Come in. Let me put some clothes on."

"I'd make a suggestive comment, but I'm too tired." He slumped into a chair with a mewling baby and a whining puppy. He was asleep by the time Hannah finished dressing.

She roused him, sent him staggering into her room, and then took both the dog and the infant and left. "This is not how I imagined having Boone in my bed," she muttered she shut the door to Serenity Cabbage a few minutes later and headed for his home.

He'd left the door standing wide open, not a surprise since he'd had his hands full, but still, Hannah shook her head at this uncharacteristic carelessness. What was he thinking? Adopting a puppy and a newborn in the same week?

She shouldn't be surprised, however. Judging by what she'd seen of him and what his friends and family said about him, once Boone McBride decided to do something, there was no stopping him or changing his mind. He kept his word and his commitments, which was a very attractive quality in a man.

And yet, a puppy *and* a baby?

He'd looked adorably pathetic standing at her doorway this morning. Guess crazy could be attractive too.

His *half an hour* of sleep stretched to over two hours, but Hannah didn't mind. She'd had no firm plans for the morning, and truth be told, she was enjoying herself.

She'd put Brianna down for a nap, and then played with the puppy and a knotted rope. He was a sweet little guy, playful and affectionate, and eager to please. "Look at those big brown eyes. Aren't you just the cutest thing?"

His coat was a darker, chestnut color. She wondered if it would change to the mahogany red she associated with Irish setters, or if this was the color he'd keep. "Either way, I'll bet you'll be a handsome fella when you're grown. You'll be all elegant and regal, and the center of attention wherever you go."

She'd seen that with the pair of Irish setters her lake house neighbors took walking every day. The rambunctious redheads literally stopped traffic. They were friendly dogs and took all the adulation as their due. Hannah pulled another toy from the basket and

326

tossed it to him. Ranger pounced, the rubber mouse squeaked, and a hummingbird buzzed by on the way to the feeder hanging from a post.

Hannah sat back in her chair, content. There were worse places and ways to spend a summer morning. Hannah loved dogs, and from childhood on, her family almost always included a pound puppy of one sort or another. They'd lost a little mixed-breed terrier shortly before the accident.

She'd sometimes wondered if having a dog to come home to after the girls died would have changed anything. Maybe a pet would have anchored her. Maybe she wouldn't have run away from home. Or maybe she'd have given the dog away.

Certainly she could not have wandered the world in the way that she'd done for three years. But maybe, just maybe, her wandering days now were drawing to a close. She cuddled Ranger against her and rubbed his long floppy ears. "Maybe someday in the not-too-distant future, I can have a cute little puppy like you. Good boy. Aren't you a good, beautiful boy?"

They played a few more minutes, then Ranger climbed onto one of the half dozen dog beds positioned around the house, circled three times, lay down, and went to sleep. With both her charges down, Hannah made coffee and grabbed a yogurt from the fridge for breakfast. She tidied up the kitchen and family room — Boone's sleepless night had resulted in a mess — and then she chose a John Sandford novel from one of Boone's bookshelves and took it and a cup of coffee onto the deck.

It was a beautiful summer morning. Sunshine sparkled like diamonds on the surface of the lake, and songbirds filled the air with music. The scent of woodsmoke drifted from the direction of Brick Callahan's campground. Eternity Springs billed itself as "A little piece of heaven in the Colorado Rockies," and Hannah figured they had it right.

Here at this moment, she felt like she'd stumbled into paradise. Metaphorically, she'd died beside Lake Winnipesaukee and wandered around in hell for three years, but now she was poised for a rebirth. Reincarnation, Eternity Springs style.

And maybe a dog.

Hannah chuckled softly at the whimsical direction of her thoughts just as sounds of stirring in the nursery emitted from the baby monitor. She set aside the novel and went to tend Boone's child. A diaper change later with nine AM fast approaching and

Boone nowhere in sight, she settled into a porch rocker with Bree and a bottle. "I do wonder who will show up first?" she said to Bree as the hungry baby latched onto the nipple. "Daddy or today's nanny?"

She'd checked the schedule Boone had posted on his refrigerator. When Ranger lifted his head from his pillow and pricked his ears, she told him, "I think I'll put my money on Sarah Murphy."

Hannah won the bet. At nine on the dot, a red Jeep sporting the Fresh Bakery logo on the side pulled into Boone's drive. Sarah exited the vehicle carrying a bakery box. Petite with dark hair worn short, she had eyes that were a similar blue to Hannah's. This morning, they sparkled. "Hello, Hannah. Don't you make a pretty picture sitting on Boone's porch with a baby in your lap? But I'm wondering, did I look at the schedule wrong? Is today not my day for day care?"

Hannah smiled and shifted Bree to her shoulder to be burped. "You're not wrong. Not about today being your babysitting day, anyway. The pretty comment, I don't believe. I didn't even take time to comb my hair this morning, and my socks don't match."

She extended her sneaker-clad feet to

display the truth of her claim, then summarized the situation for Sarah, who shook her head. "I knew that he'd claimed one of the pups and that they were ready to leave their mama. I never put that event together with Brianna's arrival. Oh, wow. Well, better him than me. These are going to be an eventful few weeks, aren't they?"

"I suspect so."

Bree let out a big burp that had both women exchanging a smile. Hannah rose from the rocker, saying, "This is probably the best time to conduct a handoff. She'll likely finish off her bottle now."

"Cool. I'll trade you a cinnamon roll still warm from the oven for one little bundle of love."

They did the switch, then Hannah peeked inside the box. "Oh, Sarah, that smells sinful. Boone is in for a treat when he comes looking for breakfast."

"I say you snooze, you lose. You should have it, Hannah. Now, while it's still warm."

She was tempted. Sarah must have read it in her expression because she encouraged her by saying, "Tell you what. I admit to being partial to my own cinnamon rolls. Why don't we split it?"

"Deal. How do you like your coffee?"

"Black, please."

The two women went inside, and Sarah settled into the rocker with the baby in the sunroom facing the lake while Hannah made fresh coffee. Hannah cut the roll in two, plated the halves, placed the plates and two cups of coffee on a serving tray, and carried it to the sunroom. By then, Brianna had sucked her bottle dry. Once she gave another good burp, Sarah placed the baby in the bouncer, which sat in the middle of the sunroom's table.

"I had one of these when my son was born. We both loved it. Baby stuff has seriously improved in the years since I had Lori. Of course, that was many years ago."

"My youngest was born eight years ago, and I thought her baby swing was pretty spectacular. The one Boone bought makes it look like a horse and buggy compared with a Ferrari."

"How many children do you have?" Sarah asked, her smile friendly as she speared a bite of roll with her fork.

It was a natural question to ask. After all, Hannah had introduced the subject by mentioning Zoe — something she couldn't believe she'd done. Telling Boone was one thing, considering the circumstances under which they'd met, but to mention her so casually to Sarah?

331

Was Hannah's broken heart truly beginning to heal?

Well, Sarah was watching her expectantly, so now was not the time to explore that question. Instead, she summoned up her strength and stated, "I had two daughters. I lost them both along with my husband in an accident three years ago."

"Oh, honey, no." Sympathy welled in Sarah's violet eyes. She reached across the table and touched Hannah's arm. "What a tragedy for you. I'm so sorry."

"Thank you." She signaled the subject was closed by licking her lips and then asking, "This roll is either heaven or the most sinful thing on earth. If I were to settle here, I'd need to establish some firm boundaries about how often I'm allowed to visit Fresh."

Sarah picked up her coffee mug and grinned over its top as she quipped, "Many have tried, few have succeeded. So you're thinking of staying in Eternity Springs permanently?"

What? I blabbed that too? "No. No. I have no plans. Still trying to figure life out."

"Hmm. What about Boone? Is something —"

Crash. "Yelp. Yelp. Yelp." In the great room, Ranger darted away from the brass table lamp, now lying in the middle of the floor, giving Hannah an excuse to hop up from the table and evade Sarah's interrogation.

Startled, Brianna let out a wail.

Instinct had Hannah immediately turning back to the baby, but once she realized that Sarah had Bree, she focused on the lamp disaster.

The lightbulb had broken, the lampshade bent, but the base appeared undamaged. Hannah retrieved a broom and dustpan from the kitchen and set about cleaning up the mess, a challenging task since Ranger had decided he needed to help and kept tangling himself around her legs, yipping and nipping at the cord. "Stop that, Ranger. Down. Stay down."

Boone walked into the house just as Ranger managed to knock the dustpan from Hannah's hand and send the glass shards flying. "Ranger!" the man snapped. "Bad dog."

Unfazed, the puppy ran to him to say hello by jumping and nipping and yipping. Boone let out a long, heavy sigh, bent down, and scooped him up.

"Uh . . . hello, ladies."

"Hi, Boone," Sarah said. Then she waved Brianna's arm and added in high-pitched voice, "Hi, Daddy."

Hannah folded her arms. "Gotta love a man who manages to squeeze a half-hour nap into three full hours."

"Guilty as charged, and I humbly beg your pardon." He eyed the lamp and then winced. "It's been that bad, has it?"

Hannah sniffed. "Brianna is an angel. Ranger hasn't been bad. He's just a puppy. It's not his fault that you don't have the sense God gave a goat."

"I know. I know. Ranger and Bree at the same time is a bit too much."

"Ya think?"

He flashed that boyish grin that lately seemed to make Hannah's heart give a little flutter. "No worries, though, because I figured out what to do to fix it."

Hannah sent Sarah a droll look and stated, "Now, why am I not surprised?"

Sarah asked, "Are you sending the puppy back to Mac?"

Hannah shook her head and said, "No, he won't do that."

Simultaneously, Boone said, "No, I wouldn't do that."

Sarah settled Brianna back into her bouncer. "So how are you going to fix it?"

"He's cooked up a scheme," Hannah said. She had a sneaking suspicion that she knew exactly what it was too.

"It's not a scheme. It's a solution to a problem. I'm going to hire a night nanny for Ranger." He turned a puppy dog look toward Hannah. "Want the job?"

Bingo.

When Hannah didn't immediately respond, Sarah scoffed. "A night nanny for a dog?"

"Why not? It makes perfectly good sense. These first nights away from his mother are hard ones for Ranger, and he's going to require attention. I physically can't give him the attention he'll need because I'm already sleep-deprived thanks to Bree. The last thing I want is to stretch myself too thin and have an accident of some sort. Last night I scared myself. A night nanny takes care of that problem. And since I have help with the baby during the daytime, I'll be able to work with Ranger on the training he needs."

His smile hopeful, he asked, "What do you say, Hannah? The pay is good. *Really* good." He paused, waggled his eyebrows, and added, "Comes with *benefits.*"

Hannah snickered.

"I'll bring him over to the Cabbage every evening just before I take over daddy duty solo." Oblivious to their audience, Boone sauntered over to Hannah and placed his hands on her hips. "What do you say? Will you be our night nanny?"

"For how long?"

"I think it's usual for puppies to cry at night for a week or two, but Ranger is a smart dog. He might make the transition in a few days."

"What if I say no? Do you have a backup plan?"

"I always have a backup plan, but I hope I won't need it. Say yes, Hannah. Please? I want you."

Yes, well, she wanted him too, didn't she?

"Okay. But I'll need a crate and food and whatever else he needs before you bring him tonight."

"Deal. We'll do that after our lunch date."

"You still want to do lunch?" she asked, surprised.

"I do. As long as . . ." He turned toward his babysitter. "Sarah? Are you good holding down the fort here for a few hours this afternoon?"

She'd been watching Boone's and Hannah's exchange with avid interest. "Of course. That's why I'm here."

"I'll pick you up at noon?" Boone asked Hannah. She shook her head. "I'll meet you at the Moose. I have an errand or two I'd like to do this morning, so I'll be on my way."

"Okay, then." He leaned down and gave her a quick kiss on the lips. "See you at noon. Thanks a million for the assist this morning. I wouldn't have made it without you."

"Glad to help. Just don't make a habit of it."

"Yes, ma'am."

Smiling, Hannah crossed to where Sarah sat holding Brianna. She bent and kissed the baby on the back of her head, then said to Sarah. "It was nice visiting with you. The cinnamon roll was spectacular. I hope you enjoy your baby day."

"I plan on it."

"Cinnamon roll?" Boone repeated in a hopeful tone. Hannah laughed. "You snooze, you lose, McBride." She was grinning as she exited the house and shut the door behind her.

Inside, Boone spotted the bakery box and sighed to see it empty. Sarah said, "So, you want her, do you? As something more than a dog sitter."

"Definitely more."

"Are we talking something permanent? Is the most eligible bachelor in Eternity Springs off the market?"

Boone dragged his thumb through the dribble of icing at the bottom of the bakery box, then licked it off. "Yes, I think so. If I can persuade her to hang around, then I think it's a real possibility."

"Oh, wow. A scoop! A baby, a puppy, *and* a wife! Is this public news? Can I share?"

"That would be premature. I'm not one hundred percent certain I'll be able to pull this one over the finish line."

Sarah shook her head. "You're Boone McBride, Eternity Springs' own silver-tongued, silver-eyed juggernaut. I'm betting on you. And I can speak for the entire babysitters' brigade that we are ready to assist in any manner possible. We excel at interventions when they're necessary."

"Thank you. I'll keep that in mind."

"So when should we plan for a wedding? And where? Here? Texas? Her hometown?"

"I'm not going to rush her."

But he was going to charge his batteries. He'd need 100 percent power to light her way to life, happiness, and love.

Probably wouldn't hurt to have a backup battery, come to think about it.

He and Hannah were meant to be. He'd known it the moment she'd asked him to make love to her. Call it kismet or karma or fate or even a sprinkle of Celeste Blessing angel dust, meeting her that morning up at Lover's Leap had been more than chance. It had been destiny. *Be a light.*

What he hadn't realized was that illuminating someone else's world would light up his own life too.

Boone scraped one more puddle of icing off the bottom of the box and took the delicious sugar hit. "I won't rush her," he repeated, "but I'm thinking a candlelight service here in Eternity Springs on New Year's Eve."

"That's moving at a snail's pace where you're concerned. A New Year's Eve wedding sounds fabulous. I suggest you phone Celeste this morning and book the Honeymoon Cottage at Angel's Rest."

"I'm on it." Boone watched through the window as Hannah Dupree, dressed in black and mismatched socks, walked the path between his home and Serenity Cabbage. "I'll get Tucker's wife to work on finding the perfect wedding gown for Hannah too."

"Wait a minute!" Sarah exclaimed. "Your cousin Tucker? When did he get married?"

"That's a whole different story, but it's a good one. Why don't you hand me my baby, and we'll sit outside in the sunshine and rock for a bit? I'll tell you all the grubby details about Tucker and Gillian's romance."

He did exactly that, and had her in stitches about the wedding vows that the Elvis impersonator had instructed Tucker and Gillian to exchange. After he'd told the entire story, and with Brianna snoozing peacefully in his arms, he brought the conversation around to the earlier topic. "Sarah, about those interventions you mentioned. Do you think our babysitters' club would be willing to play matchmakers from time to time?"

"Honey." Sarah patted his knee. "This is right up our alley. Tell me what you're thinking."

CHAPTER SIXTEEN

Hannah raved over her sandwich at the Mocha Moose, and afterward, she and Boone spent a couple of hours exploring available commercial properties should he proceed with his retail shop idea. Despite the successful date and Sarah's enthusiastic support for his romantic endeavors, Boone uncharacteristically second-guessed his decision to persuade Hannah to marry him.

Was this relationship happening too fast? Should he apply the brakes?

Sarah was right. A baby, a puppy, and a prospective fiancée were a lot to tackle in a week.

Could he be wrong about his feelings?

Uncertain and uncomfortable because he rarely suffered doubt once he'd charted a course, Boone scheduled a video conference consultation for later that evening with two recent experts on the subject of love and marriage — his cousins Jackson and

Tucker. After showing off Bree and introducing Ranger to the family, he posed his problem.

"Wait just one minute," Jackson said, holding up one hand palm out. "Before we get started, I want to take a moment to savor what's happening here, Tucker. Mr. Know-It-All is coming to us for advice, and not advice on just any topic, but on *women.*"

"It's a miracle," Tucker agreed.

Boone flipped them the bird. "The miracle is that both of you losers found fabulous women who are willing to put up with you. In my defense, I'm not at the top of my game because I'm running on fumes due to nighttime feedings that average every two hours, so I'd appreciate it if you'd quit busting my balls and tell me what you got for me."

Tucker snorted. "Fine. Fine. Fine. I'll take point. You are looking for a romance battle plan. You got a name for your operation?"

"A name? Why do I need a name?"

"It helps. Believe me. You've called looking for advice. Take my advice. Give it a name."

"Did you have a name for your plan to win Gillian?" Jackson asked.

"I did. I came up with it when I spied a

342

critter as Gillian and I were hiking the canyon." He paused dramatically. "Operation Horny Toad."

While Boone and Jackson snickered, Tucker continued, "I also think you need a two-pronged strategy. If you can get Hannah to fall in love with Eternity Springs, it'll make it easier for her to fall for you."

Boone bounced the eraser of the pencil he held on his desk. "I agree. That's why I enlisted the help of the babysitters' club."

Seated on the lanai of the hotel where he was honeymooning in the South Pacific, Jackson observed, "Actually, he needs a three-pronged plan. It'll help him if Hannah falls for Brianna too."

"Good point," Tucker agreed. He was using the computer in his office at Enchanted Canyon Wilderness School in Redemption, Texas.

Jackson continued, "The problem you have, Boot, is that new babies have a way of dominating everything. Juggling romance and parenthood is gonna take some planning. Hannah needs to know that you want Hannah for herself, not because you want a mother for your child." He paused a moment, then asked, "I have that right, don't I? You're in love with her?"

"It's only been three weeks," Boone hedged.

Both his cousins snorted. Jackson said, "When was the last time it took Boone three weeks to make any decision of consequence?"

"Good point," Tucker repeated. "You're in love with her."

It was the reassurance Boone had wanted from the men who knew him the best.

"I am. You'd tell me if you thought I was making a mistake, right?"

Jackson nodded. "We'd tell you. You wouldn't listen, but we'd tell you."

"We're not telling you," Tucker assured him. "Hannah was a hit with everyone at the wedding. You two were quite the topic of discussion with the Texas contingent. Maisy invited her to visit Redemption this fall once the weather cools off."

"I told Hannah we should go in October." Boone rubbed his tired eyes. He'd managed to nap for an hour after his date, but he was still sleep-deprived.

Sleep deprivation was probably why he was having this moment of insecurity.

The cousins spoke for only a few minutes more before signing off. After all, both Tucker and Jackson were newlyweds and had better things to do than talk to Boone.

After ending the call, Boone kept his seat for a few minutes, bouncing the pencil eraser and planning. Soon he had a battle plan, but he still needed a campaign name. "Horny Toad," he muttered, his lips twisting in a rueful grin. Yeah, he could definitely go with something along similar lines. Operation Stiff Stick. Blue Balls. Only something more refined. Something about light maybe. Operation Blue Lantern.

Oh well. Something would come to him. In the meantime, he had arrangements to make.

He found Sarah in the nursery, preparing to give Brianna a bath. "Want me to do that?"

"Oh, please allow me. Bath time is too much fun."

"Be my guest. Now, about our list of babysitters. Do you have someone to suggest I contact for overnight care on Friday? I'd like to take Hannah glamping."

"At Brick's river camp?" Sarah asked, referring to Brick Callahan. "Ooh, good romance move, McBride."

"I think so. I checked the weather forecast. Supposed to be a cloudless night. Hannah has a thing for stars."

"Well, if she didn't already, I expect after a night with you she will." Sarah considered the list of overnight babysitter volunteers. "I wouldn't ask any of our shopkeepers. They all need to be fresh for Saturdays in June. I think Caitlin Tarkington put her name down for overnights. Her day care is closed on Saturdays. I'd try her first, and then maybe Hope Romano."

"You don't think any of them will judge me for being away from Brianna overnight so soon?"

"No. Not at all. In the cause of romance, the wives of Eternity Springs are all on board."

"Perfect. I'll make my calls and then run the pup over to Hannah. I promise to be back before the end of your shift at nine."

"Sounds like a plan."

Five minutes later, all the arrangements were set. As he secured the leash to Ranger's collar, he heard Sarah talking on the phone. "Yes, Cam. I will. And don't let Devin leave without the Star Wars Lego sets we're donating to the camp. They're in that box in the mudroom."

Star Wars Lego sets. Boone wore a self-satisfied smile as he scooped Ranger into his arms and headed for his back door. *Operation Lightsaber commences.*

By Friday, Hannah was a bundle of excitement, anticipation, and nerves. Tonight was the night. Boone had invited her on an "overnight excursion," and she'd accepted. He hadn't told her where he intended to take her, though he had explained that he had arranged thirty-six hours' worth of both child care and dog sitting. He was picking her up after Brianna's sitter arrived at nine. They would drop Ranger off at Lori Timberlake's vet clinic on the way to . . . wherever.

He'd instructed her to wear clothing appropriate for outdoor activities and bring something "nice" to wear to "dine" at an elegantly rustic place. Or rustically elegant. He wasn't sure of the appropriate term.

He had her hooked at that.

He also had her making her way to the Angel's Rest Boutique for something to wear. Thursday afternoon, Hannah had stepped inside the shop to find Celeste working the afternoon shift. She introduced Hannah to another customer, her cousin Angelica Blessing, who had long fire-engine-red hair and a devilish twinkle her eyes. A McBride family friend, Angelica had traveled from Texas, where she managed the bed-and-breakfast the McBrides owned in Enchanted Canyon. "I believe we met at the McBride wedding, didn't we?"

"Briefly, yes. It's nice to see you again."

"Right back at you. I'm stoked to meet Bree. I'll be the first of Boone's Texas family to meet her. That's buckets of fun for me. I'm also playing nanny for the weekend while you and Boone are off scr—"

Celeste interrupted in a warning tone, "Angelica!"

Her eyes sparkled, and she gave her hair a toss. "Stargazing."

Celeste sighed and stepped out from behind the checkout counter. "How can I help you today, dear?"

"Well, I was wondering . . ."

"The sundress? I put it back for you."

"You did?" Hannah laughed. "You had more faith in me than I had in myself."

Angelica waved a dismissive hand. "That's Celeste's MO. I've seen that dress, and you'll definitely knock Boone's socks off. And the rest of his clothes too."

"Angelica." Celeste sighed.

A day later, as Hannah carefully folded the sundress, she recalled the moment she'd first tried it, and the image of herself in the boutique mirror. Celeste had told her the dress was right for the woman she was becoming.

"The woman I'm becoming," Hannah repeated now as she placed the dress into her overnight bag. It was a hope. A promise. A vow.

The heeled sandals she packed along with the dress were pure temptation. Angelica had talked her into buying those.

She wore her favorite pair of jeans, hiking boots, and a new shirt when shortly after nine, a knock sounded on her door. She opened it to discover a road-worn Jeep in front of the cottage, and Ranger pulling at his leash at Boone's feet. "Good morning, Hollywood. You ready?"

"Good morning, Texas. I'm as ready as I'll ever be." She picked up her bag from beside the door where she'd left it.

"Excellent. Here, I'll trade you the dog for your bag."

As they walked toward the battered vehicle, she observed, "That's not your usual ride."

"Nah. Took the Land Rover into Josh Tarkington's garage for a tune-up. This is my project car. It's fun to drive in the mountains." She waited until they were in the Jeep to ask, "So we're going up out of the valley?"

"We are. We're headed for Brick Callahan's Stardance River Camp."

Hannah thought of her dress and heels and frowned. Had she misunderstood him?

"We're going camping?"

"Not in the traditional sense, no." He glanced at her and added, "Nice shirt, by the way. Pink looks good on you."

"It's not pink. It's watermelon."

"Now you've done it. There's nothing like the sweet taste of watermelon on a hot summer day." His grin went casually wicked. "Hope it's on the lunch menu. I'll be dreaming about taking a big old bite."

"Corny, McBride." Nevertheless, a shiver raced over Hannah's nerves at that.

After they dropped off Ranger at the vet's, and while driving past the Angel's Rest resort, Hannah told Boone that she'd met Celeste's cousin. "I love Angelica," he said. "She's a hoot. She'll say anything, and she's often a little risqué. Yet she has a heart of gold. Tucker says she's like Celeste's evil twin."

Hannah laughed at the description, but having met the woman, she could agree. For the next half hour as they drove into the mountains above the valley that sheltered Eternity Springs, he entertained her with the tale of how his family had come to inherit the Enchanted Canyon property. He painted a vivid picture of their discoveries inside the old brothel, saloon, and dance hall that they'd remodeled and opened as the Fallen Angel Inn and Last Chance Hall.

"We saved what furnishings we could and used them in both the inn and the restaurant — the Saloon. We found a lot of junk, but some nice pieces too."

"I'll bet it was a treasure hunt."

"It truly was. It just so happens I brought one of them along with me today to show you. It's in the glove box. Look."

She did as he asked and discovered a leather-bound book.

"It was inside a box along with a harmonica and a pocket watch," Boone told her. "Jackson kept the first, Tucker the second. The journal came to me."

Hannah opened it and flipped through the pages. "The handwriting is beautiful. A little hard to read but gorgeous."

"It's difficult reading at first, but once you power through the first few pages, your eyes and brain adjust, and you get the rhythm. Comprehension gets easier. The author is a woman, an ancestor of mine named Ellie McBride. In the introduction to the journal, Ellie wrote that she intended to record the stories that her father told his children about Comanche raids, outlaw deeds, and cattle drives of his youth."

"I'll bet it's interesting."

"It is, but not in the way I originally

thought it would be. It turns out that the tales Ellie recorded in the journal are more often about her mother than cattle thieves and Indian raids. Adelaide Throckmorton lived quite the life. I think you might like to read about it."

"I'd love to read it. You've got me curious now. Though I hope my eyes are up to deciphering her penmanship by the light of a campfire."

"You'll have lamplight. We won't be roughing it at Stardance River Camp."

"Okay, I'm dying of curiosity. Tell me about this place we are going."

"Okay, but first, let me take care of something that I can't seem to put out of my mind." He pulled his phone from his pocket as he maneuvered the Jeep onto the shoulder of the road. As he thumbed through his contacts and placed a call, his gaze lingered on her breasts. "G'mornin'. This is Boone McBride. I'd like to add fresh watermelon to the lunch menu if that's doable?"

Hannah shivered. She hadn't experienced this much sexual tension since her teenage years, and she was glad he'd chosen the romance route, after all. She resisted the impulse to arch her back and squirm in her seat.

"Great. Perfect. Thank you." He listened a

moment, then responded. "No changes to our schedule. We should be arriving in fifteen to twenty minutes, so I think we're good to go."

The call ended, Boone pulled the Jeep back onto the road. He picked up the conversation as if he hadn't just lobbed a heat grenade between them. "Are you familiar with the term *glamping?*"

"It's upscale camping, right?"

"Yes. Luxury camping. I think the term evolved from *glamorous camping.* River Camp is a glamping resort. I've been up here a few times, but I've never stayed overnight. It's been on my to-do list. I'm thinking of adding a glamping component to the Enchanted Canyon offerings. Utilize the ghost town as a base."

"What's it called again? The ghost town?"

"Ruin. It was an outlaw enclave. The brothel sat halfway along the road from Ruin to Redemption, or, vice versa, depending on your viewpoint."

Hannah gave him a teasing smile. "So this isn't a date, but a business trip?"

"Two birds, sweetheart. And just so you know, I definitely mean business."

She darned sure hoped so.

At a discreet sign that read STARDANCE RIVER CAMP, he turned off the paved road onto a dirt one. She soon saw why he'd brought the Jeep. Four-wheel drive was required to get up and down and around the hills. She began to wonder how much "luxury" they'd find at Stardance River Camp.

When the curve of a switchback revealed an alpine meadow covered in a sea of yellow wildflowers and ringed by snowcapped peaks, she decided luxury didn't matter. "Oh, wow. That's breathtaking."

"Pretty piece of land. It's a shame Brick got to it before I set eyes on it." He motioned up ahead of them. "We're looking for a small sign that reads SHANGRI-LIL. If you spot it, shout out. I think we should be coming up on it soon. When you can read it, tell me which path to take."

"Shangri-lil?"

"His wife's name is Lili. We're staying at their personal retreat."

Hannah tried to place Lili Callahan. Had she met her at the wedding or the baby shower? She'd met so many people that she had trouble putting faces to names. Spying the sign he'd mentioned, she pointed toward the left. "There it is."

Moments later, Boone pulled the Jeep to a stop at a campsite. And wow, what a campsite. The tent was made of canvas and sat on a large wooden platform with a front porch, including rockers. Hannah said, "Oh, wow."

"Go check it out. We don't have to stay if it doesn't appeal."

"Not appeal? I'd have to be crazy." Hannah scrambled out of the Jeep and hurried toward the porch steps, passing two mountain bikes parked in a bike rack made of logs along the way. She ducked past the tent flap and gasped aloud. To the right sat an old-fashioned heating stove and to the left, a desk. Sitting in the center and dominating the space was a luxurious king-sized bed. "Okay, then," she murmured.

In the far left corner sat a big, comfy-looking chair with a table and reading light next to it. The other corner held a bookcase. Hannah walked past the bed to peer behind another set of flaps and discovered an en suite bathroom. "Oh, wow," she repeated.

The floor was tiled. The walls, metal. Two sinks. A commode. A separate shower, and a soaking bathtub big enough for two. What was the term he'd used? *Rustic luxury.*

It was fabulous.

She heard Boone enter the tent and she turned to greet him. He stood watching her across the ocean of the bed. His silver eyes burned with the kind of fire she hadn't seen in a man's look in, well, ever. His voice was gravelly with desire as he asked, "So, Hannah. Are the accommodations acceptable?"

Her pulse quickened. Heat flooded through her and pooled low in her belly. "They are."

He prowled his way toward her, his gaze locked onto hers. An arm's length away, he stopped and held his hand out to her. "In that case, Hollywood. Make love with me."

"Yes." She stepped into his arms. "Oh, yes."

Cradling her face, he kissed her slowly, reverently, and with care. Taking his time, he pushed her to the very brink and she moaned against his lips.

"You taste so good," he whispered, slipping his hands down to unbutton her shirt. "I want you."

He slid his hands around to explore her bare skin, pulling her closer. He rested his forehead on her shoulder and inhaled a deep, bracing breath. "I don't want to rush, but hell, Hannah. I can't seem to help myself."

"I can tell," she replied, arching against his lower half and feeling just how much he wanted her. "And I want you too. I suggest we enjoy the rush."

Her assurance was all he needed. Boone

tumbled her onto the ocean of the bed and dove in after her. Together they sank beneath a wave of hunger and desire that was new and fierce and exultant.

When finally they surfaced and Hannah lay naked, panting, and replete with Boone's large hand resting heavily on her belly, his thumb tracing lazy circles around her navel, an emotion stirred within her heart that she'd almost forgotten.

Hannah was happy.

CHAPTER SEVENTEEN

Boone was exhausted.

He had an inviolable rule against falling asleep on a lover in the aftermath, but this was the first time he'd been with a woman since becoming a father. Turned out that midnight, two, four, and six AM feedings were a challenge to a man's stamina.

But damn it, he wouldn't fall asleep on Hannah. With superhuman effort, he pried open his eyelids. Seeing her lying on her back beside him, smiling like a cream-drunk kitten, was worth the effort. "You rock my world, Hannah Dupree."

"It got a little shaky for me too."

Her soft laugh held a note he couldn't quite place. It intrigued Boone and gave him enough energy to turn his head. "Just a little?"

A twinkle entered those gorgeous Liz Taylor violet eyes. "Fishing for compliments, Texas?"

"Maybe. I wouldn't mind a little re-assurance that I'm not imagining how great that sex was." The truth of the statement surprised Boone. He wasn't needy in the bedroom.

Maybe tents were different.

Hannah was definitely different.

I'm losing it. He cleared his throat and elaborated. "I'm running on fumes, and you scrambled my brains, so my judgment may be off."

She stretched slowly and sinuously, no kitten here, but rather a sleek and powerful cat. "Your judgment is just fine."

"Good." His eyelids drifted closed. There was something else he should tell her, something that was vital she understood. "I didn't plan this, you know."

She snickered. "Yeah. Right. I have a bridge to sell you."

"No, I mean it. I had no intention of falling on you like a ravening beast the moment we arrived." *Ravening beast? Where did that come from?* "I promised you romance. I keep my word. I have a whole day of romance planned."

"I'm sure you do." Hannah rolled onto her side and up onto her elbow. "No worries, Boone. For one thing, the ravening beast thing worked for me, and it was most definitely romantic."

"Good." Boone relaxed. Sleep was a siren calling to him, and he valiantly fought the song. "That's good to know. You'll like the rest of what I have planned. I'm confident of that."

"I'm excited." She snuggled against him and lay her head atop his chest. He trailed his thumb up and down the valley of her spine. "Boone?"

"Mmm?"

"I don't want to ruin any of your plans, but I'm feeling awfully lazy right at the moment. Do we have time for a little nap?"

A nap.

She wants to take a nap.

I have found the perfect woman.

"The schedule is flexible," he murmured and drifted off.

Boone slept hard and woke to find the bed beside him empty. He sat up, dragged his hand down his face in an effort to scrape away the cobwebs, then shook his head like a sleepy old hound dog and took stock. His clothes lay strewn across floor and furnishings where he'd flung them in his haste to get naked with Hannah. His duffel now sat beside her quilted overnight bag on the bench at the foot of the bed. She'd brought in their things.

He wondered if she'd even napped or if that had been a goodwill gesture on her part. His exhaustion must have been obvious. He snorted with disgust. *Some stud you are, McBride.*

He rose, scooped up his clothing and duffel, then strode into the bathroom, where a damp towel and the scent of lemon shampoo informed him that she'd bathed. How the heck had he slept through that?

"Damned shame," he muttered as he switched on the water. They could have practiced water conservation and shared. Of course, it probably would have killed him, but like they say — what a way to go.

A few minutes later, bathed and refreshed and feeling like a new man following his — Boone checked his watch and groaned — ninety-minute nap, he exchanged text messages with Angelica about Bree. He then exited the tent in search of his date. He found her down by the creek, where a wooden glider was perfectly positioned to watch the sunset while listening to the music of water babbling over the stone. Hannah stood lobbing pebbles into the white foam.

Boone's heart went *thunk-a-thunk* at the sight of her now interposed with the memory of the way she'd risen above him on the bed, her cheeks flushed with passion, the rosy nipples on her full breasts hard and damp with moisture left by his mouth. She'd changed from her watermelon-colored top into one the color of a coconut-blue Popsicle.

His mouth watered. Wonder how soon he could coax her back into bed?

"Hey, Hollywood," he said as he approached. "I'm sorry I zonked out on you. I wish —"

She turned and met Boone's gaze. He halted abruptly in his tracks as all thought of sex evaporated like mist. Her eyes were big blue pools of sorrow, and she had tear tracks on her cheeks. "Honey? What happened? What's wrong?"

She gestured toward the glider. Boone spied Ellie McBride's journal lying on the seat. She said, "It's heartbreaking."

Crap. Had he made a tactical mistake here? The journal wasn't supposed to make her cry.

Boone's cousin Jackson swore that the harmonica that had come to him from the treasure box they'd found in Enchanted Canyon had played an important role in his romance with Caroline. Tucker said the same thing about his watch and his relationship with Gillian. Therefore, Boone didn't doubt that the treasure box journal had a role to play for Hannah and him. His instincts had told him that this was the right time to share the story of Adelaide Throck-morton. Had he been wrong?

Maybe. Maybe not. Whatever the reality, he hadn't wanted to make her cry. He'd brought her to Shangri-lil for the sex she'd requested and the romance he'd promised. Not tears.

Well, nothing to do now but attempt damage control. He would try to tease Hannah from her tears.

"C'mere," he said, clasping her hand. He tugged her over to the glider, sat, and pulled her down beside him. "I'd come looking for you intending to wax poetic about our interlude," he said, draping his arm over her shoulder. "Now I think my nap blew the mood. I don't know what it is about you, woman. You somehow manage to take sandpaper to my suave, and yank the deb right out from beneath my onair."

She drew away. "What are you talking about?"

"I'm ordinarily the suave and debonair McBride. With you, I'm an awkward, stum-bling snooze."

"Ah." The corners of her mouth lifted slightly, rewarding him. "I won't argue the

363

snooze, but you have an excuse in Bree."

"Sleep deprivation is a killer. How long does this part of parenting last?"

"Depends on the baby, but as a rule, the first three months are the most challenging."

"I still have a way to go then."

"I think it's probably good for you to work naps into your daily schedule."

"Naps? Plural? So I've had my morning nap. Are you suggesting an afternoon nap, maybe? Following some strenuous and satisfying physical activity, perhaps?" He waggled his eyebrows.

Her smile broadened, and she shrugged. "Maybe."

"Dang, woman." He slapped his thigh. "Okay, that's it. There's only one thing to do. Will you marry me?"

At that, she laughed, and the last of her melancholy appeared to fade away. Humor sparkled in the gorgeous blue eyes she turned toward him. "I don't think I'm ready for six feet and two hundred hard-body pounds of charisma, but thanks for the offer."

Well, now, that comment made Boone want to preen. He said, "I'm heartbroken, but fair warning. I'll likely ask again. Also, I'm six two and a half. The half matters because it makes me taller than Tucker and Jackson. And I maintain around one ninety, depending on how often I drive to Gunnison for Mexican food."

"I apologize, and I stand forewarned."

"Actually, you're sitting forewarned." He nuzzled her hair and murmured against her ear. "I'd suggest an early-afternoon nap, but our lunch is due to be delivered soon. Want to go for a walk? There's a meadow not far away. Brick told me the wildflowers are spectacular right now."

"I'd love that."

They detoured by the tent to drop off the journal, and then Boone led the way into the forest. "Smell that," Hannah said once trees surrounded them. "There's a reason air fresheners and household cleaners are given a 'pine-fresh scent.' I do love the fragrance of a forest."

"I know. It's almost as good as the aroma of brisket on the Green Egg."

"The what?"

"Not a barbecue woman?"

"Oh, the smoker. My mind went to Dr. Seuss. However, you shouldn't compare the fragrances of nature with food aromas. It's apples to oranges."

"You have a point." Boone grabbed her hand, pulled her toward him, and kissed her. "You smell better than pine forest and brisket put together."

Her laugh was a little breathless. "Now, there's a compliment I've never heard before."

"Stick with me, Hollywood. I've got a million of 'em."

"I'll just bet you do."

A few minutes later, they broke from the forest at the edge of an alpine meadow. Hannah abruptly stopped. "Oh, wow. It's even more gorgeous than the last meadow we saw."

"It's a little early in the season to see so much color. Conditions have been perfect this year. Makes you want to don a wimple and twirl like a nun, doesn't it?"

" 'The hills are alive,' " Hannah sang, picking up on the reference to *The Sound of Music.*

Before them, wildflowers painted a carpet of color across the land, mostly orange, yellow, and blue, with a few pinks scattered about. Above them, puffy white clouds floated lazily across a summer-blue sky, their gray-tinted bottoms teasing afternoon showers. Craggy mountain peaks with patches of snow clinging to the crevices rose in the distance. "It's a postcard, isn't it?"

"It's a beautiful spot." Boone scanned the

meadow for wildlife. While he'd love to be able to point out an elk or antelope to Hannah, he hoped not to deal with bears.

"Thank you for bringing me here," Hannah said suddenly. "It's perfect. It's exactly what I needed. The hills are alive — and so am I."

He brought her hand to his mouth and kissed her knuckles. "You're welcome, and you are. Very much so."

"My heart is full of emotion. I think that's why reading your journal brought on the waterworks."

The journal. *I did my best with damage control distraction, and now she brings it up?* Well, okay. Maybe the book's juju was meant for this moment after all.

Nevertheless, Boone had the sense of stepping out into a minefield as he observed, "The story didn't strike me as heartbreaking. I thought it was triumphant."

"Really? Adelaide Throckmorton was mourning her husband's untimely death when her house caught fire, and she was unable to save her invalid son. She almost threw herself in front of a stagecoach! That's not heartbreaking?"

"But she didn't fling her life away. She didn't quit. She chose to go to Texas and start over. Lots of people did. That's why

367

Texas came to be called the land of beginning again."

"She went to Texas only to suffer more tragedy," Hannah argued. "Diphtheria and tornadoes and rattlesnakes. Comanche raids and crop failures."

"Yes, and she also taught school for forty years before dying at the age of ninety-two surrounded by her eight living children and nineteen of her thirty-six grandchildren. That woman *lived*. Life gave her lemons, and she made —"

Hannah interrupted. "Lemonade. It's not that simple."

"I know that. That's why I had no intention of saying lemonade. I like to think I'm better than clichés. I was going to say limoncello. Sweet, but intoxicating. The way I see it, Adelaide created for herself a limoncello life."

Hannah sniffed.

Boone added, "She was strong, Hannah. Just like you are."

He could tell in that instant that he'd said the wrong thing. Her spine snapped straight. Her mouth set in a grim line.

"Strength is exhausting," she said. "I might be ready to live again, but I'm done with being strong. I intend to embrace my inner wuss and emote whenever the hell I want to emote and fold like an origami figure if the spirit moves me. From here on out, I will live life in all my wussified glory."

"Whoa," Boone said. "Where did that come from?" For a long moment, she didn't respond, and a momentous tension hovered in the air. Boone wasn't at all sure he wanted to hear the answer to his question, but he knew she needed to tell him. This was the journal kismet at work.

Finally, he pressed a kiss against her hair and surrendered to the inevitable by softly encouraging, "Tell me."

She exhaled a shuddering sigh. "Yes, I think I need to do that. I think it's time. But let's walk. I can't do this standing still."

She bent and picked a trio of Indian paintbrush wildflowers before continuing along the path. They walked half a minute more before she plucked an orange petal from one of the flowers and tossed it. "Adelaide's story struck a nerve because I too had a sick child I was unable to save. Only, my house fire was my husband. Andrew was brilliant, a chemical engineer. He loved his work. He loved our children, and he loved me."

Boone told himself he wanted to hear this. Nevertheless, jealousy stirred in his blood, which only made him feel stupid. Andrew was dead. Boone was here, walking beside Hannah. Loving Hannah.

"Andrew was a good man." She plucked another petal off of the flower. "We had a good marriage and a happy, comfortable life. We were thrilled to find out we were expecting. I closed my practice when Sophia came along. I loved being a stay-at-home mom. Two years later, we got pregnant with Zoe, and life was even better."

Practice? What practice? What sort of work had she been doing?

"When we went in for the anatomy scan at twenty weeks, we didn't anticipate any problems. Oh, you always worry, but we already had one healthy child." She denuded the Indian paintbrush of its remaining petals and tossed the stem away. "They saw a blockage in Zoe's intestines, which led to further testing and eventually a diagnosis. Zoe was born with cystic fibrosis."

Boone winced. He was familiar with the genetic disease, having assisted in local fundraising efforts for the CF Foundation in Fort Worth. Though cystic fibrosis remained a serious, life-threatening disease, recent medical advancements had taken the word *fatal* out of the diagnosis. Progress in ongoing research offered real hope that a cure would come in the not-too-distant future.

Nevertheless, learning that your child would carry that burden had to have been a blow. "That must have been scary."

"It was terrifying." Hannah twirled a second wildflower stem between her thumb and index finger. "We couldn't do anything but power on. We were careful with Zoe. Followed the guidelines our doctors gave us to a T. For the first year, things went fairly smoothly. Still, every little hiccup in her health put Andrew, especially, on edge. Being an engineer, he approached everything with logic and reasoning. He wanted to find a 'fix.' But you can't do that with this disease. Medicine is headed there, but it isn't there yet. Zoe was eighteen months old the first time she was hospitalized. That was the first time her father fell to pieces. He didn't deal."

"So you had to," Boone said.

She shrugged. "Having to be the strong one all the time gets tiresome."

"I imagine so."

They walked on for another full minute before Hannah resumed her tale. "Zoe was a tiny little thing. Getting her to eat was always a battle. She was stubborn. Oh, the girl was hardheaded. I always thought that

371

was a good thing, though, because she needed to be a fighter. She was going to face many challenges. We tried to give her as normal a life as was possible, but certain things weren't safe for her to do. She didn't understand. She was still too young."

Boone ached to take Hannah into his arms. She had a fragile air about her now, a brittle note to her voice. He wanted to touch her, hold her, rock her in his arms, and murmur words of comfort against her ear. But because the story was not yet completed, he settled for resting his hand at the small of her back.

Hannah briefly leaned her head against his shoulder before saying, "Sophia, on the other hand, was the most biddable girl. Sweet as sugar and had a heart as big as the sun. She was a little mother who sang lullabies to her baby dolls every night while rocking them to sleep. She'd tuck them into their bed with a kiss. When Zoe had coughing fits, Sophia would go sit beside her and pat her foot."

"What a sweetheart," Boone said.

"She was. When she wasn't comforting her sister, she was comforting her dad. The year Zoe turned four was tough. As careful as we were, we made three trips to the hospital in the first six months. The third time, Andrew quit coming along to the ER. He didn't even visit once she was admitted. He just couldn't do it. Seeing her lying in a hospital bed hooked up to machines was more than he could manage."

Prick, Boone thought.

Hannah started tugging petals from the third flower. "He, um, pulled away from us. From me. He took on a new research project and all but lived in his lab. Not that he disappeared from the girls. He didn't. He was still a good daddy who read bedtime stories and played hide-and-go-seek with the girls in the backyard. But every time Zoe had a setback, he fell apart. It was up to me to put him back together each time. But that was just a Band-Aid, and he was hemorrhaging."

Boone didn't think he'd ever felt as much animosity toward a dead person in his life. Andrew Dupree had left Hannah to do all the dirty work by herself.

"Shortly before Zoe's fifth birthday, we had a particularly scary incident. She had RSV, which is a serious viral respiratory infection. For two days, it was touch and go. I seriously thought we might lose her. But like I said, she was a fighter. She pulled through, and I brought her home. Andrew was there, waiting with ice cream."

Isn't that special.

"It's the days and weeks that followed that haunt me still today. I knew something was wrong with Andrew. I thought he was having an affair. I thought he'd needed someone to lean on, and I hadn't been there for him, so he found someone else."

Yep. Definitely a prick.

"I didn't call him on it. I didn't have the energy. I had my hands full trying to help Zoe. She was weak as a kitten, and she desperately needed to put some weight back on. Also, Sophia was extra needy during that time. I think she sensed things weren't right between her dad and me."

Boone was pissed and trying not to show it. *Who was there for you to lean on, Hannah? Damn Andrew Dupree.*

"I let it ride. I was exhausted, and I didn't have the energy to confront what I thought was wrong in my marriage." Hannah dropped the wildflower remnant and clasped her hands. Her knuckles went white. "Then I caught the flu. It knocked me flat. I checked into a hotel to quarantine myself from the girls, and Andrew stayed home with them."

Well, I should hope so.

Boone sensed she was coming to the apex of her tale. He wanted to shush her, to tell her she need not say the words out loud, that he didn't need to hear them. He didn't *want* to hear them.

He knew he had to hear them.

"I was dead asleep when he called. I think he'd called more than once before I woke up enough to answer. He was babbling. Panicked." She closed her eyes and repeated. "Panicked."

Boone gave into his desire to drape his arm around her shoulders.

"He said that Sophia had a fever of a hundred and five, that he needed me to come home and help. But I was running a hundred-and-two temp myself, so . . . I . . . I . . . told him to take her to the ER."

She looked up at Boone, her eyes hollow and watery with grief. "The hospital was on the other side of the lake. Andrew drove off the bridge."

CHAPTER EIGHTEEN

"Oh, honey. No," Boone murmured, his voice rough.

"The girls were strapped in their car seats. The autopsy showed that at some point before her death, Sophia had a seizure. The police theorize it happened during the drive, and that's why he lost control."

He wrapped both arms around her then and held her tight. His face buried in hair, he said, "What a horrible, tragic accident"

She pulled away, and met his gaze. Fiercely, she declared, "One that never should have happened! The man was in the midst of a full-blown panic attack. I should have told him to call nine-one-one. He had no business driving. Actually, he had no business caring for the girls at all that night. I should have called a sitter."

"Whoa. Whoa. Whoa. Hannah, you were ill. Your plate wasn't full; it was overflowing. He could have called a sitter. He could have called nine-one-one."

"No, I don't think he could have. That's what keeps me up at night. It's so easy to see in hindsight. There was no affair. Andrew was depressed. He had an anxiety disorder. Boone, I should have caught it. Before I quit working to raise my babies, I was a therapist."

"Ah, Hannah."

"I was a professional, and I didn't pick up on the clues. My babies died. Their father, who truly was a good man, died. I failed my family."

"That's not fair, Hannah. You're being way too hard on yourself."

"Maybe so, but for the past three years, it's been my reality. I'm no Adelaide McBride, pioneer wonder woman. I'm Hannah Dupree, screwup."

"I repeat, bullshit. You are Hannah Dupree, modern wonder woman. The fact that you are here with me right now proves that. Look at what you went through. Look at what you survived. You *are* strong, Hannah. You're strong and resilient and courageous, and I wish you would recognize that. What you are *not* is omniscient. Andrew wasn't your patient. He was your husband. It seems to me that you did the best you could in a trying situation, and you need to cut yourself some slack."

Boone shoved his fingers through his hair, betraying his frustration. "This has gone off the rails. It's not how I planned today. Today was supposed to be romance and relaxation. Instead, it's revelations and recriminations. I wish I'd taken that journal and thrown it off Lover's Leap!"

"No. I'm glad you brought the journal." Recognizing the truth of the statement, Hannah took his hands in hers. These next words were important. She wanted him to know that, so she squeezed his fingers as she said, "This was the right time for me to read it. Adelaide's story opened a door for me, Boone. I needed to show you my wounds. I needed to confess my mistakes and share regrets. Confession *is* good for the soul."

Frowning, he asked, "So you feel better?"

"I do. My heart is still heavy, but the burden is lighter now. The darkness isn't so dark."

"Be a light," he softly murmured.

"This is the first time I've told the story. You are the first person I've wanted to hear it. How you responded, what you said, it was exactly right. It's what I needed to hear. Here and now. Today."

"Good. Because everything I said is true."

378

"The problem is that what I know in my mind doesn't always jive with what's in my heart. I know I did my best, but nothing can change the fact that if I'd done better, I might have saved Sophia and Zoe. That's my harsh reality. I haven't been able to forgive myself for that."

"Well, it's time you did."

"I think you're right. I think I'm ready to cut myself the slack you mentioned. Accident or not, what happened was tragic. I had a part in it, but so did Andrew. So did fate. It's not all on me."

"Exactly."

She showed him a bittersweet smile. "It's been a long time coming, Boone, but I think I can do it. I think I'm finally ready to forgive myself."

He looked at her, studied her hard. After a long moment, he nodded. "Good. That's good. I'm glad."

"Me too." She went up on her tiptoes and kissed his cheek. "It's because of you, Boone. My world was black. You changed that. You brought color back to my world. You brought light into my life and led me to this good place, this bright, colorful world where I'm alive."

Tenderly, he cupped her cheek. "Hearing you say that makes me very happy, Hollywood. I'm glad I brought the journal along."

"I am too."

"Nevertheless, before we move along, I want to circle back to the strength issue, because I see something different, and I think you need to hear about it. Hannah, I don't think you're ready to embrace the wuss. I think you don't want to be strong alone. You want someone to be there for you. You want someone you can lean on when you need support."

She tilted her head as she considered that. "You may have a point."

"After this little walk of ours, I'm certain of it. And this is my response. I'm here." He poked his chest with his index finger. "I've got broad shoulders, and I've spent the past five years sinking deep roots. I won't blow over. Lean on me, Hannah. When you're tired of being strong, lean on me. If I had my guitar with me, I'd break out into that seventies tune by Bill Withers. We all need somebody. Let me be your somebody. I will be there whenever you need me."

"You are really very sweet, you know."

"Thank you. I think."

"Sweet as Sarah's strawberry pinwheels, in fact."

"Now you've done it. I'm hungry." He held out his hand toward her. "We should probably make our way back to camp. Lunch will be delivered soon."

"Sounds fabulous." She placed her hand in his, and they turned to retrace their steps through the meadow. Before they entered the forest, she said, "Boone, I find your broad shoulders attractive for many reasons, but I want to be honest with you. While you've been busy sinking roots, I've been sleeping. I'm slowly waking up from a three-year nap. I'm just beginning this living business. It'll probably take me a bit of time to figure it out."

"That's okay." He laced their fingers and brought her hand up to his mouth to kiss her knuckles. "Take all the time you need. But promise me you'll stay in Eternity Springs while you're doing your thinking. Give this thing between us a chance. Give *me* a chance."

"I don't know if that's smart. I may have shed a bag or two, but my cargo hold is still packed full. It's not just you. It's Brianna too. That may be a hill too high for me to climb, not without a lot of time and therapy, anyway."

"I understand baggage, Hannah. Believe me. See, I'm a multitasker. While I've been sinking roots, I've also been sorting through my baggage. I promise you that you won't find a better place to unload. No one will rush you. You'll have all the time you need to tackle the task. And as far as therapy goes, you could go to the ends of the earth, and you won't find a better counselor than Celeste Blessing."

She wanted to say yes. She yearned to say yes.

She was afraid.

But she wanted to live. She wanted to keep the color in her life.

She wanted Boone McBride and the chance at happiness he offered.

But right this moment, she needed to take a step back. The man would steamroll right over her if she allowed it. So she avoided making any agreement by teasing, "Oh, I know what's going on here. You just want to earn your wings."

"Excuse me?"

"Your Angel's Rest blazon. You're such an overachiever, McBride. It's not enough for you to be Brianna's light. You want to be my light too, and earn your wings."

"I won't argue that. So what do you say?"

She dropped his hand, lifted her arms, and laced her fingers behind his neck. "I say is that a Zippo in your pocket or are you just happy to see me?"

He snorted.

Encouraged, she added, "I'll be the candle, and you can light me up."

His silver eyes glittered as his hands slid around her waist. "Did you really just say that?"

"Too much corn? Unfortunately, I don't have your smooth-talking gift, Boone. Flirtation does not come naturally to me, and I'm rusty at romance."

"I disagree. No rust on you, Hollywood. You might not use words to flirt, but those eyes of yours? They say more than *War and Peace.*"

"War and Peace?"

"Longest novel that comes to mind at the moment." He held her gaze, his own steady and sure. "So that's a yes? You'll stay in Eternity Springs?"

He *was* strong. "You're a steamroller."

"No. I'm a lawyer."

She'd have to be strong to be with him.

"Say yes, Hannah."

She pursed her lips. "You promise you'll be patient with me?"

"Sweetheart, when it comes to you and this relationship we're building, I have the patience of a saint. Say yes."

I am strong. "Yes."

Triumph blazed in his expression.

When he yanked her tight against him, his

eyes alight with a wicked gleam, Hannah added. "There's nothing saintly about you, Texas."

Just before his lips captured hers, he murmured, "Aren't you glad?"

Happiness rose within her right along with desire. The blaze of it all but blinded her. *Yes.*

The next few weeks passed in a sleep-deprived and sexually sated haze of happiness for Boone, as he and Hannah officially became a couple to his friends in Eternity Springs. Their welcome to Hannah as the town's newest resident could not have been warmer. In a development that both pleased and annoyed him, Boone sometimes found himself competing for her time.

The babysitter brigade happily endorsed and encouraged the romance, which aided Boone's attempt to find a balance between "couple" and "family" time. He was careful not to foist too much motherhood on Hannah. Yet with every day and week that passed, she assumed that role more and more often.

Toward the end of July, as the nanny's start date approached, Hannah moved in with Boone to free up Serenity Cabbage for the nanny, Serena Whittaker. In early August, Hannah joined Boone, his nanny, and his daughter on the trip to Las Vegas for Tucker and Gillian's wedding vow renewal. That's when the beans about Brianna officially spilled to his sisters. With his parents due home from their cruise less than two weeks later, he trusted them to keep their mouths shut that long.

What he didn't anticipate was his mother having Facebook-friended Gillian's mother. She posted a candid shot from the festivities, including one of Boone bending down to kiss Hannah while he was holding Bree. Luckily, he was tending to the two AM feeding when his mom's ship-to-shore phone call occurred, so he was already awake, and the ringing didn't disturb Hannah.

He told his mother the whole story. She honestly seemed as excited about his relationship with Hannah as she did about Brianna joining the family.

Boone's parents arrived back at DFW in the middle of August on a Friday morning. They didn't leave the airport before taking the next flight to Colorado, arriving in Eternity Springs in time for Brianna's bath.

Nana was in heaven. Hopeful mother-in-law-to-be struck just the right chord with Hannah too. They stayed for three nights and bought a small vacation home before returning to Texas. Boone was okay with that. He wanted Brianna to know her grandparents.

The day following his parents' departure, Boone met with a client in his office in downtown Eternity Springs. After listening to Benjamin Karr's request, Boone slowly shook his head. "Ben, you don't want to do this."

"Sure I do." The gray-haired man lifted his chin and spoke with belligerence in his voice. "It's a good cause. Do you know they rescued almost three hundred dogs last year? And the people who run it are all volunteers. They're good people."

"So is Melissa."

Ben scowled. "She had them take away my driver's license!"

Boone hesitated. Hannah might like to call him a smooth talker, but he wasn't so certain. Meetings like this one required that he dust off persuasive skills honed by years of argument before a jury and now gone rusty with disuse. "Ben, you love your daughter, and your daughter loves you. Melissa isn't trying to punish you. She's trying to do what's best for you and everyone around you. You'd be devastated if you ever inadvertently caused harm to another. You know it. She knows it."

"Anybody can hit a deer," Ben defended glumly. "Happens all the time."

Boone chastised him with a look.

"It's my arthritis, my hip. I just need to change my medicine, and I'll be able to move a little quicker."

"That's between you and Doc Cicero. I'm your lawyer, and I'm advising you that disinheriting your daughter due to this disagreement would be a mistake. I'll draw up a new will if that's what you insist, but I want to be perfectly clear. I will not defend you in a vehicular manslaughter case."

"Manslaughter!"

"Deer aren't the only things that dart into the road. How old are your grandchildren, Ben?"

The octogenarian glared at Boone for a long moment before dropping his chin to his chest. "Damn it, it's hard to get old."

Boone knew his client well enough to silence the better-than-the-alternative quip some people might have appreciated. Benjamin Karr was a proud man. Losing his driver's license was a blow to his independence, and Boone respected that. "You are managing better than most, Ben. May I make a suggestion?"

Ben shrugged.

"Write a check to the boxer rescue group,

and add the Uber app to your phone. We have half a dozen drivers in the area now. They'll get you where you want to go PDQ as a rule. You won't have to depend on Melissa or anyone else's schedule."

Harrumph. "My girl told me about Uber. Sounds expensive."

"You can Uber for six months for what it would cost you to have me rewrite your will."

"You're just a thief in a fancy suit, aren't you, McBride?"

Boone grinned and lifted his hands in a gesture of surrender.

Ben sneered at him, then sighed heavily, reached into his pocket, and pulled out his phone. "Since this is just a consultation, and you're not billing me for the time, would you get me set up and show me how it's done? This Uber thing?"

For just a moment, Boone zoned back to the Fort Worth courtrooms where he'd tried murder cases. *This is what I've come to professionally?*

Yes, it is. And you, Boone McBride, are a blessed man.

Twenty minutes later, Boone watched from his window while Benjamin Karr climbed into the back of a high school senior's Jeep for a ride home. He returned to his desk, thinking he'd knock out revisions on a real estate contract he was doing for Celeste when his office phone rang. "Busy morning," he murmured as he answered the call. "Boone McBride."

"It's me," Hannah said. "Do you have a few minutes if I stop by?"

"For you? Always."

"Good. I'm downstairs now. I'll be right up."

Now, this was the way he liked to keep busy at the office. Boone heard her footsteps on the stairs as he opened his door, and when she first came into view and glanced at him with those big blue eyes that this morning glittered with happiness, his heart did a little *doo-wop*.

She'd taken the two AM feeding this morning and forgotten to turn down the monitor. He'd woken to the sound of her cooing praise at Bree and calling her "my little love." Boone had wanted to vault onto his feet, do a fist pump, and shout "yes." Instead, he'd waited for her to get the baby to sleep and return to bed, and then he'd made slow, sweet love to her.

He was so far gone over Hannah Dupree that there was no coming back.

"Hey, Hollywood. This is a nice surprise."

"I saw Ben Karr leaving, so I hoped you'd

389

have a few minutes." She paused to kiss him — no quick buss, but the real deal — then breezed into the office and took a seat in his guest chair.

Boone reached behind him and locked his door. Hannah had visited his office a few times, but he'd never made love to her here. Time to break in his desk.

Hearing the distinctive click of the lock, Hannah shook her head. "None of that, McBride. I'm here on business."

"Monkey business?"

She chastised him with a look, then gestured toward his chair. "Have a seat."

Well, well, well. The woman was full of surprises today.

She reached into the tote bag she carried and pulled out a manila folder. She slid it across his big desk.

"What's this?" he asked, flipping it open.

"A business plan."

Boone looked up from the pages and met her gaze. Damn, but those eyes of hers sparkled. He arched a brow. She explained, "Claire and Gabi and Caitlin helped me write it."

All three women operated businesses in Eternity Springs. Claire Lancaster owned Forever Christmas. Gabi Brogan owned Whimsies, a gift shop. Caitlin Tarkington owned Gingerbread House, a day care center. "Oh, yeah?"

Boone looked back down at the file and scanned the page. Maternity Springs. *Hot damn!* "What are you proposing here, Hannah? Cut to the chase for me?"

"A partnership. I invest my own money, and I have a controlling interest in the business. I want to manage it, and I want the space next door to the Christmas shop."

Boone's head jerked up. "That property isn't on the market."

Self-satisfaction glimmered in her grin. "It will be tomorrow — unless I exercise the purchase option I agreed to this morning with Celeste."

"Location. Location. Location," he breathed. That spot was perfect for a children's store.

He slammed the folder shut. "It's a deal."

"You haven't read my plan."

"Don't need to."

"What sort of businessman are you?"

"I'm not a businessman. I'm a lawyer and a lover." He swept the file off the desk onto the floor and reached for her, glad he had an extra-large desk. However, if he was going to start conducting business in the office with Hannah, he probably should bring in a couch.

Feeling like a million — no, ten million — bucks, he hummed his way through the chamber of commerce luncheon at noon. As he sauntered back to his office afterward to prepare for his two o'clock appointment, he whistled "We Are the Champions." Reaching his building, he bounded up the stairs, unlocked his door, and stepped right over the pile of mail the postman had slid through the mail slot.

"No time for losers," he sang as he stooped to pick the envelopes up.

One in the middle of the stack gave him pause. WAGGONER, THOMPSON, AND COLE. "Huh."

In the past, receiving a letter from his old law firm had driven him to drink, but he'd put that old ghost to bed with Brianna's adoption. Right?

So why was apprehension slithering up his spine like a rattlesnake?

He reached across his desk and removed a letter opener from the drawer. Propping a hip on the desk, he slit the envelope open and removed a letter. Recognizing Ashleigh Hart's handwriting, he almost tossed the paper in the trash. No, it was time to move on. Time to finally forgive.

He scanned the page. His stomach took a tense roll. So Ashleigh had news related to

Bree? What was it about this woman and the children in his life?

He picked up the phone and placed a call to his former law firm and requested to be put through to his former friend.

"Boone?" came her hopeful voice a few moments later.

"What do you have to tell me about my daughter?"

"First, I'm going to talk about Mary. I'm sorry, Boone. I'm so very, very sorry that I interfered in the adoption. I have attempted to atone in what ways I can, and I pray every day that you will find it in your heart to forgive me."

Boone closed his eyes. "Why did you do it?"

"Because I wasn't in my right mind. We never told you that I had a miscarriage, Boone. I really wanted the baby despite the trouble in our marriage. I knew when I lost it that Joe and I wouldn't make it. I mourned my baby and my marriage and I was jealous of Mary. You loved her and she was going to have her baby. It made me crazy. That's why I meddled. It's no excuse, but it's the reason. I'm terribly sorry."

Boone sighed heavily and rubbed the back of his neck. What a crappy set of circumstances. People acting badly all the way around in those days — himself included. "I forgive you. I hope you'll forgive me too. I was wrong to shut you down when you tried to talk to me, Ash."

"My heart was broken. It's still broken."

"You should pay a visit to Eternity Springs. This place works wonders on broken hearts. Now tell me what you know about Brianna?"

As Ashleigh relayed the story, Boone felt the blood drain from his face. No! No. No. No! Be damned if he'd let this happen. No way. Period.

Hannah would cut and run, and he couldn't blame her.

No way was this gonna happen. Neither he nor Hannah was going to lose another child.

CHAPTER NINETEEN

Hannah couldn't believe she'd had office sex. Morning office sex. This, after middle-of-the-night sex. The man was an animal.

And she loved that about him. She loved a lot of things about Boone McBride. His shoulders and his smile. His generosity and the way he filled out his jeans. Definitely the way he went gooey over Bree. The truth was, she was more than a little in love with the whole enchilada.

It scared her. She'd never dreamed that she would fall in love again, certainly not in a minute and a half, which is about how long this summer seemed to have lasted. Days that dragged by before she'd arrived in Eternity Springs now flew past in an instant. Who knew that living life rather than slogging her way through it could alter time?

She was falling in love with Boone Mc-Bride. Even more frightening, she was mush for Brianna Claire. The pair had brought light and color back into her world, and Hannah's senses reeled with the pleasure of it. She loved it. She loved.

Which meant her vulnerable heart was at risk again.

Hence, the scary part.

However, now was not the time to dwell on fears. She had shopping to do!

She'd turned down Boone's invitation to join him at the chamber luncheon because she already had a lunch meeting with Celeste at the Angel's Rest Boutique. Hannah was buying an entirely new wardrobe, and Celeste was giving her first shot at recent arrivals.

The door chime sounded as she stepped into the store at precisely twelve o'clock. Celeste set a small flower arrangement in the center of a small bistro table set for two, glanced up, and met Hannah's gaze. A smile of welcome wreathed her face and warmed Hannah's heart.

"Perfect timing! My chef just brought our meal down from the kitchen." Celeste handed Hannah an OUT TO LUNCH sign. "Hang this in the window, would you please? Set the little clock to one thirty. I'm of a mind to have a leisurely lunch today."

Hannah did as her hostess requested. Then she stepped farther into the shop.

"What pretty flowers."

"Cheerful, aren't they? Nothing like daisies to brighten a table. And speaking of bright, don't you just shine like the sun today!"

"I'm having a good day," Hannah replied.

"Excellent. I'm always pleased to hear that from a customer. Happy shoppers spend more money."

Hannah laughed. Celeste grinned and motioned toward the table. "It's a cold luncheon, so we've no rush to eat. Would you rather shop first?"

"Definitely."

"In that case, come back into the storeroom with me, and I'll show you what I've set aside."

Hannah followed her into the back, where an explosion of color met her eyes. On display were a mix of prints and solids, everything from shorts, tops, and sneakers to slacks and blouses and jackets. Belts and scarves. And dresses. Casual dresses and sexy eveningwear.

Red lingerie.

If Celeste had missed a single color in the spectrum, Hannah couldn't say what it was. "If I were to buy all of this, I'd need to raise the limit on my credit card. On all my credit cards."

Celeste's laughter jingled like Christmas ornaments on a tree. "No pressure, dear. I wanted you to have lots of options from which to choose. Now, how shall we tackle this?"

"I don't know!"

"I'd suggest you begin by choosing a casual wardrobe, then throw in a few business things, and finally, dressy attire. You'll notice this is mostly cooler-weather items. Winter arrives early here in the mountains. Luckily, here in Eternity Springs, we tend to carry our fall color all the way through the spring. And of course, I have resort wear. I suspect you and Boone will want to go somewhere warm on your honeymoon."

"Our what?" The belt Hannah had been inspecting slipped through her fingers and spilled onto the floor.

"Bella Vita Isle is popular with our winter honeymooners. It's in the Caribbean. Lovely place. Talk to Gabi about it. That's where she met Flynn. Cicero is from there too."

Hannah bent to retrieve the belt. "Celeste, you are way ahead of me here."

"Yes, it's what I do." Celeste reached into one of the racks and pulled out a yellow polka-dot bikini. "I insist you try this. It's so retro, and you'll look stunning in it."

She handed the swimsuit to Hannah, who

soon ended up with a dressing room bursting with clothing to try on. It took over an hour to work her way through all the options. When she was done, her "keep" pile was twice the size she'd anticipated.

Celeste pulled salads from the break room refrigerator and set them on the table along with bread and iced tea. "So I take it Boone agreed to your proposal for the shop?"

"Enthusiastically," Hannah replied, her cheeks warming with a blush. "You were right. Boone wanted the property. It was quite a coup for me."

Celeste studied her. "You sparkle when you talk about him. Tell me you're not blind to the feelings you have for Boone."

Hannah delayed her response by taking a sip of her iced tea. "It's complicated."

"Love always is. If you care to talk, I'm here to listen."

Hannah's lips twisted in a rueful grin. "Boone told me you're an excellent therapist."

"Unlicensed, but I do have a good sense of direction when it comes to life trails. You've traveled far since you arrived in Eternity Springs, Hannah. Tell me, what is preventing you from reaching your destination?"

"I'm not a speeder. Before my life fell

apart, I was the driver who set the cruise control for two miles per hour beneath the speed limit. Slow and steady, that's me. But this thing with Boone — and with Bree — I feel like I'm strapped into the driver's seat of a car. Boone is riding shotgun. I'm bearing down on the gas, and right ahead of me is a collapsed bridge. My instinct is to stomp on the brake this very second because I've made this jump before and crashed, but Boone is beside me saying, *Jump it. Do it. Do it. You can do it.*"

"Boone does have a convincing manner."

"I know! And he lives this large, movie-fantasy life where the cars all jump the bridge and make it safely to the other side. Sometimes in slow motion. He's convinced we won't crash, and he's trying to get me to believe. I haven't managed to say no to him yet. Not that it even matters, because I *want* to do it."

"So go for it, Hannah. We have a saying here in Eternity Springs. Leap like a lunatic."

"Celeste, I'm driving a Prius!"

"Oh, honey." Celeste sat back in her chair. "Boone McBride wouldn't be caught dead in a Prius. He's a Maserati man all the way."

"I know. That's why this is hard. The crash hurts, Celeste. It hurts real bad. I know that if I slam on my brakes now, I'll slide up to the edge, but I won't go over. I'll live."

"You'll live." Celeste nodded. "But will you be alive?"

"No." Hannah shut her eyes and slumped back in her chair. "What do I do?"

"Why, you get out of that Prius." Celeste rose and asked, "Have you finished your lunch?"

Hannah had barely started it, but her appetite had disappeared when she started talking about her fears. "Yes."

"Then come with me."

Celeste led her outside of the boutique and along the path that led through the Angel's Rest rose gardens and toward the hot springs. But instead of veering left to the pools, she went right. A moment later, they arrived at the structure that once had been a carriage house. Celeste opened a door on the side and pressed a button. As a machine began to hum, a wide door opposite them began to rise. The sunlight revealed a trio of gleaming vehicles. "My babies," Celeste said. "My Gold Wings." Hannah had heard that Celeste rode a motorcycle, but she'd never seen her out and about on one.

Celeste crossed to a storage rack containing a selection of helmets and clothing. Lifting a helmet, she held it toward Hannah. "My dear, your healing heart is holding on to fear. That's understandable, but for you to be free, to be alive, you must conquer your fear. Come join me on a ride."

Hannah took a physical step back. "I couldn't. I don't know how. I've never ridden. I'd crash. Motorcycles are dangerous!"

"Hannah, you're driving a Prius."

"Not in real life."

"Aren't you?" Celeste's blue-eyed gaze became knowing. She placed a helmet in Hannah's hand, along with a gold leather jacket and a matching pair of chaps. "Allow me to share a little bit of history with you. Many, many, many years ago, I drove a Ford Pinto. It was a hand-me-down car from my sister who bought it thirdhand from a nun who had purchased it from a grad student at Clemson. It was powder blue and had yellow shag carpet inside. I did a lot of living in that car. It was a fine vehicle — until it caught fire. It was a fuel tank design flaw."

"Oh, no. Were you injured?"

"Superficial burns. I will say it was an exciting moment in my life, my own crash below the bridge, so to speak. What changed my life was the man who helped me escape from the burning Pinto. My hero rode a Hawg."

"A hog?"

"A Hawg. A Harley. That ride was the closest thing to flying I'd found on earth up to that moment."

Celeste chose a helmet for herself and pulled on a white-fringed leather jacket. "It's why I ride. Traveling in a car is like watching the screen in a movie theater. The screen can be huge with surround sound or even three-D effects, but you're still a passive observer. Traveling on a motorcycle turns you into a participant. You are *in* the movie, no longer watching it."

Yearning rose inside of Hannah, but fear held her back. "I kind of think we're getting our metaphors and our realities mixed up here."

"Not really. I'm inviting you to step out of the movie. Ditch the Prius and climb onto a Gold Wing and experience the life you are living." Celeste laughed a soft, tinkling sound that reminded Hannah of wind chimes. "My message to you, Hannah Dupree, is that I ride not to escape life, but so that life doesn't escape me. I leaped like a lunatic from the back of a Pinto onto the wings of a Hawg, and I've been soaring ever since."

"You've never crashed?"

"I choose my route with care. I follow the

rules of the road. But life is hard. Crashes happen. None of us get through without a spill or two, so you wear a good helmet and a good set of leathers for protection and hit the road. Then if you lose your balance or run into an unexpected obstruction and literally hit the road, you get up, dust yourself off, and climb back into the saddle."

Hannah stared at the helmet, jacket, and chaps. She licked her lips.

Celeste said, "We will take a spin around the grounds of Angel's Rest while I give you a safety lesson, and you grow accustomed to the ride."

Hannah filled her lungs with air, and exhaled in a whoosh. "Does a Gold Wing go fast?"

"I'll answer you this way. You can keep up with a Maserati if you want."

Maserati Man.

Yes, she wanted. She absolutely positively wanted. *Leap like a lunatic.*

Slowly, deliberately, Hannah strapped on the chaps, slipped into the jacket, and pulled on the helmet. She slung one leg over the saddle of a silver motorcycle and met Celeste's gaze. "So tell me how to start this thing."

It didn't take Hannah long to learn to

404

handle the Gold Wing, and Celeste led her on a mostly back-roads ride through the mountains. Eventually, the drive took them around Hummingbird Lake. When the road to Boone's home came into sight, Hannah gestured that she wanted to turn. They stopped the cycles in front of the house. Spying the nanny pushing Bree in a stroller along the path around the lake, Hannah waved.

She removed her helmet and stared out at the lake. "Thank you, Celeste."

"So you enjoyed our ride?"

"I did. I loved it. I'm reminded of the advertising poster for Refresh that's posted around town. It's a photo of a white-water rafter with the caption LIFE BEGINS AT THE END OF YOUR COMFORT ZONE."

"You found your wings."

"I did. I have." She gave Celeste a sidelong glance and asked, "So does the Angel's Rest Boutique sell wedding gowns by any chance?"

Celeste clicked her tongue. "We've sold a few. But you'll want to make a trip to Redemption, Texas, and shop at Gillian's Bliss Bridal Salon. Her mother is a genius. She'll find you the perfect dress."

"Hmm . . ." Hannah nodded. "Boone is taking me to see Enchanted Canyon in

October. Can you buy her gowns off the rack, or do you need to order ahead?"

"I'm sure Bliss Bridal will provide whatever you need when you need it."

"That's good." A wistful smile spread across Hannah's face. "My girls would have loved Hummingbird Lake, loved Eternity Springs. I will miss them every day for the rest of my life."

"Yes, you will." Celeste linked her arm through Hannah's. "I have a theory about the littlest angels, you know. My theory is that they are made guardians for new souls. They're closer to the work. Experienced, so they know what to watch for."

"You're saying Zoe or Sophia might be Brianna's guardian angel?"

Celeste's blue eyes twinkled. "It's a lovely thought, isn't it? And speaking of little angels, here one comes now."

Serena pushed Brianna's stroller up the sidewalk toward the deck. Focused on the waving fist within, Hannah said, "I love her, Celeste. I love her so much already, and it scares me half to death."

"Well, it's a mother's lot to worry about her children. That never ends."

"But at least Bree has her guardian angel, doesn't she?"

"Or angels. They sometimes work in pairs."

Celeste spoke with authority. Hannah wasn't about to refute the claim. "I'd like to spend a few minutes with Bree, if you don't mind delaying our ride for a bit?"

"Actually, I need to get home. I have another appointment this afternoon. I'll go on, and you can return the bike and retrieve your purchases at your convenience."

"You think I'm safe riding solo?"

"Sweetheart, you have your wings and my Wing mastered. Which is why I have something to give you." Celeste unzipped a pocket on her jacket and removed a delicate chain and pendant. Hannah recognized it right off. Delight washed through her. "The Angel's Rest blazon?"

"For those who have embraced love's healing grace. Congratulations, Hannah. Welcome to Eternity Springs." She fastened the chain around Hannah's neck.

"Oh, it's beautiful. Thank you! Boone is going to be *so* jealous."

"I know." Celeste laughed cheerily. "Isn't it fun? Now, there is no rush on the vehicle switch. You take all the time you need. I'll have all your purchases boxed up and ready when you come."

"Thank you." Hannah threw her arms

around her friend and hugged her hard. "Thank you for everything."

"My pleasure, dear. It's my job."

She finger-waved goodbye, and moments later, Hannah heard the engine on one of the Gold Wings fire up and depart. She went forward to meet Bree and Serena. "How's everybody doing?"

"Fabulous," the nanny replied. "We've had a nice walk, and now our little angel is ready for a diaper change and a nap."

"Let me do it," Hannah said. "I need a little Bree time."

"She's all yours. It will give me a chance to grab a glass of iced tea, sit on the deck, and call my mother. I promised her I'd check in today. Holler if you have any problems."

"I will. I'll give you heads-up when I leave."

Hannah focused on the baby, speaking to her while she lifted Bree from the stroller. "Hello, beautiful. Did you enjoy your outing? I'll bet you did. It's a beautiful day."

Brianna let out a few fussy cries as Hannah carried her into the house and then into the nursery. "It's okay, baby. You're a tired girl, aren't you? Let's get this diaper changed, and then we'll rock. Mama has a story she wants to tell you."

With practiced hands, she quickly changed the diaper, keeping up a gentle patter all the while. Hannah offered Bree a pacifier, which the infant latched fast, and then they settled into the rocking chair. Ordinarily, when she rocked Bree, Hannah would sing. Today she placed the baby against her shoulder, patted her back, and said, "Go to sleep, little love. No worries. You know why? It's because you have your own special guardian angels watching after you. Isn't that awesome? Let Mama tell you about your sisters, Sophia and Zoe."

Hannah held Brianna long after the infant drifted to sleep, rocking her, remembering, crying just a little bit, laying her ghosts to rest. Eventually, she kissed Brianna's brow, rose from the rocker, and carried her to her crib, where she ever-so-gently lay her down. "Sweet dreams, precious."

Hannah fingered the pendant around her neck and whispered, "Andrew, accident or not, I forgive you. I forgive me."

She sent a text message to Boone before she left the house. Climbing onto Celeste's Gold Wing, she took the road back to where it all began and waited for her future to arrive.

■ ■ ■ ■

Boone was a wreck.

As he drove his truck up toward Lover's Leap, his mind whirled like a top. He'd spent an hour working the phone, to no avail. It was a Saturday afternoon in August. Offices were closed. People were on vacation. Hell, half of Texas found the way to southern Colorado this time of year. If he scouted the campgrounds and fishing spots, he might find the people he needed to contact.

He was almost ready to try it. Anything would be better than facing Hannah with the news that had slithered through his mail slot today.

He'd considered keeping the news to himself, but that would only delay the inevitable. Hannah needed to know.

Oh, God. Please, God. Give me the right words.

He'd rehearsed a dozen different ways to say it after he received Hannah's text, distracted shortly by the fact that she was riding Celeste's motorcycle up to Lover's Leap and wanted him to meet her there. Hannah on a bike? Another day, another time, he'd think that sexy as hell.

410

Today all he could think about was hanging on to his girls.

He didn't speed. In fact, he took his time, making a full stop at every stop sign and driving well below the speed limit. He added five whole minutes onto the usual drive time from town to Lover's Leap. Nevertheless, he did arrive.

She was sitting beyond the stone wall in the same spot where she'd sat the first time he'd met her. The sight of her took his breath away. So beautiful. So alive.

Probably wouldn't hurt anything to move her back away from the edge before he shared his news.

Not that she'd jump, but during times of emotional distress, accidents happened.

He shut off the engine and climbed out of his truck. Better if he eased into this slowly. Better for him, anyway.

"Hey, Hollywood."

The smile she turned toward him was as pretty as a sunset against a field of bluebonnets. "Hello, Texas."

"You're wearing leather chaps."

She laughed. "I am. I have a leather jacket too. It has lots of zippers."

He strode toward the wall and took a seat. "How do you feel about role-playing in the bedroom, Biker Girl?"

411

"Well, it would be a new experience for me, but I've discovered I'm game for new things."

He patted the space beside him. "Join me?"

She repeated his gesture. "How about you come to me?"

"Ah, hell, Hannah. Any other time. Any other place." He rested his elbows on his knees, leaned forward, and dropped his chin to his chest. "I gotta tell you something."

Following a pregnant pause, he heard her stand and move toward him. "Sounds like a confession," she said lightly. Sitting beside him, she added, "Does it have anything to do with New Year's Eve?"

He gave her a sharp look. "What have you heard? No. Wait. That can wait. I gotta tell you this, and get it out there."

Her smile faded, and concern creased her brow. "What's wrong?"

"You have to trust me."

Her hand clutched his thigh. Her tone intensified. "Boone, what's happened?"

"It'll be okay. Truly, it will. I've been down this road before — well, a similar road, anyway — and I have experience. I know what I'm doing. I'm a good attorney, an excellent attorney. This won't happen. I don't want you to freak out and . . . and . . .

412

oh, hell, Hannah. I'm scared."

Hannah closed her eyes. "It's Brianna, isn't it?"

"Yeah. I'm going to be sued for custody."

"Rachel changed her mind?"

"No. It's the grandparents. The father's parents. I got a letter from Ashleigh, and then I called her. She gave me the details. The woman knows everything that's going on in the legal field in Fort Worth. Somehow, the grandparents found out about Brianna, and they've decided they want her. We'll fight it, of course. They won't win. I *will not* let them win. But things might be, um, unsettled for a while."

"Will we have to give her up to someone?"

"I cannot see that happening. I will not allow that to happen. I know the attorney representing the grandparents, so I tried to reach him but couldn't. Honestly, I'm hopeful that this is a shot across our bow. I'm guessing that these are grieving parents who lost their son and want to know their granddaughter. They think this is the way to ensure that it happens."

"Well, that's stupid. All they had to do was ask. Right?"

"Right."

"So why are you scared?"

Boone shoved to his feet and began to

413

pace back and forth in front of her. "I'm afraid that my patience is going to bite me in the ass. I haven't had time to lock this thing up. Under the circumstances, I wouldn't blame you for running for the hills. You need to protect your heart. I get that. But, ah hell."

He went down on his knees in front of her and took her hands in his. "Don't leave us. Please, Hannah, don't leave us."

"Oh, Boone."

"I know you've bonded with Bree already. You love her. I see it in your eyes as you gaze down into hers. I hear it in your voice when you speak to her. You struggled to resist her, but she's irresistible. She won your heart. Now it's my job to make certain it doesn't get shattered again. I will do that, Hannah. Your heart is precious to me. I love it. I love you. I will protect your precious heart. You have my word. You can trust me. You can lean on me. I am here for you and Bree and for our family. Because that's what we are — a family. Maybe we don't have a legal license yet, but we are a family. You and Bree are my family. And I will protect our family with my life. I'll be your strength. You have my word on that. So don't leave us, Hannah. Please, don't leave us."

She reached out and tenderly cupped his

strong chin in the palms of her hands. She stared deeply into his silver-gray eyes. "I'm not going anywhere."

Tension began seeping from inside him like air from a slowly leaking balloon. "You're not?"

"Except maybe to Texas if our fight for our family takes us to Fort Worth. I love you too, Boone."

He exhaled a heavy breath and rolled back on his heels, rubbing his hands up and down his thighs. "Whew. Okay. I knew you were falling for me. Wasn't aware I had a one hundred percent commitment."

"Then why have you reserved the Honeymoon Cottage at Angel's Rest for New Year's Eve?"

"Where did you hear that? No, doesn't matter. We can talk about that another time."

"Now is good. We are not going to lose Brianna. I have total confidence that Boone McBride, Esquire, has what it takes to settle the situation with her grandparents in a way that's good for everyone involved. I also have it on good authority that Bree has two little guardian angels watching out for her."

Sophia and Zoe. One corner of Boone's mouth inched up as he pictured older sisters with wings fluttering over Bree's crib.

"You and I are meant to be Brianna's parents," Hannah continued. "She is meant to be our daughter. We will fight for her. Fight for what is best for her. And we will win. I have no doubt, so we don't need to discuss it any further at the moment. I want to talk about this wedding. I'll have some say-so in the planning. Frankly, New Year's Eve in Eternity Springs doesn't work for me."

Wedding. Planning. She said *wedding* and *planning*. The last of Boone's tension disappeared in a blast of joy. She loved him. She'd said it. She couldn't take it back. Then, because a man must do what a man must do, he rolled to his feet and faced her, his stance wide, his arms folded. "Marrying me on New Year's Eve in Eternity Springs doesn't work for you? Why the hell not?"

She shrugged nonchalantly. "It's cold."

"I'll keep you warm."

"And I don't like snow. Oh, flurries are fine, and a storm or two is okay, but feet on the ground for months on end?" She wrinkled her nose. "Not a fan."

Boone was tempted to lean down and nip at that cute little nose. "Well, that's a bit of a problem for someone who has moved to the mountains and started a new business, don't you think?"

416

"It is. Luckily, I've thought of a way to fix it."

"You have, have you?"

"Yep. Consider it as an addendum to my business plan. I've already talked to Angelica about it."

Now, that one shocked him. "Angelica!"

"Seems the children's store in Redemption is up for sale."

"Wait a minute." He held up his hand, palm out. "A moment ago you said you weren't going anywhere. Now you want to leave Eternity Springs? You want to move to Redemption?"

"From October to March sounds good. Maybe April. Come home to Eternity Springs for the good weather and the tourist season."

"Oh. Well . . ." He slowly began to nod.

"Your cousins and their new wives have both settled in Redemption. It's an easier trip for your parents to make from the ranch. Brianna should grow up with family, don't you think?"

"I do, but —"

"Of course, our friends here in Eternity Springs are family too. It's the best of both worlds, the way I see it. I realize this schedule could pose a problem with your legal practice, but frankly, from what I've seen, you don't do all that much work."

"Hey!" he protested. "It takes a lot of effort to keep Benjamin Karr from disinheriting his daughter."

Hannah rose from her seat atop the rock wall. She faced him and reached for his hands. "Teleconference. It's all the rage."

Boone gazed down at their linked fingers, and his heart swelled. "I am so lucky. So blessed. It scares me to think I might have driven right past you that morning in June. I love you. With all of my heart and soul, I love you. You've changed my life, Hannah. You've completed my world. You've completed me. You are who and what I came looking for when I moved to Eternity Springs."

The time had come to do this thing right. Unfortunately, he didn't have a ring in his pocket, but that was a minor issue. His grandmother's engagement ring was at home in his safe. He'd cook up some real romance for this evening and present it to her then.

His fingers tightened on hers as he moved to go down on one knee. Her tug halted the movement.

Love shone in Hannah's eyes as she held his gaze. "On a morning not too long ago, I found myself here at Lover's Leap in the middle of nowhere. Today because of you, here in the middle of nowhere, I have found myself. I have a heart that is mended and whole and ready to be shared. And I have wings to wrap around my loves as shelter from life's storms. Wings that on clear days will enable me to soar, to leap like a lunatic and land safely with you beside me."

Hannah caught Boone totally by surprise when abruptly, *she* went down on one knee. "Will you marry me, Boone? Will you marry me in October in Texas, at the Fallen Angel Inn in Enchanted Canyon, with Tucker and Jackson as your best men and Brianna and Haley as our flower girls? Will you dance a first dance with me at the Last Chance Hall and skinny-dip with me in the moonlight pool beneath the waterfall?"

She'd rendered him speechless. For the first time in Boone's entire life, his facile tongue failed him.

He didn't say yes. He just stood there staring down at her like six feet two and a half inches of tongue-tied Texan fool.

Hannah giggled. "Are you going to leave me hanging here, McBride?"

Finally, he managed, "This is wrong, so wrong. It's backward. I'm supposed to be the person down on one knee! I've been planning. It's Operation Lightsaber. I was going to do a big, over-the-top proposal. That's the way we do it in Eternity Springs."

"Beat you to it. You snooze, you lose. Besides, it's a brand-new world, Texas. A brand-new life. So what do you say? Are you going to live it with me?"

"On one condition." He tugged her back onto her feet. His arms slid around her waist.

"What's that?"

He pulled her hard against him. "You don't breathe a word about the way this happened to Jackson and Tucker. They'll give me hell."

She giggled again. "Nope. No conditions. No negotiations. Yes or no. What's your answer?"

"Unbelievable," he grumbled. "Outmaneuvered by a Yankee. I'm going to have to turn in my cowboy card."

His lips swooped in and captured hers in a long, steamy kiss. When he finally broke to breathe, he gasped, then said, "My answer is yes. Yes. Yes. Oh holy hell, yes, I'll marry you whenever and wherever you want, although I really like your suggestion. Now let's go home where we can roll around naked without having to worry about rolling right off a cliff, shall we?"

"I like that plan, but first, I have something

to give you to mark the occasion." She picked up the leather jacket and tugged open one of the zippers. She placed something gold and lightweight in the palm of his hand.

Boone stared down at the chain and pendant in shock. He recognized it, all right. "An Angel's Rest blazon? Where did you get an Angel's Rest blazon?"

"Celeste gave it to me."

"Celeste gave it to you," he repeated. "You got one, and I didn't? What the heck? That's not the way it works!"

"Take it up with the angel, McBride. Later. Let's go somewhere and make love."

"The Angel's Rest blazon." He scoffed. "Well, that solves one problem, I guess." He began tugging at the buckles on her motorcycle chaps.

"What are you doing?" she asked, slapping at his hands.

"I'm going to make love to you. Right here."

"No, you're not!"

"Right now." He estimated he could carry her to the backseat of his truck in two point seven seconds.

"This is a public place. You're an attorney! Besides, what about the rolling-over-the-cliff thing?"

"We'll be fine, Hannah." He dangled the Angel's Rest pendant in front of her eyes before swooping her up into his arms. "After all, we've got wings."

EPILOGUE

REDEMPTION, TEXAS

On the morning of his wedding day, Boone met his cousins Jackson and Tucker for a motorcycle ride through Enchanted Canyon. Just as he'd done on their first visit three years ago, Tucker led the way out of Redemption on his H-D Road King. Jackson followed on his Harley Fat Boy, while Boone brought up the rear on a Kawasaki Ninja. They made the fifteen-mile trip to the canyon at a leisurely pace, though they gunned their engines and stirred up dust just for fun when they turned onto the original narrow dirt road that cut through the scrub brush and flat, rocky terrain.

It was a perfect day for a ride, not a single cloud in the brilliant blue sky, and the current temperature hovering in the sixties. The forecast for this evening was for clear skies and temps in the seventies — perfect for an outdoor wedding and the wedding night he had planned for them beneath the stars. Hannah had enjoyed their visit to Stardance River Camp so much that he'd decided to create their own luxurious glamping tent here in the canyon. He'd finally found a purpose for Ruin, the outlaw conclave at the far end of the canyon, and renovating it into a glamping resort would be his next big project. Once he felt like tackling big projects again, that is. For the next little while, he intended to concentrate on his little family, his wife and child, Hannah and Bree.

Life was good for Boone McBride, and he was a happy man.

Where the road curved and the canyon first came into view, the three men cycled to a stop, switched off their engines, and climbed off their bikes. They stood shoulder-to-shoulder gazing out toward where the earth had fallen away.

It was a beautiful spot. Jackson had a vivid way of describing Enchanted Canyon that had always stuck with Boone: "It's like God plunged his fingers into flat, barren land, ripped it asunder, and then breathed life into it."

Below him, patches of summer green clung to life amid the changing colors of autumn. Listening hard, he could hear the distant roar of a waterfall, and he knew if he paid attention as he descended to the canyon floor, he'd see a variety of wildlife. Enchanted Canyon was different from Eternity Springs, but every bit as beautiful. How lucky was he that he'd get to live in both places with the people who mattered most to him in his life?

Jackson interrupted Boone's reverie by saying, "That first time we rode out here, I was so damned miserable. I'd just lost the custody battle for Haley, and I couldn't write a decent song to save my life. But the instant I laid eyes on this place, I experienced the weirdest sensation. I knew that my life had irrevocably changed, but I never would have guessed that the change would be so huge. I never dreamed I could be this happy, this blessed. Married to the most fabulous woman in the world, Haley living with us, and a new baby on the way."

"Plus, you are writing kick-ass songs, and your vision for the dance hall has proven to be a huge success," Tucker offered. "Good job, cuz."

"Good job, yourself," Jackson replied. "You're not doing too shabby either."

"That's the damned truth." Tucker shoved his hands into the back pockets of his jeans as a slow, satisfied grin spread across his face. "Who would have thought that a rough old army man like me would become so enthralled with satin and lace? Gillian rocks my world."

Boone eyed Tucker thoughtfully. "So are the two of you thinking to give little Caroline Junior a cousin anytime soon?"

"Emma," Jackson said. "We've settled on Emma."

"Emma McBride. Beautiful family name. Excellent choice, Jackson." Tucker's grin widened, and a gleam entered his brown eyes as he added, "Actually, Gillian doesn't want to steal any of Hannah's thunder, so we're waiting until after your wedding, Boone, to make any announcement."

"Hah!" Jackson said. "Awesome." He clapped Tucker on the back.

Boone snapped his fingers. "I knew it. Gillian didn't drink any champagne at the rehearsal party last night. I bet Hannah five dollars that you'd knocked her up."

"Don't be crass. Like Grandma used to say, she's in a family way."

The three men shared a grin, then Boone punched Tucker's shoulder in the way that substituted for a hug among the McBride cousins. "I'm really happy for you, Tucker. Congratulations."

"Thank you."

"So all three of us will have little ones

close in age," Jackson pointed out.

Boone nodded. "History repeating itself. How about that? Maybe Tucker and Gillian will have a girl too. Brianna, Emma, and Gillian Junior."

"Haley will be in heaven," Jackson observed.

"Four girls." Tucker frowned. "That scares me to death. Imagine what it'll be like if our girls want to date guys like us."

"Won't happen," Boone declared. "We'll choose their boyfriends for them."

Sagely, his cousins nodded in agreement, then they resumed their ride.

Boone reflected on the changes in his own life as they snaked their way down to the canyon floor, retracing the path of their first visit. He recalled that on the very day when he'd received word that Great-Aunt Mildred had bequeathed this property to his family, Celeste Blessing had offered some profound advice.

And remember, Boone, she'd said. *The trick to breaking the chains of the past is to reject it as your master and embrace it as your teacher.*

Well, he sure hadn't rushed that particular task, had he? Nevertheless, breaking those chains had taken the exact right amount of time. In less than eight hours, he was going

427

to stand up in front of friends and family and marry his soul mate.

What better place to do it? Hadn't Celeste always said that Enchanted Canyon was where troubled souls came to find peace? He was determined that his soul mate would find not only peace in Enchanted Canyon, but everlasting happiness and joy too. And when Boone made his mind up about something, he made it happen.

He intended to make Hannah the happiest woman in Texas, Colorado, the United States, then the entire world. Hell, he'd make it his life's work to make her the happiest, most joyous woman in the universe! She was his soul mate.

His soul mate.

The words echoed through his mind shortly after six o'clock that evening. A string quartet played Bach, and roses perfumed the gentle evening breeze. With Jackson and Tucker standing beside him, Boone watched Brick Callahan seat Quetta McBride in the right front row of the white garden chairs next to Boone's father. Then Gabe Callahan escorted the figure whom Hannah had chosen to serve the role of the bride's mother up the aisle. Once Celeste was seated in the left front row, the bridesmaids dressed in autumn gold gowns started up the aisle — Caroline, Gillian, and his sisters, Lara and Frankie.

Boone's heart swelled when a beaming Haley started up the aisle, pulling a wagon filled with roses and mums and Bree seated tall in her Bumbo.

Seated behind Boone's mother, Brianna's grandmother let out a little happy sob.

Then finally — finally — Hannah stepped into view, and Boone's knees went weak. Gone was the woman who always wore black. This Hannah — his Hannah — wore the bright red-orange of the Enchanted Canyon maples in October, and she was glorious.

He loved her beyond measure with a heart that was whole.

After their vows were spoken, after they'd danced at the Last Chance Hall and skinny-dipped beneath a harvest moon beside a rushing waterfall, Boone made sweet, tender love to his new bride long into the night.

Eventually, exhausted and replete, beneath the star-filled Texas sky, Boone and Hannah drifted into sleep in each other's arms.

Elsewhere in Enchanted Canyon, Jackson and Tucker also slept peacefully in the loving embrace of their blissful wives.

The McBrides of Texas had finally found their happily-ever-afters.

ABOUT THE AUTHOR

Emily March is the *New York Times* and *USA Today* bestselling author of the heartwarming Eternity Springs series. A graduate of Texas A&M University, Emily is an avid fan of Aggie sports and her recipe for jalapeño relish has made her a tailgating legend.